Saint
Christopher
and the
Gravedigger

ALSO BY CATHERINE COOKSON

The Kate Hannigan Series

Kate Hannigan

Kate Hannigan's Girl

The Mary Ann Stories

A Grand Man

The Lord and Mary Ann

The Devil and Mary Ann

Love and Mary Ann

Life and Mary Ann

Marriage and Mary Ann

Mary Ann's Angels

Mary Ann and Bill

The Mallen Novels

The Mallen Streak

The Mallen Girl

The Mallen Litter

**FT
Pbk**

PRAISE FOR

'Humour, toughness, resolution and generosity are Cookson virtues . . . In the specialised world of women's popular fiction, Cookson has created her own territory.'

—Helen Dunmore, *The Times*

'Queen of raw family romances'

—*Telegraph*

'Catherine Cookson soars above her rivals'

—*Mail on Sunday*

'Catherine Cookson is an icon; without her influence, I and many other authors would not have followed in her footsteps.'

—Val Wood

The Bonny Dawn

The Branded Man

The Desert Crop

The Lady on my Left

The Blind Years

Riley

The Solace of Sin

The Thursday Friend

A House Divided

Rosie of the River

The Silent Lady

Non-Fiction

Before I Go

Our Kate

Let Me Make Myself Plain

Plainer Still

Her Way

Children's Books

Bill and the Mary Ann Shaughnessy

Matty Doolin

Joe and the Gladiator

Saint
Christopher
and the
Gravedigger

Published by Lake Union Publishing, Seattle
www.apub.com

Amazon, the Amazon logo, and Lake Union Publishing are trademarks of Amazon.com, Inc., or its affiliates.

ISBN-13: 9781477823910
ISBN-10: 1477823913

Cover design by Lisa Horton

Printed in the United States of America

We wish to thank The University of Newcastle upon Tyne for the picture of Catherine Cookson used in this book. While every effort has been made to trace copyright sources, Amazon Publishers would be grateful to hear from any unacknowledged copyright holders.

Chapter One

The crossroads were under repair and a big red board proclaiming DANGER – ROADWORKS AHEAD brought the cortège to a halt. The cars following the hearse drew close together and waited in dark solemnity until six other cars, in colours varying from red to pale primrose, were waved on their careless, heedless way with never a thought for 'the poor swine' lying there. So was the private comment of Broderick McNally as he stopped his drill in deference to the dead. He showed this deference by standing with head bowed and one hand, palm outward, behind his back, while the other supported his machine.

With the signal to go, the funeral procession wended its way tentatively past Mr McNally on the narrow piece of road he had left them, and not until they had gathered speed, as if in a hurry to reach their destination, did Broderick speak. 'There goes another one for Gascoigne to shovel the muck on. Oh, it's happy he'll be the day,' he remarked caustically.

The man at his side, leaning on his shovel, laughed and said, 'You don't like Gascoigne, Broderick?'

'It isn't that I don't like him,' said Broderick, bringing his drill between his feet again, 'but some way or another I seem to get under the man's skin and sour him. That's not saying we haven't been good neighbours for the past sixteen years . . . though, mind, he'd have me out of me house if he could the morrow, the pigheaded old swine, and all on account of me nationality. Aye, would you believe it? An' his old mother's worse than him, if that's at all possible. But, mind, for the rest of the family you couldn't find a nicer.' A grin spread over Broderick's large, flat, red countenance and, bending forward, he whispered, 'And I'll tell you somethin'.' His lips went close to the other man's ear and the effect of the words pouring into them caused the man's eyes to stretch.

'You don't say?' he exclaimed.

'I do.'

'Well, I'd like to see the end of that.'

'You will, please God and His Holy Mother.' Broderick nodded once before pressing a lever and the noise that followed only allowed the two men to smile at each other by way of communication. The repair of the crossroads between Battonbun and Downfell Hurst on one road and Biddleswiddle and Befumstead on the other, was once more under way.

Downfell Hurst cemetery supplied the needs of the four villages and was commonly referred to as 'Fell Bottom', because that was where it was placed geographically, clustering at the foot of a fell. In attendance at the burials in the cemetery there would be either of two Reverends: the Reverend Collins, who ministered to Battonbun and Biddleswiddle; or the Reverend Bailey, who ministered to Downfell Hurst and Befumstead. Then there was Father Stuckly, who saw to the passing over of the scattered Catholic fraternity, and a Mr Hope, who was also a Reverend but no one used his title because he saw only to the laying aside of, as the gravedigger John Gascoigne summarised them, 'the neither one thing or t'others'.

But whatever their denomination, the dead were the dead and were all the same to John, or at least they had been up to this last month or so. Before that, he had thrown the dirt onto them with the comment, and this to himself, that 'such was life' or, when feeling very talkative inside, he might add, 'When their number's called, even the deaf hear.'

But this was before he had witnessed the accident at the crossroads.

He had heard the screams as far away as the back cemetery gate and when he had reached the scene it was to see a woman running around half-demented and splashed all over with blood. And two cars looking like one, so closely were they tangled, with a dead man lying in the middle of them. The only things that were left whole from either car were two dangling effigies. The three-inch figures, identical in pattern, stared at each other from their scaffold of tortured iron and the sight of them had raised a comment in John's mind. 'All this mess,' he had thought, 'and them never touched.'

That was John's first acquaintance with St Christopher.

The second time was when young Steve Morton ran his motorcycle at a telegraph pole. He no doubt thought it was the lesser of two evils, the other being a head-on collision with a very merry car driver. But it hadn't worked out that way, for Steve had died, in spite of the St Christopher medal dangling from a chain around his neck.

The third meeting had come about through Mrs Wheeler, who helped her man to run a smallholding up Biddleswiddle way. You would have thought anyone would have been safe enough feeding chickens in a field, and that with a rail round it. But no, this time one of the St Christopherites had brought his car over the ditch, through the railings, over a hen cree and onto the petrified woman. Mrs Wheeler had got off with a broken leg, but Mrs Wheeler's broken leg had cost the driver of the car his neck, and around it was a medallion of . . . that bloody Saint, as John called him.

This last meeting with the Saint had set John's mind working.

John was a man of few words and many grunts and one of his grunts could express a volume. He had a variety of them which he adapted as the situation arose. But they all seemed to express his view on life, the principle of which was, 'you leave me be, and I'll leave you be'; except perhaps in the case of his neighbour, Broderick McNally, and at odd times his own mother. These two people alone had the power to turn John's grunts into words, and the words were such that they never failed to set the sparks flying in both quarters, even if along different lines.

John had lived for over sixteen years in Downfell Hurst, and with regards to the village – that was fast becoming a town with its blotches of new bungalows that created controversy, especially among the residents who took pride in tracing their ancestors back for 300 years – John took no part. When there were meetings to protest against this or that erection, no one said, 'Are you coming along, John?' for they knew it would be useless. Even such a colossal event as the visit of a Member of Parliament to the Downfell Hurst Church Hall tomorrow, who was coming to answer questions on the proposed revolutionary scheme to turn the disued chapel into a cinema to supply the four villages with films at least twice a week, evoked no response from him. Either to the one side – who asked, with dramatic gestures, could any suggestion be madder with television aerials going up like nine pins all round the countryside – nor to the other: the more youthful members of the community, who said, 'We don't want to be born and live and die inside four walls, we want to get out.'

'Out' for them, apparently, meant going to the pictures and sitting in the dark, which of course was different to the dark of the front room where they only rubbed shoulders with the family. This section wanted a darkness that licensed them to rub shoulders with a stranger, or better still, with the love of the moment. They wanted to sit in a darkness that was different; a darkness through which new worlds flicked before their eyes and of which they could take their choice – a new world twice a week.

No, not even this interesting battle stirred John. One might think that John never pondered, but he did. He was thinking and pondering all the time; not about coffins and graves and funeral services, these were everyday things and became monotonous, but about things that went much deeper. So deep that he wasn't always conscious of thinking; so deep that he often became lost in a maze that was so filled with questions, there was no room for the answers.

But that was John up to the first time he became aware of the St Christopher effigies and medals. To the outside world he remained the same, but John knew that he was no longer the same. For now there was a battle raging inside him, a talking battle, and his opponent was a man in a long robe with a staff in his hand.

This was the man who, up to a comparatively few years ago, had been an obscure saint, but who was now a power that was creating a mass superstition the like of which had not been known since the Dark Ages, or so reasoned John. And he saw this saint as something more terrible than anything in the Dark Ages, for then people could be forgiven for thinking that even a piece of wood touched by a wandering friar held enough power to alter their destiny. But the wearers of the effigy today were no longer souls petrified by the vast unknown; they were educated and supposedly enlightened people. But despite this, the superstition had flooded high schools, grammar schools and colleges, and had bemused not only the scholars but those who taught them.

This subject had hit John with such intensity that he could no longer remain unaware of his deeper thinking. He became so much aware of it, in fact, that he was worried by it and therefore he was determined to do something about it.

This breaking out of his cocoon did not surprise John, for being the least introspective of men, he had not been aware that he lived in a cocoon.

At this particular moment, John was standing out of sight of the cortège as it came through the cemetery gates, but it wasn't out of his sight, and as he looked at what he termed the latest victim of this St Christopher racket, he muttered, 'Something oughts be done about this,' and he nodded once to himself in answer. 'Aye it should that.'

John had never spoken aloud to himself before. This was a momentous event.

Florrie Gascoigne had painted her kitchen doors yellow and the walls mauve. She had pink-patterned curtains on the oblong window and thick, serviceable, coloured crockery on the delft rack. She liked the effect and considered it the bonniest kitchen in the village. It was an old-fashioned kitchen and was large enough for the table to be in the middle and this offered a double service. The food was prepared on it and eaten off it, and now Florrie was moving back and forward between it and the gas stove, which stood cheek by jowl with the modern water-heating range. She was setting the table for the evening meal in between keeping an eye on the pan on top of the stove, which she stirred at intervals.

At the sink below the window stood her second son, Frankie. He was nineteen and worked on the buildings, and he was a talker. Frankie was always talking. He was an observer of life but so voluble was he that he didn't allow his observations time to sink any deeper than the skin. It would appear that he took them in through his eyes and they slid down the back of his nose and out of his mouth in one motion. He was 'the talker' of the family, and as he could not possibly have inherited this from either parent the obvious suggestion was that he took after his paternal grandmother. Frankie didn't take to this suggestion because he didn't take to his grandmother.

Sitting on the couch was Linda, reading *Woman* magazine. Linda was plump, with the transitional curves of a seventeen-year-old, and pretty. She took after her mother not only in looks but in character, for her manner, like Florrie's, held some restraint and a suggestion of secretiveness, which didn't help her in her job of selling things in Twait's drapery shop.

Then there was the eldest son, Arthur, but he wouldn't be in until eight o'clock tonight, it being Friday. He always worked late on a Friday getting the last batch of dough ready for the ovens in the bakery.

Florrie knew almost to the minute when each member of her family would walk in through the back door, and now she turned from the stove, looked at her husband, gave a small smile and made the usual remark of 'Another one over?' as he came into the kitchen.

The evening procedure was that John would walk the three steps from the kitchen door to the cupboard where the work clothes were kept and there deposit his coat, and on the journey he would answer his wife with the syllable 'Aye', and from the inflection that he gave to his reply she was able to judge the quality of his day. But tonight he didn't answer her with the brief 'Aye' and her head came round sharply to him when he repeated her words with heavy stress. 'Another one over,' he said. And now he brought her mouth agape with the addition of 'Aye, and completely over for some folks.'

Florrie, spoon held in mid-air, continued to gape and Frankie, too, gaped. If his father had rolled into the kitchen paralytic drunk, he could not have looked more amazed. His father's reply, especially at this precise point in the evening, amounted almost to loquaciousness. Frankie often considered that his father was the most suitable man in the world for the post of gravedigger, for he was dead mute most of the time. Then just as he was getting his mouth to close and his tongue was flicking preparatory to questioning his father's last remark, his grannie entered the kitchen from the hall.

Old Mrs Gascoigne was like nobody but herself. Her white hair was so sparse that it had its work cut out to cover her head. On some parts of her scalp it failed to do this, and patches of grey-pink bareness showed through. It would appear that she had no cheekbones for her eyes lay flat upon her face, the skin dropping from the lower lids direct to her upper lip, which was short and curved inwards. But it was her chin that drew a newcomer's attention. Looking at it sideways, they would have sworn that her jaw was dislocated for the whole of her chin and the lower lip protruded a good half-inch beyond the flat surface of her face. Her nose was of no account, for it was lost in the no man's land between the remarkable chin and two round, hard, blue bullet eyes. After looking at Gran's face, no one bothered to look at her figure, of which there was little to remark on anyway, being just a bone structure on which she hung her numerous out-of-date blouses and skirts. Gran was seventy-nine and looked ninety, but she had the clout-clipping tongue of a harridan of twenty. It was to her only son's advantage that in looks, personality and approach to life he in no way resembled her.

'What's the matter now . . . you brought a funeral in with you? All standin' round like a lot of stuffed dummies.'

Her greeting returned the atmosphere to something of normality. Florrie began ladling out portions of sauce-covered tripe and onions, and in the middle of each plate Linda placed a diamond of toast, before carrying it to the table where Gran and Frankie were already seated. As Linda placed the plate in front of her grannie, the old lady offered no word of thanks but turned her eagle eye on her grandson and asked abruptly, 'What's up with you? Sickening for somethin'?'

Frankie brought his gaze from his father, who stood at the sink, back turned, methodically washing his hands, and answered, 'No. What makes you think that?'

'Bein' in the room nearly three minutes and I haven't heard you open your mouth.'

'Coo!'

'Coo' was an exclamation that Frankie resorted to when things got beyond him, and this was such a moment. Picking up his knife and fork he attacked his high tea, only to bolt his first mouthful as his father's voice hit him with the expressive word, 'Hungry?'

'Yes, Dad . . . Aye.'

'So am I.' John sat down at the head of the table and Florrie, whipping off her apron, joined them.

John said, 'Now.' Whether he was going to add 'We can start', or had been about to further surprise his family with a wordy sentence, is a matter of conjecture, for his mother at this point raised a bony, blue-veined finger and cried, 'Ready, set . . . go.' Her chin moved twice, once up and once down before she continued, 'Since when did we start to eat to order? Now,' she mimicked her son, then repeated again, 'Now.'

John levelled his gaze at her with anything but filial love.

'Now, Gran, get on with your tea, do,' said Florrie in a soothing tone, as she pushed the cruet towards her mother-in-law. 'And you, Frankie, if you're in a hurry to eat, get on with it an' all.'

'But, Mam . . .'

'No "but Mam"s. Get on with your tea.'

They all began to eat and as the meal went on and the silence became more constrained, Florrie found that the tripe, tender as it was, was sticking in her throat. There was something up with John. She had noticed it from the moment he came in the door. His face had looked different but she hadn't realised it fully until he had spoken.

Florrie loved her husband; at one time she had worshipped him, but now the emotion held no ethereal quality, it was settled on the solid basis of understanding. This love, had it been evident to her family, would have amazed them, but then she knew things about her husband that they were unaware of, things that evoked admiration, things that no one, no one but herself could give him credit for. She alone knew the character of John Gascoigne. It was this knowledge that made her so patient with his mother.

Sometimes she thought that his feelings for his mother had passed from mere dislike into hate and this worried and upset her, for she had the old-fashioned idea that no one could hate their parents without sinning deeply. But she knew it was almost an impossibility to find a likeable trait in old Mrs Gascoigne. And yet . . . This 'and yet' presented itself to her from time to time, for she thought that if the old woman had it in her to care for anyone it was for Florrie herself. And this suspicion

9

of warmth in her mother-in-law helped Florrie to keep applying the soothing oil of patience to her, and also to the unlucky member of the family who was unfortunate enough to be under her attack.

Florrie's pondering over the sudden change in her husband was abruptly checked by the kitchen door opening and the head of her eldest son, Arthur, appearing round it. And not only did she turn towards it but so did everyone at the table.

'You're early, aren't you?' she said.

'Yes, I asked off.'

Silence greeted this remark and Arthur, avoiding the eyes directed at him, withdrew his head into the scullery again and there, taking off his coat, he threw it over the gas boiler. Then, stepping outside the back door, but keeping under the porch so that he wouldn't be observed by the neighbours either to the right or the left, he banged himself violently all over with his hands.

Arthur was assistant to Mr Duckworth who had the monopoly of baker shops in Downfell Hurst – his being the only one. Moreover, Mr Duckworth lived next door, on the left side of them; moreover still, Arthur was entangled with Henry Duckworth's only daughter, Joan. How this had come about Arthur couldn't rightly explain. Perhaps it was the subconscious desire to be a master baker and have his own shop one day that had been the prod which had pushed him on to ask Joan Duckworth out, and eventually to mention marriage. Or, he was asking himself often now, was it he who had first mentioned marriage or had she? What he knew she had mentioned, and quite a lot, was that one day he'd be head of Duckworth's. But this prospect looked at in broad daylight, which was a different light from that of Potters Lane in the dark, was very far ahead. Henry Duckworth was hale and hearty at fifty, and Arthur could see him living to ninety, and if he did die young there would still be Mrs Duckworth, for Arthur could never see Mrs Duckworth dying. And still moreover, Arthur had a strong suspicion now that he didn't even like Joan, that he never had liked her and never could like her, but they were going to be married on 25 August.

Arthur banged the seat of his pants, his knees, his calves and finally his head, and as he turned to go indoors, he admonished himself for his past weakness by saying to himself, 'You don't want your head banged, you want it lookin' at.'

When he was seated at the table and his mother had found sufficient tripe still left to give him a meal, he was really taken by surprise when his father addressed him quietly saying, 'Not bakin' the night?' It was usually Frankie who asked the questions.

Arthur kept his eyes on his plate as he answered, 'Aye but he let me off . . . there's a social on in Biddleswiddle.'

'Huh,' said Gran.

The Gascoignes would appear to be experts in the use of expressive monosyllables and this one brought a deep rose hue that tinted Arthur's pale skin.

It would seem that this reply now prompted John and Frankie to place their knives and forks slowly on their plates as they looked towards Arthur, but naturally it was Frankie who spoke first.

'The game the morrow?' he asked. 'He's not keeping you on the morrow?'

Frankie was now leaning across the table and Arthur, his eyes still cast down, said flatly, 'Aye. He wants to play.'

'Why the peg-legged old . . .'

'That's enough, Frankie.'

'But, Mam, he can't play for taffy apples. Look what he did last week; he lost us the game, and that was just a friendly. But the morrow . . . And them coming from Battonbun and the pitch perfect.' Frankie half rose from the table now crying, 'You go and tell her what to do with that social. The game's more important than any social.'

'Madam Joan said social and social it shall be.' Gran's chin seemed to have jutted another inch and Arthur, raising his eyes to her, said reproachfully, 'Now, Gran.'

'Don't "now, Gran" me, that won't make me shut me mouth. That madam's got you under her thumb now and the minute you put the ring on her you'll be flat on your face for the rest of your life, with her heel stuck right in your neck, me lad.'

The prospect of lying under the weight of his future wife's anatomy was too much for Arthur as he pushed his chair back from the table and, getting up, went quickly from the room.

John, looking at his mother added, 'Can't you mind your own business for once, Mother?'

'It is me business. If you haven't got the spunk to say anything about it, and tell him what he's in for, then don't criticise me 'cos I have.'

'Your spunk means mischief, Mother, it always has and it always will.'

Florrie stared fiercely at her husband. Whatever was the matter? There was something different about John tonight. His words were coming easy. Always before she had seen him stop and think before speaking, even to his mother.

'Well, I think Gran's right.'

This was quite a short statement for Frankie but it took some courage to make it, for it put him in open opposition to his father and Frankie, for all his bumptiousness, was afraid of his father. He could talk big behind his back but he had never yet been able to do it to his face without a tremor of fear running through his thin body. Now, having taken the side of his grandmother – at least in this small instance – he was straightening his shoulders under the momentary flush that courage brings, when his grannie floored him with, 'When I want you on me side I'll ask you, me lad. Until then speak for yoursel' and you'll find you have enough to do.'

'Coo!' Frankie was reduced to his syllable and Gran – as was her wont – did a repeat with, 'Coo . . . aye . . . coo.'

At this point in the proceedings, Florrie sighed deeply, which John noticed, and the sigh brought his mind from Frankie's provoking remark to her. How she put up with his mother all day and every day he just didn't know. Did she do it because she thought she had to . . . sort of payment like? He had asked this question of himself before, and the answer was the same now. He shook his head. Yet only a saint could put up with his mother and not retaliate.

John thought the world of his wife, but he wasn't sure if she cared a straw for him. He'd had the idea for years that the affection she showed him might only be gratitude. It was hard for a man to tell the difference between gratitude and love. Yet she had seemed to love him when they were first married. He remembered it as an intense, almost embarrassing emotion, but in these latter years there had been none of that. He supposed that was the way of marriage, any marriage. But theirs hadn't been just any marriage. He rose from the table, his mind still on her, and so deep had his thoughts, for the moment, gone into the past that he had to drag his mind back to take in what his ears were hearing. He turned slowly to the table again and, looking across at Frankie, who was talking to Linda, asked him, 'What did you say there?'

Frankie, putting his head back, looked up at his father as he said, 'What d'you mean? About the motorbike? I said I'm savin' up for a motorbike.'

'You're what?'

'Well . . . well, you heard me, Dad. What's wrong with that?' Frankie sidled slowly to his feet. 'Savin' up for a motorbike.'

'You'll have no motorbike while you're in this house.'

'But why? I've been on about a motorbike for ages.'

'Well, you can forget about it from now on.'

Florrie, dragging her eyes from her husband, turned to Frankie and said soothingly, 'Your dad's afraid of you having an accident. There's been so many latterly, you know there has.'

'But, Mam, all the fellas have motorbikes.'

'And all the fellas carry St Christopher medals with them, don't they?'

Now Frankie's eyes were wide and his mouth hung open in perplexity as he looked at his father. 'Aye, they do. What's wrong with that?'

'Nowt's wrong with it if you look on it as a passport to the other side. People are dying all over the country because you and the likes of you carry bits of tin on yoursel's that you think gives you a licence to say "Scram out of it, I'm a St Christopherite, the road's mine!"' John thrust his finger towards Frankie's chest. 'You're carrying the medal so you're all right, Jack. But the other fellow. Oh, him! "Skedaddle chum if you don't want your brains splattered all over the place."'

Florrie gaped at her husband.

Gran peered at her son, and Frankie and Linda gazed at their father.

Not one of them spoke a word, but they watched him as he filled his chest with air and made one more statement before marching from the room. 'Let that be the last I hear of that,' he said.

Florrie slowly sat down in her chair and Gran, leaning towards her daughter-in-law, said grimly below her breath, 'If we didn't know him, I'd say he was bottled.'

Frankie, looking towards the door through which his father had just gone, muttered with a kind of sympathetic awe, 'It's the gravediggin'. Uncle Brod's always saying gravediggers and hangmen go loopy in the end.' Then turning slowly towards his mother he made a half-hearted apology by adding, 'Sorry, Mam. But there's somethin' up with him, isn't there? I've never heard him talk so much in me life. And such rot.'

Florrie did not answer, but Gran put in comfortingly, 'Anyway, that's put paid to you and your motorbike, me lad.'

'Oh, for crying out loud, Gran, shut your mouth will you.'

'Frankie!' Florrie got to her feet. 'Now I've spoken to you a number of times already the night.'

'What's wrong with everybody? Why should everybody pick on me? I'll tell you what it is, Mam. I'll go into digs, I will; I'll not put up with it.'

Florrie closed her eyes. Gran gave her derisive 'huh' and Linda, after watching Frankie dash towards the cupboard and pull out his shoes, jerked her chin upwards once before leaving the room unobtrusively and going up the stairs.

Linda's room was so small that if she sat on the deep windowsill and put out both hands she could touch the foot of her bed and her chest of drawers at the same time. She had been sitting on the sill for some minutes before she reached out and pulled open the top drawer of the chest, and after groping knowledgeably she lifted out a felt bag and gently shook a medal onto her palm. She gazed at it tenderly for some time then turned her eyes in the direction of the house next door, the McNally's house, and sighed.

A year ago, after Patrick McNally was divorced and had gone to lodge as far away as Befumstead, she had bought the medal and every night she had asked St Christopher to guide his steps back to his home next door. It had seemed an impossible request for the McNallys still considered him married. Then his wife that was had died. About this latter happening Linda's conscience wasn't entirely at ease, for at times it reminded her of her mixed assortment of prayers. But now Patrick had returned home and she had no longer to walk nearly to Befumstead to catch a glimpse of him; she saw him every day, and they talked. Linda hugged herself, and as she did so she dropped the medal, and when she retrieved it, she pressed it tenderly to her cheek. St Christopher had done all this, and then for her father to go on like that about him. Well, she wagged her head defiantly, nothing that he could say would make her stop praying to St Christopher, so there. What did her father know about him anyway? He was old – not St Christopher, her father, she laughed to herself . . .

Across the landing John too sat looking out of the window and he also was thinking about St Christopher. It seemed monstrous to him, in fact a personal affront, that this figure of superstition should have penetrated his own door. Motorbike indeed! He thrust out his lips, and they remained out for some time before subsiding on the thought. 'But why had I to go for the lad like that?' Seemingly the question disturbed John for he rose to his feet and stood staring through the window, not seeing, as he usually did, through the gap between the two cottages opposite, the village green in the far distance and, on this particular night, its roped-off sacred centre patch. No, the whole window seemed to be taken up with Frankie's face, and John asked himself once again, 'Why did I do it?'

His reactions towards this particular son had been the main problem of John's life, for Frankie irritated him, whereas Arthur didn't. John did not think of loving Arthur, that quality was kept alone for Florrie, but he would have said he had a dull affection for Arthur. And Linda? Yes, he was fond of Linda and she had her own particular corner in his heart. But Frankie . . . well, Frankie. The situation troubled John, had troubled him for years, for under the circumstances, the very odd circumstances, he knew it was most unnatural to dislike Frankie and love – well, say, Arthur.

A tap on the door broke into his thinking and when Arthur's voice came saying, 'Can I come in, Dad?' he answered abruptly, 'Aye.'

Arthur was dressed for outdoors and he appeared very presentable. If his expression had not been one of deep solemnity he could have looked attractive, for his face, although not good-looking, was open, his grey eyes had a foundation of kindness and his mouth spoke of generosity. The combination did not make for strength and determination and his voice bore this out when he said with half-averted gaze, 'I'd like a talk with you, Dad, sometime.'

John, looking full at his son, asked briefly, 'Anything wrong?'

'Lots. But I'd like to talk about it on the quiet.' Now Arthur was looking at his father and as John jerked his head in the direction of the Duckworths' house, Arthur, lowering his eyes towards the floor, answered the silent question with a small nod.

'You're working the morrow and it can't be the morrow night, so Sunday it'll have to be . . . mornin'.'

'Yes, Dad, that'll do.'

'I'll be goin' up to the shed around eleven, there's another one on Monday, early.' John was referring to a funeral. 'You could take a dander up then.'

'Aye, Dad, I will; that'll be fine . . . Thanks. So long.'

Arthur had the doorknob in his hand when John checked him with, 'Just a minute.' He turned round and waited.

'Look, tell me . . . What do you think about this St Christopher lark?'

'St Christopher what?'

'This St Christopher business. Imagining you can get protection from a piece of tin with his face stamped on so you can drive a car like you were always drunk, or a motorbike . . . oh, motorbikes.'

Arthur screwed up his eyes as he looked at his father a moment in silence, then he gave a small laugh as he said, 'Well, havin' had nothing faster than a bicycle I don't have much need of him, do I?'

'But if you had a motorbike would you depend on him to get you from here to there instead of using caution, like, and your common sense?'

Arthur's eyes screwed up still more as he answered. 'Well, as I say, I've never had a bike so the occasion has never arisen . . . I've never thought about it . . . or him.'

'No, that's everybody's trouble – they don't think about it, or him, until it's too bloody late.'

After watching his father turn to the window again, Arthur, greatly puzzled, went out and slowly down the stairs. What was up with his dad? 'Until it's too bloody late,' he had said. He could count on his two hands the times he had heard his dad swear, and never in the house . . . never.

As his grannie was in the kitchen, he made no reference to the incident. He had more sense, but passed through the room with,

'I'll be seeing you, Mam.' Then as he reached the back door his grannie's words, like hard peas, seemed to hit him in the neck, saying, 'Goodnight, Gran, I'll be seein' you an' all.' And he turned somewhat wearily and said, 'Sorry, Gran. Goodnight.'

Gran's only reply was a loud sniffing 'Huh' and when Arthur reached the back porch his terse comment on Gran was checked by Frankie who was polishing his shoes vigorously.

'What's wrong with St Christopher? The old man's up the lum, did you hear him going on about me getting a bike? Between him and Gran this house will drive me barmy . . . You're lucky you'll soon be out of it.'

To this statement Arthur made no comment whatever. He just straightened his tie, stretched his neck out of his collar and walked quickly down the back garden path, along the few feet of dividing fence and up the next path to the Duckworths' back door, and as he did so he repeated the word . . . lucky. Then, not unlike Gran, he added . . . Huh. He'd swap places any day with Frankie . . . Dad, St Christopher . . . and Gran thrown in. Boy, he would that . . . Lucky.

Chapter Two

'I think,' said Broderick McNally, 'your peas have a touch of the blight, John.'

John gave no indication that he had heard this remark but went on steadily hoeing, trying to ignore the great bulk of his neighbour where he sat in a dilapidated deckchair among the high grass that took up much of the space in his garden. But although John had not spoken, he was answering Broderick rapidly in his mind, saying, 'And what else can you expect with the weeds and grass seeds blowing about all over the place? Why don't you get a shovel in your hand, you big lazy galoot, and get your patch cleaned up? It's a disgrace to the street.'

Broderick was talking now as if he were answering a comment of John's. 'Aye, it's a beautiful mornin' . . . Y'know, John, I look forward to Saturda' mornin' from Sunda' night. When the old drill is blasting me eardrums apart I think to meself, come Saturda' mornin', Broderick lad, you'll be sittin' at peace in your own back garden and, God willing, he'll set the sun flamin' down on you . . . and he has.' Broderick thrust his hands between his shirt and his trousers top and patted his large stomach. He turned his head lazily round to John again and asked with a broad grin, 'Don't you get tired of mucking about with the earth, John?'

John paused long enough to look at Broderick under half-raised lids before continuing the prodding movement with his hoe.

'But there, I've always held the notion you like shovelling muck.'

'Then you've noticed wrong.'

No sooner were the words spat out than John could have kicked himself for having risen to Broderick's bait. His only defence now was to turn his back completely on his neighbour, and as he did this, Broderick, wriggling into an upright position in his chair, cried, 'Well now, you surprise me. I somehow had the idea that it must give you a sort of delight to chuck on the first shovelful. The sound of it going plonk on the coffin lid, I told meself, must be like music to John's ears.'

John, after closing his eyes for a moment, was on the point of straightening his back preparatory to retreating indoors when Katie McNally's voice came from her kitchen door crying, 'Will you give over, you wobbling lump of Satan you, and stop tryin' to get John's goat. Take no heed of him, John . . . Would you like a cup of cocoa?'

John forced himself to turn his face towards Katie McNally and he shook his head as he said, 'No, thanks, I've just had a cup of tea.'

'Good enough, John. But it's no use asking his nabs there if he wants one, he could drink a swill bucket full. Here, Moira, take that to your da.'

As Moira came down the path carrying the mug of cocoa to her father, Katie shouted to John, 'It's a grand day for the match, isn't it? The lads were saying this mornin' that the ground's just Arthur's cup of tea. He could get a hundred the day and no bother at all.'

'He might if he was playing, but he's not,' Moira said.

Not only did Broderick and Katie say, 'What's that?', but John turned and looked at Moira over the fence. How did she know that Arthur wasn't playing? Nobody in the house had said a word, he was sure of that; not even Frankie. For after a lot of to do about going out last night, he had gone to his room in a huff, and stayed there, expecting somebody, as Gran had said, to go and 'tice him out of it. Moreover,

Linda hadn't left the house either. It wasn't likely that Arthur himself would have spread the news. Being used like a puppet between father and daughter wasn't anything to talk about. As for it coming from the Duckworths, they never opened their mouths to the McNallys, any one of them.

'Where did you hear that?' asked Broderick.

Moira wobbled her bottom and turned her saucy glance towards John as she replied, 'Oh, a little bird told me.' Then depositing the cocoa in her father's hand, she moved towards the railing and leaning on the top of it she put her dark shining head on one side and asked with subtle simplicity, 'He's not playing, is he, Uncle John?'

The fact that he was 'Uncle' to all the McNallys annoyed John. He had never even been able to call Broderick Broderick. He had always been McNally, and he had addressed Katie all the years as Mrs Mac. 'Is he, Uncle John?' repeated Moira.

'Well, since you know it all, Moira, why ask?'

Moira was not put off by John's answer. She was used to Uncle John, and she enjoyed teasing him as much as her father did. Now she said under her breath, 'He had to take dear Joanie to a social last night, hadn't he? Because Papa Duckworth wanted to play the day, didn't he? And there you've got the whole set-up.'

John kept his eyes from the sweatered bust resting on the rails and looked at the merry, vivacious face. Here was a minx if ever there was one; she had all the makings of a piece. McNally would have trouble with this one, he'd bet his bottom dollar. But how had she come to know why Arthur wasn't playing?

Moira dropped her eyes and her face assumed an innocent childlike expression as she muttered, 'Don't look now, Uncle John – speak of the Devil and his imps will appear. Here comes Joanie and her dear mama, and they look happy – oh, ever so happy.'

John took Moira's word for it that Mrs Duckworth and Joan were coming down their pathway. He couldn't hear their footsteps, for the

Duckworths' trim garden was divided by a grass path, but when a few seconds later his own garden gate clicked open, he was forced to turn his head towards it, and from there he met the superior glance of . . . the snipe, as he thought of Mrs Duckworth.

He was about to give his brief greeting of 'Mornin'' when Broderick's voice sailed over his head crying, 'Good mornin', Mrs Duckworth, and you too, Joan. Isn't it the grandest mornin'? The air's nearly as strong as a Burton, you can feel it puttin' a jig into your legs, can't you, now?'

Accompanying her husband's greeting came Katie's laugh, a deep sharking bellow, and the lighter, more telling laugh of Moira. And when both Mrs Duckworth and her daughter went up the path without returning the greeting in any way, Moira turned from the railings and giving a simpering imitation of Joan's walk, lisped, 'Today I am so happy, as it happens, so happy, today I am so happy, I'm almost fit to burst.' The last word came on an explosive yell as Broderick's large hand caught her a slap across the buttocks, and he cried in mock firm tones, 'Away in with you and don't make game of decent people.' Then, his voice taking on a low, chuckling, confidential note, he asked John, 'How d'you feel, John, about your family bein' tied up with the sourpusses?'

John stopped his hoeing and, looking at Broderick, he said grimly, 'Do you ever do anything but ask questions, McNally?'

'Begod, y'know I do. I'm the hardest worked man in the village. But what you don't seem to understand about me, John, is that I take an interest in life, and what is life but people?'

John groaned inwardly as he watched Broderick heave himself out of his chair and come sauntering across the tall grass towards the railings. McNally goading him from the centre of the garden was one thing, but his great bulk leaning over the fence spraying him with jam-coated vitriol was another, and unbearable. It was almost with a smile that he looked towards his own kitchen door and Florrie standing there beckoning him. 'Can you come a minute?' she called.

Without a word John turned his back on Broderick, who had just settled himself, with the support of the fence, into a talking position, and went steadily up the garden towards his wife.

One look at Florrie told him that there was trouble and she indicated as much by a backwards warning jerk of her head. When he followed her into the kitchen it was made evident by the expression on the faces of both the mother and daughter confronting him.

John's own nature was quiet, yet he prided himself that he could see the funny side of things, and often he had a quiet laugh to himself. But he had always doubted if either Mr or Mrs Duckworth had ever laughed, inside or out, in the whole of their lives – and it was evident that their daughter had inherited this sombreness in a double dose. With her it had taken on the form of sullen peevishness. What on earth did Arthur see in her? He hadn't yet got over the surprise of the first time he had seen them together. Arthur was a good lad, a nice-looking lad, and to John's mind was worth something far, far better than Joan Duckworth, but he was quite aware that the Duckworths had the same feeling about their daughter and they did little to hide their opinion. To them the whole thing was unbalanced. Joan would one day own the business and she should find a partner who would bring something to the firm. What would Arthur Gascoigne bring? Nothing but his hands. It wasn't good enough. But as Mr Duckworth had said, his daughter's happiness came first, and they mustn't let position stand in the way. This last comment, John knew, did not refer to Arthur's position only, but to his own as a gravedigger.

'Do you know anything about this, Mr Gascoigne?' Full titles were still used between the Duckworths and the Gascoignes. For in spite of the engagement, the social gulf must still remain unbridged, or so at least thought Mrs Duckworth. 'Mrs Gascoigne says she knows nothing whatever about it.'

'About what?'

'About putting off the wedding for another three months.' Mrs Duckworth's thin nose twitched. She looked affronted; gravely affronted. 'Everything's settled, hall and everything, and Joan's dress on the way.' She glanced at her daughter and Joan drew her small full mouth to the prune position, and naturally she too looked gravely affronted.

'Why has he done it? That's what I want to get clear. Why?' Mrs Duckworth was now looking straight at John, and as he returned her gaze he thought, 'This is what the lad wants to see me about.' He did not now answer Mrs Duckworth but, looking towards Joan, he asked, 'What reason did he give you?'

'He said he wanted to save a little more.' Joan's voice was as thin as her face.

'And that's all my eye.' The use of such an idiom did not go at all with Mrs Duckworth's voice or manner. The expression seemed very much out of place. 'Aren't we paying for everything? Hall, reception and everything. The lot.'

Florrie was biting on her lip when John said, 'Well, perhaps that's just what he doesn't like. He wants to stand his share.'

'Nonsense. When will he be able to have enough money to meet them?'

'When you give him a rise.' Florrie's retort cut off John's reply and brought Mrs Duckworth's eyes wide, and a gaping, pained look from Joan.

'Well, I like that. Talk about imposition. Still . . .' Mrs Duckworth sighed. 'It's no more than I expected . . . But, anyway, that's all beside the point and I can see that we're not going to get near that here.' Mrs Duckworth turned to her daughter. 'I'll see Arthur myself; this has got to be put straight.'

At this point, Florrie, hearing Gran's door closing above, said, 'I'd do just that, Mrs Duckworth.' And to intimate that there was no time like the present, she marched stiffly towards the door. There remained nothing for Mrs Duckworth to do but make her exit, which she did after throwing one disparaging glance in John's direction. Joan followed her mother, but she paused for a moment in front of John and, her grey calculating eyes hard on him, said, 'It was set for August 25th and it stays August 25th, so there.'

Poor Arthur. John was scratching the front of his head when Florrie came back into the kitchen, but they hadn't time to exchange a word before Gran was on them. After a quick glance round she asked of no one in particular, 'They gone?'

Florrie, knowing her mother-in-law, was not so silly as to ask, 'Who do you mean?' but said, 'Yes, they've gone.'

'What does Madam Duckworth want at this time of the mornin'? Not yet ten.'

Florrie glanced at John, then sitting herself at the table remarked, 'Oh, on about wedding arrangements.'

'Like to bet ye tuppence that it doesn't come off.'

On this remark, John did not look in the direction of his mother but made straight for the hall door and the stairs.

Gran, casting her eyes ceilingward and with her head on one side, listened for a moment to his steps before turning to Florrie and stating, 'Y'know summat? he's gone up them stairs in his gardenin' boots.'

Florrie drew in a deep breath before saying, 'Yes, I know he has, Gran.'

A silence followed Florrie's remark, then Gran, sitting down by the table, made another statement. 'I knew somethin' was afoot,' she said. 'I knew it, and this is only the beginning. I had a feelin' last night things were gonna happen. It's gonna be one of them weeks . . . You mark my words.'

There was no cricket pavilion in Downfell Hurst; the pitch being on the village green, the players got changed in Raglet's barn. This was situated behind the village hall and the village hall was almost in a line with the wickets. The hall, moreover, had the advantage of having a wooden veranda along its front. This position was sacrosanct to the cricket scorers and the elite of the village. If it was too hot or too cold, the privileged few dissolved into the village hall and watched the game from the two windows that flanked each side of the door.

It was the custom too for the wives of the players to provide tea for the visiting team and they always did this in the village hall. But today the custom had been broken. 'Did you ever know anything like it?' was the general gist of conversation. 'To hold a political meeting on a Saturday. That's your ruddy Conservatives for you, just to be awkward,' said the Opposition.

'Don't be silly,' said the Conservatives. 'It's the only day our Member could come. He has to go abroad next week and will be away for a fortnight, and then there are the holidays, and this business of the picture house must be seen into, and at once. It's as much to your advantage as ours.'

The Conservative Member of Parliament was young – well, at least he was young enough to still be enthusiastic. Moreover, he had a theory: 'You look after the villages and the towns will take care of themselves.' So from eleven o'clock until he adjourned for lunch at Hurst Lodge with Colonel Morgan, he had answered questions on the seemingly vital subject of, 'Are we going to have our village desecrated with a picture house and be guilty of the sacrilege of using what was once a house of God for the purpose?' The Member was wholeheartedly with his constituents. And as he could not wend his way Londonward until this evening, he did not see why he should not set the seed for the hay to be gathered at the coming election, by giving an informal address that afternoon, and bust the cricket match – this latter was a very private comment.

And so it came about that, while the cricket match was in progress, the Member addressed the devout and staunch Conservatives of Downfell Hurst, of which there were more than a few. As he mouthed set phrases and put over set patterns of policy with as much verve as to make them appear original, his voice was sometimes drowned by concerted cries of:

'Lbw . . .'

'Caught out . . .'

'Oh yes, it was . . .'

'God above, what do you think of that now . . . ?'

'Well, of all the barefaced, bloody twisting umpires . . .'

The latter statement came from just below the veranda. The elite not being in evidence on the sacred platform, some of the locals – of the opposing political party, it must be stated – had taken up their position on the edge of the grass by the side of the narrow road, and during lulls, although they had their eyes directed on the game, their ears were straining to catch some remark that would give them food for ribald comment.

About a dozen yards from this particular group, and still within earshot of the speaker, was John. He was seated on a bench under a horse chestnut tree, and he too had his eyes on the game, but his mind was on the speaker. No one in the village had ever been able to find out to which party John gave his vote. When some of the bright sparks asked him outright, he had answered blankly, 'A vote's a man's own business.' And as John worked alone and under no pressure from workmates he was able to keep his political bias to himself. Although this was a great achievement, it meant he could not belong to either the Conservative or Labour clubs without giving himself away. John had never found any limiting factor in this restriction, that was until last night when he had got stirred up about the St Christopher business.

The thought had come to him in bed that it being a national superstition it should be dealt with nationally, and who better to do it than a Member of Parliament? And wasn't there one speaking in the village tomorrow? There was nothing to stop him from going to the meeting and saying, 'Look here, I want to bring up a question. It's my belief that half the accidents that are happening on the road the day are caused by hair-brained drivers who rely on nowt more than this here St Christopher medal for protection', and so on and so on.

John knew that he had only to bring from his mind into his mouth the thoughts that were there and he would be able to convince anybody that his statement was true. But even with the smooth solution that a one-sided conversation and a comfortable bed brings, John was forced to see the impossibility of himself doing anything in a big way about the matter. If he went into that meeting he would be stamped right away as a Conservative, and some of the folks that didn't like him because of his lowly occupation might start to cotton on just because they thought he thought like them and he didn't want that; he had no use for turncoats of any sort. Then some of the folks that did like him would say, 'Well now, would you believe it? Him on their side.'

But the prime obstacle against the whole idea, one that always confronted him . . . talking. Opening his mouth. Yet he had opened it in the kitchen last night all right and not only surprised his family but himself, hadn't he now? Aye, but to open it in public. Ah! That was a different kettle of fish altogether. He knew that he was no more capable of going to the meeting than he was of taking off and flying by flapping his arms. Even if it had been what could be called a sensible question he was putting, still he knew he couldn't have done it.

So John was not enjoying the game as he sat looking intently at it, for his mind was not on it, but on him there – that Member in the hall, and the question he would like to put to him . . . if he had the guts. If he had the guts he would go ahead and air his views even if he was laughed at, as he surely would be if he set out to attack a harmless saint. One, moreover, who was known to protect travellers.

Aye, and how did he protect them? By dulling their minds with a false security; by sapping their wills until they no longer thought for themselves, but relied upon his myth, upon this alluring superstition that relieved them of responsibility – of even thinking – until in a lightning flash their power to think was wrenched from them as their brains were spread around the car. John was not actually thinking these thoughts, rather he was feeling them as they moved restlessly here and there in the top layer of his subconscious.

'Four . . . four . . . boundary. Oh, good shot!'

That was the second boundary that Reverend Collins from Battonbun had achieved. Twenty-eight he was on, which made their score sixty-two and the game had only been on half an hour. John brought his mind back to the business of cricket. Battonbun would wipe the village team off the map the day, and good luck to them an' all. There might have been some hope if Arthur had been playing, but that pot-bellied Duckworth running round there like a barrel on stilts . . . If the ball was skinning his nose he couldn't catch it.

Usually when Arthur was playing he was supported by the entire family, but today John was the only one who had turned up, mainly, so he told himself, to see Duckworth make a mess of the team. And John considered he had gone a long way towards it for he had missed two catches already, and if the Reverend Collins stayed in, there was every likelihood of him missing more. The parson might look like a reed but he was swinging his bat like a seasoned player. He wasn't playing to hold the side; he was playing for runs. John watched Joe Anderson bowl a loping overarm and said to himself, 'That one's asking to be bashed.' And it was bashed. The Reverend Collins took such a swipe at it that for a moment he appeared to be airborne. As the ball soared upwards, the crowd gave a concerted 'Ooh' and at the same time the Member's voice came through the open windows of the hall asking earnestly, 'Now, any more questions?' It was at this exact moment that it happened.

John saw it coming; he put up his hand to try and stop it. He remembered blinking his eyes rapidly and then . . . bang. It was as if someone had hit him in the face with his own shovel. One instant he had been looking at a level green with white-clad figures dotted here and there, the next instant the white-clad figures were revolving in green circles, each one separate from his fellow, and rising with terrific speed heavenwards. In a strange flat silence, John watched them go, and just when he thought they were about to disappear, they began their return journey. But they came down more slowly than they had gone up and not until the field had settled itself level once more was he able to hear anything. And then, as if a switch had been released inside his head, he was almost deafened by the roar of voices and he was certainly bewildered by the swarm of faces all flooding round him.

'Are you all right?'

'Look at the lump rising.'

'Get back and give him air.'

'Where's Mrs Gascoigne?'

'Did he faint?'

'It was enough to brain him.'

'Dear, dear, dear. Oh, I am sorry. Come along try to stand.' It was the Reverend Collins' concerned voice.

John blinked up at the thin face bending over him then he put his hand up towards his head. It seemed to be expanding at least a foot on each side of him.

'It's bound to be very painful. Come into the hall.'

John felt the Reverend pulling him up from the seat and, when another voice bawled over his head in pompous tones, 'I'll see to him, he's a neighbour of mine. Come on, John, up you get', John thrust out his arms and almost pushed Henry Duckworth on his back; he was saved only by the press of people around him. Then, depending on the sole support of the minister, John set out on very unsteady legs towards the hall.

The Member of Parliament himself was waiting on the veranda and he tut-tut-tutted at the sight of John's steadily rising forehead, and his voice was most kind and solicitous when he said, 'Good gracious, you have caught it. I think it would be wise to see a doctor.' He looked at the faces about him. 'Is there one in the village?'

'No!' It was a chorus from all sides. 'Dr Sanderson's on holiday and Dr Spencer only comes on Tuesdays and Fridays.'

'Cold water compresses, that's all that needs.' It was Mr Duckworth again to the fore. 'I've sent for his wife.'

'Damn and set fire to it, what do you want to go and do that for? You'll scare the wits out of her. Bloody silly thing to do.' There was no tremor resulting from shock in John's voice. His tone was firm and his voice louder than he had ever heard himself use in public. 'And look,' he addressed those about him, 'get on with the game and leave me in peace, will you.'

There was a look of sheer relief on the Reverend's face as he bent over John. 'You feel all right, Mr Gascoigne?'

'Yes, I'm all right, sir,' said John.

Slowly, somewhat reluctantly, the crowd dispersed.

'He's all right.'

'Take something to knock him out.'

'Be in the papers the morrow "Parson hits gravedigger on conk. Gravedigger conks out."'

At this, laughter burst out and spread, at least among those outside the hall and on the veranda. Here, surrounding the Member, everything was decorous and this gentleman turned and looked at John and remarked pleasantly, 'So you're a gravedigger?' and John, returning his look with a steady stare, replied, 'Aye, and you're a Member of Parliament?' Now there was a titter among the elite and the Member actually laughed and said, 'Yes, I'm a Member of Parliament.'

'I've been wanting to talk to you.'

'Yes?'

'Yes.'

'Well, here I am. What do you want to talk about?'

'I've been wanting to ask you a question.'

The Member seated himself opposite John and said in a conciliatory tone, 'Well, fire ahead. Although, if I was in your position I'd be wanting to hold my head.'

A great many ha-ha-ha's met this witticism. Only John didn't laugh. His head felt big, about twice its normal size at least, but it wasn't aching; nor did the lump on his brow feel sore, which, he commented in an aside to himself, was very odd to say the least after the bash he had got. His head must have been knocked so numb that he wasn't feeling anything yet. That would come, but at present he felt all right, and strangely enough, rather perky.

'Well, what was it you wanted to ask me?' The Member's voice was jovial.

'About this St Christopher business.' John was leaning forward, his look intent and his voice crisp.

'St Christopher business?' The Member cast a swift glance at those about him. Nobody had mentioned anything about St Christopher to him. Was it the name of a guild or association? The fellow seemed very much in earnest; he must walk warily. 'What about the St Christopher business?'

'What about it?' repeated John. 'Accidents every week at the crossroads – two people killed recently and t'others injured. And you say what about it?' John paused but no one spoke, not a word, but every eye was on him and this strangely enough intimidated him not the slightest, so he went on. 'I saw the two dead meself, and the cars mangled and motorbikes up trees and all decorated with this St Christopher.'

'Ahh.' The Member of Parliament was beginning to see, even if vaguely. It was the St Christopher medal the fellow was on about and the Member, being more sagacious than most people would have given him credit for, thought, 'That ball has knocked him silly or else he's probing something a little beyond village depth.' And, as he continued to look at John, he felt inclined to give him the benefit of the latter impression for it was quite obvious that the company was all for the 'knocked silly' version, judging from the tittering and grins and smothered laughter around him.

'You see what I mean, don't you?' John was experiencing a feeling of elation for he saw that the Member was with him, and if the Member was with him, what did it matter what this lot of dizzy-lizzies and their menfolk thought? He knew them all for what they were worth. But the Member knew what he was getting at . . . Aye, he knew.

'Something should be done high up; it's a racket. You can go into a shop and buy this piece of tin and then it's "I'm all right, chum, 'cos look what I'm carrying . . . a saint. God's on my side, you go and climb a tree." And that's what happens in the end – somebody does climb a tree.'

The laughter now bounced off the wooden stays of the hall roof and it was joined by a wave from the veranda, which had suddenly become thickly populated. The Member was uneasy; he wanted to take this matter seriously, but it was quite evident it was a huge joke to everyone else in the room, a joke that was the outcome of a cricket ball bouncing off the head of a gravedigger. But he felt he owed it to the man before him to let him understand that he saw his point and he said just that.

'I see your point.'

'You do?' John's eyes were actually sparkling. Now . . . now let them laugh . . . the numbskulls.

'Yes . . . Yes, I do.' But what the Member was going to do about the matter at this point he didn't know. To answer the questions of this intense gravedigger could only be done after some reading up and quite a deal of thought. He knew nothing about St Christopher other than that there was supposed to be a charm in carrying him around with you. The Member blushed inwardly; he had a St Christopher ensconced, if inconspicuously, in his own car. True, he had been put there by his wife . . .

'Well?' John was waiting.

But the Member was saved further embarrassment by the crowd suddenly shuffling to make way for someone coming through. It was Florrie.

'Oh, John, what a sight.' Her voice was pitying and she put her hand waveringly towards his head only to have him turn on her somewhat impatiently and exclaim, 'I'm all right. Look, leave me be.'

'Come on home.'

'I'm all right, I tell you. I'm talking to the gentleman here.' He nodded to the Member, who had now risen to his feet.

'I think you should take your wife's advice . . . not because I want to shelve this matter. No, no, not at all.' The Member wagged his finger down at John. 'It's a very interesting point you've raised and when I'm next in the district we must get down to it in earnest. Eh?'

John, feeling now that he was being bulked at, repeated firmly, 'But I'm all right.'

'Ah . . . You might think so now, but when the reaction sets in you'll go flat. I've seen it afore.' It was Mr Duckworth making himself heard again, and John turning on him angrily said, 'Oh, you an' what you've seen and what you haven't seen. Why aren't you on the field finishing the mess you started?'

'John, John.' Florrie was both startled and worried. The ball must have knocked him silly to go on like that. She gripped his arm firmly and pulled him to his feet saying, 'You're comin' home and this minute.'

Resisting for a moment, John drew in a long breath then, sighing, he turned to the Member and said, 'Thank you, sir, at least you knew what I was getting at.'

'Yes, yes, I did . . . I . . . I do. And we'll take it up another time, I promise you. Goodbye, goodbye.'

'Goodbye, sir.'

The crowd parted and became silent as Florrie led John onto the veranda and down the steps, and he made no attempt to release himself from the embarrassing position for his mind seemed elsewhere. That is until they reached the bottom step and Broderick. Broderick stood dead in front of them and his gaze became fixed on a point about the middle of John's eyes as he exclaimed in awe, 'God in heaven, but isn't that a shiner. It's a wonder it didn't kill you stone dead, John.'

'Well, it didn't,' John growled. 'And that, no doubt, you'll think a pity . . . Out of me way.' He gestured Broderick aside with a wave of his arm, then pulling his other arm from Florrie's grasp, he added, 'And I can walk, I'm not drunk.'

Florrie could only stare at her husband in utter amazement. The quicker she got him home and to bed, the better. She gave Broderick an apologetic shake of her head which meant 'Take no notice', and Broderick, nodding back and intending to be helpful, said airily, 'I'm makin' me way home. I'll walk alongside of you, John; you might need a hand.'

John stopped dead. 'If you as much as put a finger on me, McNally, I'll lay you out, and mind I'm tellin' you.'

As Broderick's head went back to let out a bellow of laughter, Florrie grasped the front of her dress in agitation. Something terrible had happened to her John. She had never heard him talk that way in her life before. Whatever he thought of Broderick he had always managed to keep it to himself.

'Begod, it's taken a cricket ball to loosen your tongue, John, just a little cricket ball.' Broderick was shaking with his mirth. 'Begod, if I'd known that was all it needed, I'd have bounced one off your napper years ago . . . Aw, it's good to hear you retaliate at last, John.'

John forced himself to turn away from Broderick. It had always been a struggle for him to retort to Broderick's quips but now he was finding he had his work cut out to stop himself from lashing out at his neighbour, not only with his tongue but with his fists. He hastened to lengthen the distance between them.

Florrie, almost trotting to keep up with him, exclaimed anxiously, 'Are you feeling bad, John?'

'No, I'm not feeling bad.' John suddenly stopped, and swinging round, shouted at Broderick, 'And you, McNally, stop creeping along behind me if you know what's good for you, for I neither need your assistance nor your presence.'

As John marched on again, Florrie cast a glance that held an appeal for understanding back at Broderick and he signalled to her with a wave of his ham-like hand that he wasn't in the least insulted. His face bore this out for it was one great, amused grin, and he indicated to her that he would return to the cricket field for very obviously his assistance, as John had intimated, wasn't required.

As they neared home, Florrie was thankful for one thing: the street was quiet. There was nobody about . . . except Gran, who was waiting at the gate.

Although Gran's words of greeting were merely an obvious statement, they seemed to carry a trace of disappointment in them. 'You're on your feet then . . . you're not laid out?' she said.

'You another one wantin' to see me on me back? I'll buy a coffin and have meself delivered to the door for you, if that'll please you.'

Perhaps for the first time in her life, Gran could find nothing to say; not only had her son's words surprised her into silence, but the look of him was causing her some private speculation. Not merely the enormous bump on his forehead, but the expression in his eyes. Their look was no longer veiled or illusive, but was direct and alert. It was a look she had never before seen on her son's face.

She allowed him and Florrie to go on up the path for some distance before she turned and followed them into the house. She was further astounded when on entering the kitchen she saw John standing near the sink patting his wife's hand as he said in a quiet, even a soothing tone, 'Look, lass, there's nothing to worry about. I'm all right. If you feel it's got to be bathed, I'll bathe it, but I haven't got a pain or a headache. In fact, I've never felt so well in my life, and that's what it is.'

Gran watched as her son straightened up and, blinking, swiftly looked around the room as if this last statement had been made by someone else and had come as news to him. There was something funny here. Patting Florrie's hand in public, calling her lass in that voice and saying he'd never felt better in his life. Definitely there was something funny here . . . fishy. This wasn't the man she had reared, and if anybody should know him, she should. He had annoyed her almost from the day he was born, with that cool, calculating, summing-up kind of look that got under her skin. He had never spoken a word until he was turned three and then seemingly with reluctance, and this reluctance to talk had kept up all his life. It was really the main reason for her dislike of him, for dislike him she did. She often thought he could be a son-in-law such was her feeling for him. That she liked her daughter-in-law better than her son didn't trouble her. Didn't the majority care for people that were no blood bond to them more than they did any member of their family? Take the case of husbands. You married a man you didn't know anything about. In the same way you could hate your nearest kin because you knew too much about them. Aye, even your own flesh. No, she saw nothing unusual about disliking her son. But this wasn't the son she knew.

'Let me get the doctor.'

'I don't want the doctor. I don't feel ill, lass.' Now John turned from Florrie and addressed his mother, looking her full in the face as he did so. 'Do I look ill, Mother?'

It was some seconds before Gran answered. She stared hard at her son then moving her jaw bone rapidly back and forward she exclaimed truthfully, 'I don't know what you look like and that's the truth.'

As Gran sat down there came the sound of running feet up the back path and the next minute Frankie was in the room. He stopped just within the doorway and brought out on a gasp, 'They said . . .'

'Well, no matter what they said,' put in John quickly. 'I'm neither dead, daft nor drunk. I've been hit with a cricket ball and in spite of what it looks like, I haven't got a headache and I don't feel bad. Now is there anything else you would like to know?'

His mouth hanging, Frankie stared at his father. Florrie was standing behind John and she went into her signalling act, and whether it was in obedience to the signal or he was too surprised to make any comment, he let his father pass him and go out of the room, and not until there came the sound of the bedroom door banging overhead did he speak. Then he asked in an awed whisper, 'Are you going to get the doctor, Mam?'

Florrie, going to the table and sitting down and looking at Gran, said, 'I don't know what to do. I've never seen him like this before. Have you, Gran?'

'No,' said Gran truthfully.

Frankie came and stood close to his mother and, still in an undertone, he said, 'They're on about it round the green, Mam. I hadn't been to the match; I was at Norton's garage looking at the cycles when Tim Brown came by on his bike and said Dad had been hit, and when I was passing the green they were standing in groups laughing their heads off. Uncle Brod was one of them and he was roaring because some fella was saying that Dad had asked the Member of Parliament what he was going to do about St Christopher.' Frankie's voice dropped to a whisper, 'They were repeating the same things what he said to me last night. Mam . . . do you think he's going . . . ?'

'No, he's not and don't say such a thing.' Florrie was on her feet. 'Just because he said something that other people hadn't thought about doesn't mean he's going off his head and don't you dare suggest any such thing, Frankie Gascoigne.' Florrie's voice was rising and Frankie turned away muttering, 'All right, Mam, don't you start going for me an' all.'

As Florrie bounced towards the stove to put the kettle on, Gran looked towards her and exclaimed, 'Well, he may or he may not be going off his head, but there's one thing I do know and I know for sure, he's not himself, not if I know him, he's not . . . But what did I tell you this mornin'? Something's gonna happen, I said, didn't I? And I'll tell you something more now . . . This is only the start, mark my words.'

Frankie, after giving his grannie one long, baffled look, went to the mantel and rested his head against it. 'Coo . . .' he said.

When John went upstairs, he had no intention of lying down. He did not feel very sleepy, far from it, he felt . . . boiled up. Boiled up against everybody in general but against his mother and Broderick McNally in particular. It was a shame to waste two houses between the two of them he thought . . . Laid out . . . he was far from being laid out and he would let them see this an' all.

He sat down on the edge of the bed to take off his shoes, then, getting up and walking in his stockinged feet towards the dressing table, he surveyed for the first time the lump on his forehead and was made to comment to himself, 'By gum, but it is a size an' all . . . no mistake.'

He touched it and felt no pain. That was odd. He had had bashes on his head before today and they had all, he remembered, been painful; but this bump had not even given him a slight headache. He was beginning to be puzzled by this and he asked himself what he felt like, but he did not give himself the answer until he was sitting on the bed again, and then with the palms of his hands cupping his knees and his eyes staring down at the floor, he nodded as he remarked inwardly, 'I feel fine, never better, I feel . . .'

He couldn't for the moment explain exactly how he felt. There was a lightness about his head that hadn't been there this morning and a sort of brightness and airiness over the whole of his body. He knew that he was thinking more swiftly than was usual and, moreover, his thoughts were more . . . gettable. He hadn't to grope at his mind for an explanation. It was there. This feeling undoubtedly was the cause of him going off at both McNally and his mother. He wondered if it would stay or would it subside with the lump. Slowly, he lay back on the bed and rested his head on his joined hands, and he discovered that he liked feeling this way – alive and alert, and ready on the uptake. He had always envied people who were ready on the uptake.

At what point he fell asleep he didn't know but when he felt Florrie's hand on his shoulder and her voice saying gently, 'John, John, are you all right?' he opened his eyes slowly and looked at her and then he did a strange thing for he said, 'Yes, I'm all right, Florrie.'

This simple answer proved to Florrie once and for all that her John wasn't all right. His usual response if she should waken him would be a grunt; and if she said 'Time to get up, John', his reply was invariably 'Um . . . right', and sometimes it was just the 'Um'. Not that this terseness meant anything – she knew her John – but the smile that now lit up his face took her back to the early years of their marriage when even then such a smile was a rare thing. She was more upset by the smile than if he had sat up abruptly and sworn at her.

'What's the time?' He was stretching his arms above his head as she gazed at him in bewilderment.

'Nine o'clock,' she said.

His mouth stopped in the middle of a yawn and with his arms still upraised he said, 'Nine o'clock! Have I been asleep since this afternoon?'

She nodded but said nothing as she watched him swing his legs jauntily off the bed.

'Well, I can't remember ever doing that afore . . . and you know something, I'm hungry . . . starving.'

'Your supper's ready.' Florrie spoke quietly and, as she turned to go, he reached out and grabbed her arm and, pulling her to face him, he said, 'What's troubling you?'

As she looked at him, Florrie could not prevent the tremor that came into her voice. 'You are, John. What's wrong? It happened afore you got this knock on your head.' She looked at the lump where it jutted from his forehead, dark and sore-looking. 'There was something wrong with you last night, John.'

'Wrong with me?' he asked in surprise. 'Last night? What was wrong with me last night?'

She dropped her eyes as she said, 'Well, going on at Frankie like that and about this St Christopher.'

'Oh, St Christopher.' For a moment he had forgotten about St Christopher and now that he was reminded of him again he thought, 'Aye that's still got to be looked into.' But he said to Florrie, 'Just because I bring up a subject that should be looked into you think there is something wrong with me. That's daft, clean daft.'

'But, John, you never talk, not to the others you don't. You used to, to me a bit when we were on our own, but of late years you've stopped even doing that. And then to burst out like you did last night, and then today outside the hall to turn on Broderick like a wild man; and then your mother. It isn't you. You've got me worried, John.'

'Huh.' The laughter was even in his eyes as he took her by the shoulders and gave her a little shake. 'Because I start talking I've got you worried. Well, I hope I give you nothing more than that to worry about, lass. Come on, let's have that supper.'

Instead of this attitude of John's putting Florrie at her ease, it did just the opposite. She didn't know this reasonable, plausible being, this being who smiled at her when he talked. There was as much difference between this man and the John she knew as between a man in his sober senses and the same man mortal drunk. They were the same, yet not the same.

When, on entering the kitchen, John saw, already sitting at the table, Arthur and Frankie beside Gran and Linda, he exclaimed aloud, 'Well, well! Nine o'clock on a Saturday night and we're all at home.'

That John should show surprise was quite in order for it was a most unusual thing to see the two boys in before eleven at the earliest on a Saturday night; but there they were and not saying a word because his greeting had dumbfounded them. It was, Arthur commented to himself, as Gran had just a moment before said: the ball had certainly gone to his dad's head.

In spite of having heard of the reception Gran had received when commiserating with his father – commiserating was the word used when Gran was telling her tale – Arthur felt that it was expected of him to enquire how he was feeling now, so when John was seated in his place he looked towards him and asked, 'How you feeling, Dad?'

'I'm feeling very well, Arthur.'

The answer had been neither a brief 'All right' or an explosive 'Now don't start that again' but a reply that was both pleasant in voice and context. 'I'm feeling all right, Arthur.' It just didn't fit in – so thought the entire family in their varying ways.

'What was the result of the match?' John was looking towards Frankie, but Frankie at this moment had his eyes cast downwards to his plate and, not expecting a direct question from his father, he did not naturally reply.

'I'm asking you a question.'

'What, me, Dad?' Frankie's head bounced up.

'Well, I'm looking at you, lad. It could be that I'm as bats as you are all thinking I am and that I'm really talking to McNally next door.'

Arthur, suddenly seeing the funny side of the situation, choked on his food and Frankie, giving a self-conscious titter, said, 'We . . . we lost. They declared at two nine seven.'

At this moment Linda, lifting her gaze from her plate, said to her mother, 'Will you take off the ham, Mam? I just want salad.'

As Florrie complied with her daughter's wishes, John looked at Linda and remarked, 'It's a very nice piece of ham. Your mother always boils a nice piece of ham.'

'God in heaven.' All eyes lifted from John to Gran, but Gran's eyes were raised ceilingward, and she exclaimed mournfully, 'The world's coming to an end, I know it . . . Even praising the bacon.'

John, leaning towards his mother, his expression now serious but not grim, was about to retort to her quip, when his attention was caught by someone moving about in the back garden. From his position in relation to the window, the intruder was in a line with his shoulder, which meant that he must be standing dead in the middle of his potatoes. This fact brought John, almost in a jump, to his feet and he rushed towards the sink and, bending over it, peered out of the window. The light was beginning to fade and the garden was bathed in a pinkish afterglow that softened all its outlines and gave to the whole a matt effect, and there, in the middle of it, dead in the middle of it, in fact, as he had surmised, right in the centre of his potato patch, was McNally. He was taking large cautious steps; and for why? Because he was dressed up in a long white sheet with a broom shank in his hand. And he was making for the side of the house.

'By damned, he'll not get away with that.' All John's suave serenity had vanished as if it had been stripped off him by lightning. 'Get off there, you silly swine.'

As he bawled through the window, Florrie, standing at his side now, cried, 'What is it? What's the matter?'

John, flinging himself round from the sink and striding towards the back door, shouted at her, 'See for yourself – McNally trying to take a rise out of me. Dressed up in a sheet. By God, I'd know him atween the sheets however he tries to hide himself.'

'Dad, Dad, wait a minute.' Arthur caught hold of his arm.

'Leave be!'

'Look, Dad, keep your temper. He likes it when you lose your temper. You'd get one over on him if you'd laugh at him.'

John, pulling himself from Arthur's grasp, said, 'I'll laugh at him. I've stood enough of him for years. It's about time he saw who he's up against.'

Except for Gran, who was standing calmly within the frame of the back porch, the whole family was now on the garden path, but not one of them could see a sign of Broderick anywhere.

'He's run indoors like a scalded cat,' John cried, and made his way on the side path towards the fence. Leaning over it, he shouted in the direction of McNally's back door, 'If you want to play games, McNally, I'll play with you any time you like. Just name it.'

'John, for God's sake, come inside; you'll have the street out.' Florrie was hanging onto his arm now and Arthur coaxed, 'Dad, look, there's nobody here, perhaps you imagined . . .'

John turned to Arthur with a ferocity that brought at least one member of the family some satisfaction, for Frankie grinned when his father bellowed at Arthur, 'Now don't you start on the imagination stunt. Don't tell me I'm seeing things. I saw McNally in the garden with a sheet on him and a broom shank in his hand, so don't you . . .'

'Is anything the matter?' It was Katie standing on her doorstep with her son, Pat, behind her.

'Get McNally to come out here. I want him.'

Pat, stepping before his mother, asked in a voice that held the same laughing quality prominent in his father's, 'Is anything wrong, Uncle?'

'You tell your father to come out here.'

'But me dad's not in – he's down at the club.'

'Don't stand there lying to me. He's had time to get the sheet off himself now. Tell him to come out here.'

'It's the God's truth he's tellin' you, John,' said Katie. 'Brod's been down at the club these two hours and more.'

'He might have been at the club but he's back here somewhere. He sneaked through this garden just a minute ago dressed up in a sheet.'

'In the name of God,' exclaimed Katie. 'And what would he be in a sheet for, and him neither dead nor in bed?'

'He was in a sheet,' exclaimed John slowly and definitely, 'because he was trying to take a rise out of me. All because I asked a question of the Member the day concerning this St Christopher business. So he gets himself dressed up like the figure on the medals with the intention of taking a rise out of me and giving himself a helluva laugh.'

'In the name of God,' said Katie again. 'You're not yourself.'

'John, John, I beg you, come away indoors will you?' Florrie now was in tears and Frankie, taking her arm and trying to pull her from his father's side, whispered, 'Leave him be. Come inside and he'll come out of it.'

'You come out with another crack like that and you won't live long enough to come out of it.'

Once started on the hapless Frankie, it was evident he was going to continue, but Frankie was saved for the moment by Katie's remark of, 'It's the clout on the head that's done it. I'd go to me bed, John; it'll likely be days afore you're right again.'

John turned round and faced Katie. He looked at her steadily for a moment across the garden, then he closed his eyes before lowering his head and turning away. But as he neared the porch and Gran, he raised his head again and gave her a look that said, 'You open your mouth and I'll gallop plumb down your throat.'

On reaching the kitchen again, John went straight to the chair that he had left a few minutes earlier, and sitting down he waited until the family were all once more in the room. Then, placing his outspread hand with a plomp on the table, he swept them all with his eyes before saying, 'I was sitting here, wasn't I?'

No one spoke.

'I was sitting here and I happened to look out of the window.' He indicated the window. 'And there I saw McNally – don't tell me I don't know McNally – and he was creeping this way, planting his big feet atween me tatie rows. He had loped over the railings thinking to make his way down to the kitchen door here without being seen. But I spoilt his little game.'

'John, come on up to bed.'

'I am not going to bed, Florrie.' Each word carried emphasis. 'And what, may I ask, are you cryin' for?'

Before Florrie could clear her throat to answer, Gran's voice came from the back door saying, 'You're sure 'twas McNally you saw?'

'Are you trying to get me goat, Mother?'

'No, I'm not trying to get your goat or anything of the sort. Why should I when McNally has already done it? But McNally, as you say, has big feet, and if he was stepping in atween the taties there's bound to be evidence of it for the ground's soft after last night's rain, but there's not as much as a fly's footprint on the soil. And what's more you banked them up this mornin' and they're still banked up, grain on top of grain.'

John rose slowly to his feet and the look he gave his mother should have shrivelled her up.

'Go and look for yourself.'

John did not move. He knew he was being challenged and there was a very odd feeling travelling round the perimeter of his stomach. It was something very akin to fear. If it was as she said . . . But it couldn't be . . . He *had* seen McNally in a sheet with a stick in his hand. If he hadn't seen his face it could have been anybody else trying to take a rise out of him, but it was McNally. Yet the thought suddenly prodded him. Say, for argument's sake, that it wasn't McNally and it was somebody else, there would still have to be footprints in the rows between the taties to prove . . .

The odd feeling was now in the centre of his stomach, and it told him to take no notice of his mother but to go on upstairs and let her talk.

He moved, but it was towards the kitchen door. He walked steadily up the garden path knowing that the eyes of his family were watching him from the kitchen window, and when he came opposite the potato patch his steps became slower; and as he looked along each row, the sweat began to break out on him and for a moment he felt sick. The rows were as he had left them last night, as his mother had said, grain on top of grain, weed-free and symmetrical as he liked to have them. He forced himself to walk down the path again and into the kitchen and his legs almost gave way before he reached the chair. Florrie was waiting for him and she eased him down as if he was a sick old man and Arthur, handing him a glass, said, 'Here, have this drop of whisky, Dad.' And Linda, who had joined Florrie now in the weeping, kept exclaiming, 'Oh, Dad; oh, Dad.' Only Frankie and Gran said nothing. That is until John, dazedly raising his hand, moved a finger slowly round the lump on his head, and then Gran said pertly, 'Now perhaps you'll stop being so pig-headed and let her get you the doctor.'

John made no retort. He was feeling better than he had ever done in his life before, more alive, and yet there was something wrong. He was deeply shaken by the experience, but even so, somewhere inside, a voice was telling him that if he was going out of his mind, there was nothing at all to worry about; it would be a very refreshing experience, for hadn't he already admitted to himself that he had never felt so good before? But although this voice was glib and confident it brought him no comfort or even strength at the moment, and like a man in a daze he allowed himself to be led upstairs to bed, Florrie on one side of him and Arthur on the other.

It was a queer Sunday morning; John lay in bed even though the urge in him was strong to get up and go out. Yet he lay on, for the doctor was expected around about eleven. This visit was causing John almost as much concern as the memory of last night. He didn't like doctors; the only time he had been examined by a doctor, as far as he knew, was when he joined the army. He had a healthy man's dread of them, and consequently illness. And what was he to tell him anyway when he did come . . . that he had seen St Christopher running about in his tatie bed? Should he admit as much he felt he would be locked up for sure. But he had seen someone; with his own two eyes he had seen a figure moving across the garden. He turned his head on the pillow, drew in a deep breath, and tried to shut out the memory.

He became aware of the Sunday morning sounds downstairs. The oven door banging, and Linda's voice droning on in low tones, stopping only when his mother's voice pierced the floor, as if she was sending her words riding on pointed darts up through the boards. Then there were the church bells, and lastly there were the usual noises coming from the McNallys. A babble of voices with Katie's shrill laugh and Broderick's deep bellow rising above them. How was he going to have the nerve to look that fellow in the face again? He could almost hear Broderick's greeting: 'So you took me for a saint? Begod, I knew the good in me would make itself known to you someday.' Aw, he knew McNally's quips off by heart.

There were footsteps on the landing, the door opened and Arthur came in. 'Mam says you wanted to see me, Dad.'

John hitched himself up on his pillow and said, 'Yes . . . Yes, as I can't get out, we might as well have our chat up here.'

Arthur stood by the bedside looking down at his father and his feet and hands moved restlessly for a moment before he said, 'Mam says I haven't got to keep you talking.'

'Oh, for the Lord's sake.' John closed his eyes, then said in desperation, 'Sit down.'

When Arthur had brought a chair up to the bedside, John leant towards him and with his voice low and intent he went on, 'Whatever happened last night, and mind I'm not denying something did happen, I know it only too well, but whatever it was, it hasn't affected me brain. What I mean to say is, it hasn't turned it. I may be seeing things but I'm not doolally.'

'No, Dad, no. Of course you're not. It's likely due to concussion.'

John lay back and repeated, 'Aye, concussion, that's about it. Well, let's forget it for the time being and tell me what you wanted to see me about.'

Arthur looked everywhere but at his father, and John, aiming to be helpful, whispered, 'Come on, spit it out, afore I do it for you.'

'It's awkward, Dad.'

'What's awkward? That you don't want to go through with it? Not just putting it off, you don't want to marry her. That's it, isn't it?'

Arthur was looking fully at his father now and he nodded eagerly, yet somewhat shamefacedly, as he said, 'Yes, that's about it. I just don't want to go through with it.'

'Well, how do you propose getting out of it? It's going to be a damn sight harder getting out than it was getting in, mind that.'

'Don't I know it.'

'You won't only be slighting her, it's the other pair you've got to reckon with. Duckworth will take this as a personal insult. As I see him, he'll do everything in his power to keep you to your word. As for her, she's the kind that'll do a breach of promise on you without winking and she'll be ably supported by both of them. You've got yourself into a jam, boy.'

'I know, Dad, and . . .' Arthur chewed on his lip and hung his head as he muttered, 'And that's not all.'

'No?' said John enquiringly. Then he added, 'You're thinking about your job?'

'Not the job.'

'Not the job? Then what?' John was leaning forward a little, and he asked very quietly, 'Somebody else?'

Arthur nodded and John sighed and remarked, 'Well, this is a kettle of fish – who is it? Do I know her?'

Again Arthur nodded, a reluctant nod this time, and John began to think rapidly of the girls in the village round about Arthur's age, any one of whom he considered would be a better match for him than the Duckworth miss. 'Well, as you've told me so much, you'd better tell me the rest.'

'It's awkward, Dad, seeing how you feel.'

'Seeing how I feel?' John repeated slowly. 'What's that got to do with it?'

'What I mean to say is . . .' Arthur paused then stumbled on, his eyes still downcast. 'Well, you don't get on with them.'

John peered at his son. 'Who . . . who don't I get on with?'

Arthur's eyes indicating their neighbours to the right caused John to think, 'The McNallys? But what had the McNallys to do with this?' And then the answer struck him like a blow . . . Moira, that damned little bust-pushing piece. 'No. Oh no.' The last no was a deep growl somewhere in the depths of his stomach and when Arthur muttered apologetically, 'I can't help it, Dad, it's been working up for a long time,' John said in a loud, harsh whisper, 'You won't do it. You won't marry into that family; I just couldn't stand it. I would go round the bend then, and no mistake.'

'But you can't stand Duckworth either, Dad,' said Arthur, now slightly on the defensive.

'No, I can't, can you? But Duckworth's one thing and McNally another, quite another. The Duckworths would leave us alone because we're inferior – at least they think so – but not the McNallys. Once we're connected . . . Once you're linked with the McNallys, there'll never be another minute's peace in this house. They'll spread over us like locusts. It's only me stonewall attitude over the past years that's kept them on the right side of me door. No, Arthur' – he gripped Arthur's joined hands – 'don't do this, lad.'

'But, Dad, I'm mad about her, I can't get her out of me mind.'

'You mean you can't get her bust out of yer mind.'

Arthur was on his feet now. 'That's a rotten dirty thing to say, Dad.'

'Aye it might be, but it's true.'

'No, it isn't. She's got a figure, admitted, and is that anything to be ashamed of? But there's more to it than that. She's got something in her, has Moira, and what's more, she's kind.'

John sighed and dropped his chin on his chest, but it was no sooner there than it was up again and thrust outwards, as were his ears, for through the open bedroom window came the sound of Broderick's voice saying in what was supposed to be an undertone, 'Now, Florrie, what would I be wantin' rompin' round the block covered in a sheet or me nightshirt – which, by the way, I don't have as I sleep in my pelt – just to put the wind up John? Now what would I be wantin' to do that for, Florrie?'

Only the mumble of Florrie's reply reached the room, and while John was endeavouring to catch Arthur's averted glance to say silently, 'See what I mean?', Broderick's voice came again saying, 'Yes, yes, I understand, Florrie. A blow like that was enough to knock his brains out. Some people go on seeing stars among other things for days and days on end. It's a well-known reaction. I remember a mate of mine once, he slipped and ran his head into a pick, the pointed end, poor sod. Fell right on it, he did. You know that fellow saw cats flying in the air until the day he died. It was likely because it was to avoid bringing the pick down on a fleeing cat that he got it in the head himself. There's a connection, you see? It's likely the same way with John . . . Would you like me to go and have a word with him, Florrie . . . give him a laugh?'

As Florrie's quick reply of 'No, no thanks, Broderick, the doctor's on his way' reached the bedroom, John said softly, 'Do you see what I mean? Pretending to sympathise and all the time aggravatin' and suggestin'.'

'But, Dad, it's only his devilment,' whispered Arthur.

'I'm well aware of that, Arthur, and it's just his devilment that I can't stomach, and if you don't want me to leave me job and this village, forget about his girl. Anyway' – John gave a violent hitch to his hips and almost lifted himself onto the pillows – 'why am I worryin', I can't see what's going to get you loose from the Duckworths, except a miracle.'

As Arthur turned without a word and went out of the room, John lay back and repeated slowly to himself, 'Except a miracle.' And as he lay, he kept thinking of the phrase. 'Except a miracle.' Miracles were funny things. He knew he had it in his power to perform one for Arthur. But in the end would Arthur thank him? There was a question here that no one could answer but Arthur himself. But who would have to pay for the miracle . . . Florrie . . . and Florrie wasn't paying anymore. She'd paid enough.

The doctor came at half past eleven. John had never seen him before nor had the doctor seen John because he was new to the district, having been in the practice as assistant to Dr Sanderson only a matter of months. He was young and had a brusque manner and this particular morning was in a bit of a temper, for Florrie's call had broken into his arrangement for a game of golf. Yet it was evident right away that he was impressed with the size of the lump on John's head, and as he pressed his fingers gently round it he muttered, more as a matter of course than as a question, 'Sore?'

'No,' said John.

'Not sore, a lump like this?' He went on moving his fingers. 'Is it sore there?'

'No.'

'Not there?'

'No, it's not sore anywhere.'

The doctor straightened his back and looked hard at John. 'You have a headache, I suppose?'

'No, I haven't a headache.'

'Did you have one yesterday after it happened?'

'No, I didn't, nor since. I've neither pain nor ache in me head.'

This fellow, the doctor considered, was either a liar or he had been knocked so silly he couldn't feel anything. He dismissed the latter idea. He half closed his eyes now as he looked at John and said, 'Well, if you've neither ache nor pain you must be very tough. You've likely inherited a tough constitution from your country forebears.'

'I wasn't born in the country.'

'No?'

'No, I was born in Howden on the North Tyne. I've only been in the village a short time . . . sixteen years.'

The doctor raised his eyebrows as he commented to himself, a short time, only sixteen years. At least the fellow had imbibed one thing from his sojourn in the country – the insignificance of time. 'Here, put this in your mouth.' He gave the thermometer a shake before sticking it between John's lips, then sitting down by the side of the bed he felt his pulse. In a few minutes it was clear to him that both pulse and temperature were perfectly normal. He wiped the thermometer and placed it in his case on the foot of the bed, then he blew his nose, after which he gave his attention to his case again, and while he straightened an odd thing here and there, he remarked, 'Your wife was telling me you had a rather distressing experience last night.'

John said nothing.

'Is that so?' His medical case closed now and standing upright on the bed, the doctor leant his elbow on it, rested his chin in his hand and tapped one finger slowly at his lips as he asked, 'Tell me, as clearly as you remember, what you saw.'

John returned the youthful, penetrating stare as he said slowly, 'I saw a man in my garden in a white gown, or perhaps it was a sheet over him, and he had a stick in his hand.'

The doctor nodded slowly. 'You thought you saw a man in a white gown with a stick in his hand?'

'I didn't think I saw,' put in John quickly. 'I know I saw somebody there.'

The doctor dropped his head back between his shoulders, he looked up at the ceiling, he looked to the right of him and then to the left of him before once again looking at John. 'You've been concerned lately about these St Christopher medals people carry about with them, haven't you?'

'Yes, I have.'

'Well then, can't you see the connection? You get a blow on the head and things that have been troubling you acquire gigantic proportion; they even take on a form of reality. The figure that you saw last night was merely a figment of your imagination. It's nothing to worry about, it will pass as your head gets better.'

'My head isn't bad.' John now leant towards the doctor and said under his breath, 'Believe me, doctor, I have neither ache nor pain and I'm going to tell you this, I've never felt better in me life.'

The doctor's expression did not change, but his eyes slid down corner-wise as if he was observing some strange manoeuvre on the eiderdown. After a moment he said, 'That's good then.' But his tone did not imply that there was anything good in it. It rather gave the impression that the situation was anything but right and his next words bore out this impression, for rising to his feet and picking up his case he said, 'You must take it easy. Stay where you are until the end of the week. Say Friday when I take surgery here, then toddle along and I'll have a look at you again. All right?'

'I'm going to work the morrow.'

'Well, if that's the case, then you can't hold me responsible for anything that happens, can you?'

'No, that's fair enough.'

The doctor gave his patient one last look and marched out, closing the door none too gently after him.

Florrie was waiting anxiously for him at the foot of the stairs. Her eyes were asking him a question and he answered it. 'I don't think my visit's been of much use, Mrs Gascoigne. I've told your husband that what he needs is rest and quiet, and he tells me he is going to work tomorrow.'

'Oh, doctor.'

'Is he always as stubborn as this?'

'Yes, I'm afraid so, doctor. You see he's never been ill in his life before. About . . . about what he saw, doctor.'

'Oh! That was likely the effect of the blow on the head, and if only because of it he should rest, but he insists that he feels fine, never better. But I'm afraid, Mrs Gascoigne, that I don't believe him. By the look of his head that ball hit him with some force. It's a wonder it didn't knock him out altogether. But you tell me that he didn't lose consciousness.'

'As I told you, I wasn't there, doctor. They said he just swayed a bit and looked dizzy and then he came round.'

'Well, I would keep an eye on him, and if you think my presence is necessary again within the next few days, just give me a ring.'

'Thank you, doctor.'

Florrie let the doctor out and then turned to the kitchen. It was evident that the family had heard all that the doctor had said for Gran voiced her opinion straight away. 'Let him go to work the morrow. If he wants to see things the cemetery's the best place to do it in.'

'Oh, Gran, how can you be so hard?' Linda tightened her face at her grandmother. 'It's all right being like that when he's himself, but Dad's not well, and you know it.'

'I don't know it,' Gran retorted. 'If his behaviour last night is anything to go on, for I've never seen him so lively or talkative in me life. And don't forget, miss' – she wagged her finger at her granddaughter – 'I happened to know him a while afore you did.'

'Yes, I know you did, Gran, and I never heard anybody speak of their son as you do of Dad. Great Aunt Lucy acts more like a mother to him than you do.'

'Linda!' It was Florrie rapping out her name, but Linda was not to be silenced on this occasion. She was strongly in defence of her father and at this moment she disliked her grannie intensely and there was one known weapon with which to attack Gran, and that was the mention of her sister. So she reiterated, 'So she does.'

'You're not too big, me girl, to have your ears boxed.' Gran turned on Linda.

'You won't do it, Gran.' It was a defiant mumble, but Gran heard and was rearing ready to carry out her threat, when Frankie exclaimed, 'Aunt Lucy . . . coo! And I forgot!'

Florrie looked at Frankie where he was standing with his hand across his mouth and she asked, 'What did you forget?'

'About Aunt Lucy. Linda on about it just reminded me.'

'What about her?' Gran demanded.

It was to her that Frankie turned and said, 'I saw her on Friday and she gave me a message for Dad.'

'Where did you see her and what's the message?'

'I was on the lorry with Jimmy delivering bricks to the new building and I saw her standing at the bus stop and she waved to me and Jimmy stopped and she came up and said hello . . .'

'Well, after all that that tells me nothing. What was the message?'

'It was for Dad. She just said to tell him she would be over during the week to see him, the early part.' As Frankie repeated the message he also remembered something else that his Great Aunt Lucy had said . . . 'Tell him on the quiet,' she had added. 'Tell him I'll call in at the cemetery and see him . . .' Well, he had gone and done it, hadn't he? He had given it half away. His dad would be furious with him, but that was nothing new. Still, he didn't want to make him worse the way he was.

'If she comes here I'll spit in her eye,' said Gran.

'You'll do nothing of the sort.' Florrie's tone was sharp. 'I've got enough trouble on me hands. If Aunt Lucy wants to come she can come and welcome and I won't have her put off. Now understand that, Gran. Here, drink your cocoa' – she pushed the cup towards Gran – 'and let's hear no more about it.'

Gran took the cocoa and drank it, and not until she had drained the last drop did she speak again.

'The trouble you've got will be nowt compared to what you'll have if our Lucy's encouraged here again . . . she breeds trouble . . . I should know . . . mealy-mouthed . . .'

'Aunt Lucy used to come here every week before you came four years ago, and if you hadn't pretended you were going to die, Dad wouldn't have had you then . . .'

'Linda!' Florrie's cry silenced her daughter. 'Go on upstairs.'

Linda, red in the face, left the kitchen and Frankie, his eyes averted from his grandmother, followed her out.

'Take no notice.' Florrie was looking at the old woman where she sat with head bowed, quietly tapping the table. 'The young ones will say anything. I'll have something to say to her later, see if I don't.'

There followed an uneasy silence then Gran, lifting her eyes to Florrie, said quietly, 'She's right, you know.'

'Oh, Gran, Gran.' Florrie, full of pity for the moment, could not speak, but then there was no need to, for after a considerable pause, Gran added, 'But that's not to say I won't fight like hell to keep our Lucy from these doors.'

Chapter Three

It was Monday morning and the first funeral of the week was all but over. Joe Twait from Biddleswiddle walked up the cemetery path, his head bowed and his hat clasped between his hands. He was surrounded by his near relatives – they too wearing suitable expressions – but it was at the chief mourner John looked as he thought, 'Damned hypocrite, serve him right. Who will he get to look after the bairns now? Not his fancy piece, I bet. Oh no. Now he's in a fix she'll drop him like a hot coal . . . Devil's cure to him. He's asked for it if anybody has, for he's put his wife where she is at this minute.'

Mary Twait's passing had been what you would call a natural one in as much as it had no association with cars, motorbikes or St Christopher; yet it aroused John to anger. A week ago it would have been none of his business. But this morning everything seemed his business. It was just the way he felt.

As he now approached the grave, shovel in hand, the Reverend Collins, side-stepping from the path, bent his lean body forward and asked, 'How are you, Mr Gascoigne?'

'Quite all right, sir.'

John liked the Reverend Collins, he always gave him his title – not like some of them, with 'Here Gascoigne, there Gascoigne' – and he himself always gave back to the Reverend the deference due to his collar.

But now, seeing that the Reverend was looking quite concerned as he gazed at the result of his handiwork of Saturday afternoon, he went further and reassured him. 'Now, sir, don't worry at all. I'm perfectly all right. Truth is, sir, I've never felt better in me life.'

John smiled and the Reverend, straightening his back, smiled too and they both looked better-looking for the relaxation. Then the Reverend, putting his hand out and patting John's arm, said, 'I've worried all the weekend. I would have come across yesterday to see you, only you know what Sunday's like, not time to breathe.'

'I know, sir.' They nodded at each other understandingly. Then the Reverend stepped back onto the path and, his smile broadening in farewell, hurried after the mourners.

Slowly and methodically John began to shovel and his thoughts moved downwards towards the coffin as the earth fell onto it. Poor Mary Twait. He remembered her as a harassed woman always with a bairn in her arms and a couple at her skirts. Joe had kept her busy with bairns while he was busy in other quarters, blast him, and all his kin.

'*Well, at least you don't hold me accountable for this one, John.*'

John was in the act of pressing his shovel into the yellow clay. His eyes were on the shovel and he kept them there as his body became rigid. The voice was like none he had ever heard before – it was deep and soft and musical. In some way it reminded him of McNally, but he knew definitely it wasn't McNally's voice speaking to him now.

Slowly he raised his eyes from his shovel and looked straight ahead. It was a grand morning; the sun was bright and clear, there wasn't a cloud in the sky. There were no delusionary shadows that twilight creates, it was half past eleven on a Monday morning, and, John told himself, he was wide awake and filling in Mary Twait's grave.

The rigidity was leaving his body and his knees were dissolving into water when very slowly he turned to the right. The shovel dropped from his hand and slid over the hillock of clay, landing with a resounding plonk on the last exposed part of the coffin.

'*Now don't look so startled.*' The figure was speaking to him. It was the same figure he had seen in his tatie patch on Saturday night, only close to it looked gigantic. It was a man in a long white robe made of some rough material, so rough that John could see the knobbles in the weave. The head sticking out of the gown was the largest John had ever seen in his life, and it was covered with brown hair that hung down to the shoulders. The eyes too were large, the mouth was large and the nose was large. Everything about the face was outsize. John's wavering gaze dropped to the feet; they were bare, but the skin around the edges looked so brown and hard as to be made of leather, and they were not only large – they were enormous.

'*Look, let me give you a hand. The sooner you get this done, the sooner we can talk . . . And we've got to talk, John.*'

The booming soft tones seemed to penetrate John's head and then became a loud buzzing sound. The great soft brown eyes looking into his were sending his senses reeling . . . He felt himself sway, and as the great hand came out to steady him, he gave a yelping cry like a scalded cat and leapt into the air. Before he lost consciousness altogether, he knew that he was taking a header after his shovel into the grave of Mary Twait . . .

'Aw-aw, aw-aw.' John heard the groan repeated deep inside himself before he opened his eyes, and when he did and found himself looking into the kindly concerned face of the Reverend Collins, he put out his hand gropingly and grasped at the minister's.

'That's it, take a deep breath. You're all right. Just keep calm, we'll get you home.' The minister sounded definitely upset.

'Rev . . . Reverend.'

'Yes, Mr Gascoigne. Don't talk, you've had a nasty fall. I don't think you should have come to work today.'

'Reverend?'

'I think he wants to say somethin'.' The man speaking was one of two mourners from the funeral and it was evident by the clay on their clothes that they had been the means of getting John out of the grave.

'I . . . I'd rather he lay s . . . still and didn't talk until we get a doctor.' The Reverend's voice was shaking, as was his entire body.

'Where is he?' Slowly John forced the hands away from him and with an effort he leant up on his elbow and looked towards the grave; his already pale face became ashen and he spluttered, 'I . . . I . . . I . . . look, Reverend.'

The Reverend, following John's pointing finger, asked apprehensively, 'What is it, Mr Gascoigne?'

John turned his eyes up to the Reverend Collins. He was asking what it was, but that was just a figure of speech for John knew he wasn't seeing anything out of the ordinary. The Reverend wasn't seeing what he was seeing at this very moment. The great white-robed figure shovelling the clay into the grave, lifting each shovelful as if it was a bairn's spadeful of sand. John clutched at both the Reverend and the man near him as he whispered, 'He's filling in the grave.'

'There now, there now, don't excite yourself for there's no one there, Mr Gascoigne. Don't worry. It's the knock on the head that's troubling you. God forgive me that it was I who should have done it. I am indeed very, very sorry, Mr Gascoigne.'

John moved his head impatiently, then whispered in entreaty, 'Do something for me, will you . . . Go to the grave, will you, Reverend. Go and stand over yon side at the right-hand corner.'

Slowly the Reverend walked towards the grave and did as John requested him, and when he reached the foot of the grave, an odd thing struck him; he had thought it was much deeper when they had pulled the sexton out. In fact, he could have sworn you could still see the coffin lid. But he must have been mistaken, the grave was now half full. He stared at the earth and for a moment he imagined he too was seeing things for the grave seemed to be filling up before his eyes. Then a shout that was almost a scream coming from John startled him so that for a moment he almost lost his balance and fell into the grave himself.

Recovering just in time, the Reverend saw that the gravedigger was on his feet and was yelling, 'Stop it, will you, stop it.'

'You must keep calm, Mr Gascoigne. You must keep calm.' The Reverend was now helping to restrain John from going to the grave, and not until John's head dropped forward, did the minister release his hold.

'He's gone.'

Slowly but steadily, John pushed the men and the Reverend aside and made his way with heavy steps to the grave. And there he stood, perfectly still, for some moments, looking into it, before he turned and faced the minister again saying, 'I think I'll go home.'

The minister by his side supporting him with a trembling hand on his arm, he walked onto the path and towards the cemetery gates, and when they reached the little chapel near the entrance, the minister gently turned John towards the porch and eased him onto the seat. 'Take it easy, there'll be a car here in a minute,' he said.

Without a word, John sat down. He was glad to sit for he felt sick. Placing his elbows on his knees, he dropped his head onto his hands. All these years and a thing like this to happen to him. Was he going mad . . . ? Was he already mad . . . ? But the grave . . . That hadn't been half-filled in by hallucinations, that had been filled in by a pair of hands. He turned to the minister but without looking at him he asked quietly, 'Did you notice anything about the grave, sir? I had just started filling it in when I came over sort of . . . sort of dizzy.'

The minister was some time in answering, in fact so long that John looked up at him, but the minister did not meet his glance; he was looking out of the church door as if awaiting the approach of the car and he kept his back to John as he said, 'I shouldn't talk, Mr Gascoigne, I should keep as quiet as you can until you get home.'

He wasn't mad, then. The unsteadiness of the minister's voice proved to him that he had at least seen something. John drew in a heavy breath. Could he depend upon the minister as an ally? He wasn't sure. He was a nice enough fellow but he didn't look the battling, die-for-my-conviction type. He was more likely to pray about the matter, then leave it in the hands of God.

John was in bed again and the sweat was oozing from every pore in his body, for although there was nobody visible in the room, he knew he was not alone.

On Saturday night, before he had seen . . . the thing in the garden, he remembered having a feeling of well-being, an airy, free feeling, a sort of talkative feeling, and he recalled experiencing the same kind of feeling as he had started to fill in the grave this morning . . . And here it was back again. But this time, knowing what it forebode, he was prepared for it, if sweating with fear was anything to go by. Now to the alerted feeling had been added something more, a sort of awareness. It was as if he had been given another sense.

This feeling of awareness became almost overpowering, so strong was it, that it impelled him to sit up in bed, look round the room and mutter in an agonised whisper, 'You're there, aren't you?'

'*Yes, John, I'm here.*'

There it was, that voice of such a depth and softness as to hold notes of music.

In an agony of mind, John closed his eyes and his hand went instinctively to his throat. He felt he was choking and any minute he knew he was going to faint again.

'*Now don't pass out again, John. This could go on forever. There's only one way we can get used to each other, at least that you can get used to me. You must look me in the eye and take my hand . . . Here.*'

John forced his reluctant lids upwards but the moment he saw the colossal figure, hand outstretched, bending over him, he went pale to the gills, slid back onto his pillows and once more closed his eyes, so tightly this time that they became lost in the sockets.

'*Give me your hand.*'

It was a command and John, bordering on unconsciousness, made a feeble effort to do as he was bidden. Apparently the effort was enough for he felt great fingers closing around his. He felt them pulling him upright, and as he came up, the faintness vanished. It was as if he had been injected with life; quick life. Slowly John's eyes travelled down the length of his own arm to where his hand became lost in that of the other's. Then, more slowly still, they travelled until they came to the face, and there they stayed for what seemed an endless time.

'Who are you anyway? What are you?' In spite of the airy feeling John could not get his voice above a small croak.

'*Now, John, have you any reason to question who I am?*'

'Why have you come to bother me?'

'*Bother you?*' The great head went back and the laugh that came from the large mouth was an outsize of McNally's. '*I think the bothering's on the other foot, John. There you were ready to start a campaign against me and ruin the work of a lifetime, many lifetimes, and you expect me to do nothing about it.*'

'What are you going to do?' John was trembling, not only like a leaf but like a whole tree of aspen leaves.

'*Talk, just talk. Inside of yourself you've always wanted to talk, John. Now, isn't that so?*'

Yes, John supposed that was so. He'd always wanted to talk but couldn't bring himself to do it. But at the same time, he didn't want to have to go to the lengths of seeing things before he could talk . . . but was he seeing things? This fellow was as real as life itself. He made just the slightest movement forward with his head as he asked, 'Tell me, I'm not just seeing you, am I? Making you up sort of. You're there aren't you?'

'*If you mean am I a hallucination, not a bit of it. I'm as real as you are, John.*'

'Then why can't the others see you?'

'*Oh, that's easily explained, but first I'll get off my feet for a minute.*' He turned and drew a chair towards the bed with an easy, natural movement. When he was seated, his great figure blotted the room doorway from John's view, and then his face broadening into an illuminating smile, he said, '*You ask why the others can't see me? For the simple reason that I'm only allowed to show myself to two people every five hundred years.*'

'Every five hundred years?' repeated John in an awed whisper. He was staring into the wide deep-brown eyes as he stammered, 'But . . . but . . . why did you p . . . pick on me?'

'*Well, to tell you the truth, John, there are only about a dozen people in this particular country who are concerned about me and my business – adversely concerned that is. I listened to all of them but had to admit that they weren't really in earnest about me. They didn't believe in me sufficiently either one way or the other to take up the matter. Whereas you, John, you did believe in me.*'

'Believe in you! No, I didn't. Oh no, I didn't . . . I don't.' John was softly emphatic. 'Not these medals and bits of tin of you and all that superstition about you in the cars.'

'*There you are wrong, John. There is no one believes in me and the authenticity of my power more than you do. You don't attack anyone or anything that doesn't exist, now, do you?*'

John stared at the mighty head. He knew he was seeing it yet his common sense told him that it couldn't possibly be there. This experience might not come under the heading of hallucinations but he knew it wasn't normal. It was queer . . . No, not barmy. He refuted this quickly. Just queer . . . odd . . . and accepting that this must be one of those strange phenomena never to be explained, he said quietly, 'You only exist in people's heads.'

'*And in yours, John.*'

'No.' John shook his head.

'*No?*'

'No.' This 'no' came as a loud protest.

'*Don't shout, John.*' St Christopher turned his eyes quickly towards the window and in a very soft voice, which held a trace of amusement, he said, '*The window's open and McNally could be coming home any minute for his dinner, and he might hear you. And if I don't exist, you daren't be found talking to yourself, now, dare you?*'

'Damn McNally and . . .' John stopped himself just in time from adding, 'you an' all.'

'*Amen to that.*'

John's eyes widened, and in spite of himself, he found his interest in his visitor increasing. 'You would damn McNally an' all?'

'*Yes, sometimes I would, John, for he's a blasphemous, unbelieving individual. But there are other times when I quite like him.*'

John lay back on his pillows and stared at the great white-robed figure. Then after a moment he commented flatly, 'If there's anybody on this earth you take after, then it's McNally.'

The Saint again put his head back and let out a roar, which brought John upright, his eyes moving swiftly. Such a bellow could be heard the length of the street yet he had just warned John to be quiet. It was all part of the queerness of this whole business.

'*Aw, that's funny.*' The Saint exhaled a great deal of breath. '*You hate McNally from the skin inwards, you can't stand him at any price, yet you say I'm like him . . . Aw, John, that isn't true, you know it isn't, for you and I are getting on like a house on fire.*'

John was about to protest vehemently at this when St Christopher raised his hand and cautioned, '*Now don't say it, John, for you'll be wrong. Lie back and rest, and give us time.*'

John lay back and he found that his mind was working rapidly. There were questions jumping about inside his head that wanted to be asked, and as he realised they were all to do with his own preservation, he fired the leading one at his strange companion. 'How long do you intend to stay?' he asked.

'*Oh, well now.*' The Saint linked his fingers together and wagged his joined hands backwards and forwards. '*That's up to you, John. I must stay until I've convinced you that my cause is a good one; that my intention is to help people, not hurt them. You see, John, I was a very conceited man in my time. I still am as far as my job is concerned. Did you know I was really the first taxi? I was and I'm rather proud of it. Of course, they had their chariots before my time but they were horse-drawn. But I was the first self-propelled passenger transport . . . And the first amphibian. There was I, for years and years fording a river on my own two legs, my passengers on my back, and uncomfortable and heavy as it was at times, I must confess I liked it. And ever since, all down the centuries, I've made it my business to guide people. Of course, some folk ask to be guided, then go their own way – you know the type, John, you get them in every generation, and it's these very types that cause the trouble, the accidents and the killings – and you, John, you now have laid their blame on me. So to answer your question, I must tell you I'm staying until you're convinced that I have nothing to do with the slaughter on the roads in this age.*'

As John listened, a thought – again connected with his own preservation – separated itself from the jumble in his mind and presented itself for consideration. But wouldn't it be wiser to keep his mouth shut and not ask any more questions, for if he was heard talking to him people wouldn't believe but that he was talking to himself, and that would be the beginning of the end. He'd be put away. The palms of his hands were wet with sweat when he heard himself asking in a low voice, 'What happened to the last two folk you visited?'

'*Ah, well now, John, that's a very interesting question.*' The saint pulled a long face and his eyes twinkled knowingly before he went on. '*One was a nun who had private doubts of my authenticity. When I started visiting her, things began to happen. First of all, they shut her up in a cell for her unchaste thoughts.*' The Saint pointed his forefinger into his chest. '*Me, I was her unchaste thoughts. Mind you, John, in my very young days I won't say I didn't lead a bit of a life. Oh, I won't deny I was a real bad one. But that was before I found our Lord. But to blame the poor young girl for unchaste thoughts because I visited her, oh, that was too much. I had a great deal of hard work to do before I got things straightened out, but eventually she was released and she became an abbess and was looked up to and revered throughout the country. It ended well that one.'*

He stopped here and John was forced to ask, 'And the other one?'

'Oh well.' The Saint lowered his eyes. *'He wasn't so fortunate, John. You see, he was a man who drank of the mead and at least once a week he cursed all the saints, and me in particular, and so I started visiting him but I could never get him to stay put. He wasn't an amenable man like you, John. As soon as I appeared, he would take to his heels and flee, and so at last'* – the Saint shook his head sadly – *'they locked him up, chained him up to be correct. Poor soul. I visited him at regular intervals to try and comfort him but it was no use. I also did everything in my power to get him released, but I'm sorry to say I failed there, too. He lived in the East Angles kingdom near Ipswich and they were very ignorant in that quarter at that time.'*

John closed his eyes and swallowed, and it was some long time before he asked, 'And . . . this time . . . the other one . . . who's he to be?'

'Oh, I haven't made up my mind yet, John. You're enough for me to get on with at present. There's plenty of time to bother about him, or her, as it might well be. The important thing at the moment is us, John. We've got to get ourselves straightened out first, eh?'

John sat up abruptly and leaning forward, apparently without fear but urged on solely by it, he pointed his finger at the Saint and said, 'You know what's going to happen if they find me talking to you, don't you? They won't believe it . . .'

The 'it' had come to a petrified stop on John's tongue, his finger was still extended, he was still addressing the Saint, but there, looking at him from either side of the white-clad figure was Florrie and the doctor. John's finger wavered then dropped, his jaw dropped also, and weakly he lay back in the bed and closed his eyes as he heard Florrie's agonised mutter, 'You see, doctor.'

Apparently the doctor did see. He took hold of John's wrist and felt his pulse. At the same time, he pulled down his eyelid and was unable to suppress a start of surprise when he saw the eye quite consciously staring up at him.

'You'll have your own way, won't you?' The doctor's voice wasn't unkind, but when John, pulling himself up with some effort, said flatly, 'I'm all right, doctor', the doctor's tone changed and he rapped out, 'You're not all right and the quicker you realise it, the better for all concerned. You've got your wife and family scared out of their wits. You know what you were doing when we came into the room?'

John drew in his chin then he drew in his breath and pressing his lips together for a moment he nodded his head twice. And this caused the doctor's eyebrows to rise and he said caustically, 'Oh, you do, do you?'

'Yes, I do. I was talking . . . but I wasn't talking to meself.' John looked towards the now empty chair that had been pushed back from the bed.

'Then who were you talking to?'

John gnawed at his lip for a minute before saying, 'It's a long story and if I was to tell you it you wouldn't believe me. But you can believe me on this point; there's nowt wrong with me, I'm not bad or anything.'

'Do you know what happens to people who see things and won't have anything done about it?'

In spite of himself John shuddered, and for a moment he felt a tightness around his ankles and his wrists, and even round his throat. For a further moment he even imagined he heard the clinking of chains, but he answered the doctor boldly saying, 'Aye, aye, I know all right. But you needn't think you're going to have me tied up – no fear you're not.'

'John, John, dear, listen to the doctor and do what he tells you. You're not yourself, you know you're not yourself.' Florrie was stroking his brow.

John did not look at his wife; Florrie was the last person to understand about St Christopher. Anyway, when a doctor, with all his supposed knowledge, didn't understand, how could he expect her to – he didn't like the doctor, neither hilt nor hair of him. Young upstart.

'You are to stay where you are for a week at least. If you don't, I'll have you put in hospital. Now, do you understand that?'

John said nothing.

'I'll send him some pills along.' He had turned to Florrie. 'And you'll see that he takes them regularly.'

'Yes, doctor, yes. I'll see to that.' Florrie's voice was trembling; her whole body was trembling. She cast one pitying glance at John's scowling face before following the doctor out into the landing and down the stairs.

'Your husband is as stubborn as a mule, Mrs Gascoigne.'

'Yes, yes, I know he is, doctor.'

'He's in a bad way, y'know. He really should be in hospital. But if he stays quiet for a week things might settle. He's got to stay in bed and remain quiet. I don't envy you your task, Mrs Gascoigne, but it'll be your job to see that he does this.'

All Florrie could say was, 'Yes, doctor.' At the same time, she was thinking, 'He'll never stay in bed.' What was she going to do?

'Try not to worry, and if he attempts to get out or won't take his tablets, give me a ring; I'll come and settle him.'

This was meant to be reassuring but the tone in which it was delivered conjured up for Florrie a picture of an ambulance and John, fighting like a demon, being forced into it.

As Florrie closed the door on the doctor she also closed her eyes and murmured, 'Oh, dear God.'

It was four o'clock when Aunt Lucy arrived. She did not come straight in but knocked at the door and when Florrie saw her standing there, the mere sight of her brought a semblance of calm and comfort to her troubled mind.

'Hello, lass,' said Aunt Lucy.

'Come away in, Aunt Lucy,' Florrie exclaimed. 'Oh, I'm glad to see you.'

Aunt Lucy came in; straight into the kitchen she walked and looked at her sister. Gran was sitting ready for her. Her jaw was out and her eyes were narrowed as she looked at the woman who was the antithesis of herself – for her sister was large. Sloppy fat, Gran termed it. But Lucy wasn't fat. Lucy's frame, like her heart, was of an outsize pattern. Her face, to match her body, should have been fat and round but instead it was long and, again to use Gran's adjective, horse-like. This was true but its expression was that of a very kindly horse, and now Lucy addressed her sister in a pleasant tone with a hint of guardedness about it. 'Hullo there, Mamie,' she said.

Gran's answer was merely a jerk of the chin.

'We don't alter, do we?' Lucy sighed as she addressed Florrie, and Florrie, quick to change the subject said, 'Take off your things, Aunt Lucy, and have a cup of tea.'

As Lucy unpinned her hat, Gran spoke. 'And what're you after, our Lucy?' she said. 'What you wantin' to see John for, eh? More mischief you're up to?'

Slowly Lucy turned to her sister. Her face was no longer smiling and her voice was accusing as she said, 'God forgive you, Mamie. The shoe's on the other foot and well you know it.'

'Here, give me your hat,' said Florrie hurriedly. Then turning quickly to Gran she added, 'I've got enough on me plate, Gran, so give over.'

'What's the trouble?' said Lucy, lowering herself down onto a chair as far away from her sister as she could get.

'It's John, Aunt Lucy.'

'John? What's wrong with him? Is he bad?' Lucy asked anxiously.

Florrie moved the cups about on the tray then poured in the milk before she said, 'I wish I knew, but he's not himself.'

'I'll say he's not. Let's face it, in plain words, he's gone off his rocker.'

'No, he hasn't, Gran.' Florrie rounded on the old woman.

'Gone off his rocker?' Lucy looked from one to the other. 'You mean . . .'

'He's seein' things, if you want to know.'

'John . . . John seein' things?' Aunt Lucy gave a laughing 'Huh'.

'Oh, you can laugh, our Lucy. You've always thought you knew him better than me, haven't you? Oh yes you have.'

'Gran.'

Gran turned to Florrie, her tone slightly modified. 'All right, I'm not startin' anything, I'm just makin' a statement – she has always thought she knew him inside out. She had a reason for everything he did.' Gran turned and confronted her sister again. 'Now hadn't you?'

'I thought I understood John, and I still do.'

'Well, you'd better get up aloft and see if you understand him now, sitting up there talking to himsel'. But he says he's not talkin' to himsel'. Who do you think he's talking to, eh? You'll never guess, as clever as you think you are. He says he's talkin' to St Christopher.'

Lucy, her mouth open, looked for confirmation of this statement towards Florrie, but Florrie was pouring out the tea and her silence spoke plainly enough.

'Since when has this come about?' Lucy asked in an awe-laden whisper.

'Saturday,' said Florrie. 'He got a hit on the head with a cricket ball.'

'He was goin' funny afore that . . . Don't forget Friday night and him talking twenty to the dozen in this very kitchen. That ball just acted like a poultice; it drew out what was already bursting to break, just waitin' to come out . . . Like corruption.'

'But he was as right as rain when I saw him last . . .' Aunt Lucy pulled herself up too late.

'Go on, when you saw him last what? So you've been seeing him on the sly, have you? Like old times.'

'Drink your tea, Gran.'

Gran's chin was wagging like a pendulum and Florrie, grabbing at anything to ease the situation, said, 'Would you take him up this cup of tea, Aunt Lucy?'

'Yes, lass, and I'll have a word with him.'

'Do,' said Gran. 'That'll make a pair of you for you've never been right since the day you were born.'

'Gran!'

'Take no notice, Florrie,' said Lucy, making her exit with slow dignity. 'I don't . . .'

When the tap came on the door and Aunt Lucy's voice called softly, 'Can I come in there?' John sat bolt upright in bed and cried, 'Aye, aye, come on in, Aunt Lucy.' And before she had closed the door behind her, he was leaning forward with his hand outstretched, and his voice filled with welcome as he repeated, 'Come away in, Aunt Lucy . . . by, am I glad to see you.'

'Now, what's wrong, lad?' Aunt Lucy, putting the tea on the side table, pulled a chair to the bedside, sat down and took his hand in hers. Peering with her short-sighted eyes towards his brow, she remarked in an awed tone, 'My, lad, what a lump. It's as big as a turnip. It must be sore.'

'It isn't, Aunt Lucy, not a bit. And I feel all right; never better.'

'Never better?' Aunt Lucy brought her brows down questioningly, then asked, 'What's all this about, then? What's wrong with you? Whatever it is you've got Florrie in a state down there, lad.' Lucy omitted mentioning her sister's comments.

John shook his head despairingly. 'You won't believe me, nobody does, but there's one thing I can assure you of afore I start telling you anything – I'm not up the pole, Aunt Lucy.'

Lucy, looking at this man whom she loved, and had always loved, more than anybody else in the world, said, 'No, John, why of course you're not up the pole. If you were up the pole, I'd be the first one to spot it.'

John let out a long drawn breath and lay back on the pillow. Then, tapping her hand, he said, 'I feel better already. Just the sight of you does me good.'

'I got a bit of a shock when I went to the cemetery and they told me you had taken bad and gone home. I've never known you to be bad. And then when I got in I had me work cut out not to let on I had been up there and knew you were bad.'

'I'm not bad, Aunt Lucy. I wasn't bad, I just got a gliff and passed out.'

Aunt Lucy shook her head. 'I can't see you passing out, John, unless there was a good cause for it. Can you tell me about it?'

'If I can't tell you, Aunt Lucy, I can tell nobody.'

John sat up in bed again and his next action brought to Aunt Lucy her first doubts for she watched him cast his eyes furtively around the room as if expecting to see someone else there. Before starting to speak, he drew his hand down one cheek across his mouth and up the other side of his face. Then he said quietly, 'Well, it began like this, Aunt Lucy. There was a smash-up at the crossroads six months or so ago . . .'

Aunt Lucy listened without interrupting, her attention riveted on her nephew, and everything he said seemed feasible – feasible until he came to the part where the white-robed figure he took to be McNally was running about among his taties. And by the time he had reached the incident that had taken place this morning, with the reappearance of the figure at the graveside, Aunt Lucy was saying to herself, 'Dear God, dear God . . .' Then when John went on to recount in very low tones what had taken place in this very room just a short while ago, Aunt Lucy found that her vest was sticking to her back and the palms of her hands were clagged together.

When John finished, Aunt Lucy was not looking at him and he reached out to her and, gripping her wrist, he pleaded, 'You believe me, Aunt Lucy?'

She brought her eyes quickly up to him and said, 'Aye, lad. Why, yes, I believe you.' Aunt Lucy saw that it was absolutely necessary that

John should believe that she believed him – he had to trust in someone. She patted his hand comfortingly and said, 'You're not the first one that's had apparitions. If you were a churchgoing man they would say you were seeing visions and have the bishop up to you.' She forced herself to give a little laugh and punched him in the chest as she said, 'If it was happening to McNally they'd have him into the priesthood with the beer still on his 'tash, an' if it was Katie who was seeing things they'd push her straight into a nunnery.' Aunt Lucy repeated the punch and her head went back on a laugh at the thought of Katie McNally in a nunnery.

John's stomach began to shake. Oh, Aunt Lucy was a comfort and no mistake. Then returning her punch, but gently, he let his laugh join hers and when it got well under way, he leant back against the bedhead and held his side with one hand while he pressed the other over his mouth. By, it was many a long day since he had laughed. He was feeling so gay and happy you'd think he had won the sweep. Suddenly, as if he had been prodded in the buttocks, he sat bolt upright in the bed and his laughter became so throttled in his throat that he choked . . . It was when he felt like this that he got his visitor; this unusual light, airy feeling he was discovering was the prelude to his seeing . . . him. Cautiously now, his eyes slid around the room, but there was no one to be seen except Aunt Lucy, and she, he was quick to notice, had stopped laughing also.

The room was quiet now – too quiet – and John broke the silence by saying haltingly, 'Frankie . . . he . . . he gave me your message yesterday, Aunt Lucy. Was it something important you wanted to see me about?'

John's question now placed Aunt Lucy in a quandary. Yes, to her mind the reason why she wanted to see him was important, very important, but should she tell him now, in the state he was in? For although he was no more daft than she was, there was something that wasn't quite right, especially about this St Christopher business . . . It had all to do with the bump on his head, she had no doubt, and when that subsided, well, as likely as not, so would the Saint. It was to be hoped so anyway. Yes, indeed.

'Are you in trouble, Aunt Lucy, are you short of anything?'

'Short? No, no, lad. I've got what sees me through, and I'm in no trouble either. I'm only a bit worried.'

'Well, I've told you mine, why not tell me yours, eh?' John was smiling now.

Aunt Lucy wanted to say, 'It's not my trouble, lad, it's yours.' And although she could see he was in no fit state to receive any more trouble, she felt bound to tell him the reason for her visit. Nothing could be gained, she felt, by beating about this particular bush. So she folded her hands, palms upwards, in the centre of her lap and said quietly, 'Freda's in the district, John.'

John's brows puckered deeply, his lips fell slightly apart then tightened together again as he gulped. The name Freda came to his ears like an echo. He hadn't thought of it in years, except for odd moments. At one time – a long time ago – it had dizzied about in his head at all hours of the day and night and it was always accompanied by a feeling of shame, and of his own inadequacy. Even now the echo could reduce him to half the man he knew he was.

His voice didn't sound his own when he asked, 'Where is she?'

'In the new houses.'

'Here?' John's eyes were wide.

'No, them lot they've put up Biddleswiddle way. Seven, Lark Lane.'

'You seen her?' John shook his head at himself. 'That's a daft question, I mean have you spoken to her?'

Aunt Lucy nodded.

'What's she after, do you know?'

'I would like to say I don't, lad, but I've got a pretty good idea. Although when I tackled her with it she denied it flatly.'

'But he's not hers, Aunt Lucy.'

'No, lad, I know he's not, but you know she wanted him as a bairn – you don't forget she came and tackled Florrie about it, do you? And be what she may, John, she stuck to Manning all these years and she must have cared for him more than a bit to want to take his bairn when she couldn't have any of her own.'

'His bairn.' John was sitting rigid in the bed now, his face a dark, angry red. 'Did he care a damn what happened to his bairn or the lass that was bearing it? Don't you talk to me about his bairn, Aunt Lucy.'

John brought his knee up sharply and placing his elbow on it rested his face in the palm of his hand and stared unseeingly at the pattern on the eiderdown. His bairn! His bairn, indeed. He forgot for the moment he was in bed supposedly suffering from hallucinations and his mind leapt in the distance of twenty-two years. He was working in Hartlepool after having escaped from home and his mother. He remembered he had been drunk for a time with the feeling of freedom, it was as if he had just been let out of jail or some such place of confinement. Then Freda had come to lodge in the same house and that was that.

His mother had always managed to put the tin hat on any affairs he had started with a lass, but now he was on his own, he went ahead. Freda talked a lot and laughed a lot and she made him dance. He was bemused, bewildered and beguiled by her, and within six weeks of first meeting her they were married. Within six weeks of being married he was no longer bemused, bewildered or beguiled. His eyes were wide open and he knew he had made a blasted fool of himself.

He hadn't had the nerve to tell his mother what he had done, and even if Freda had been other than she was, it would have still taken some strategy to present her to his mother. As it was, he dreaded the day when they should meet. Aunt Lucy was different; she knew all about everything from the start.

And from the start he knew he was no match for Freda. She was loud, she was coarse and she was shameless – and her laugh defied him to take any action to check her. He was intimidated by her laugh until the night, the shift being cut short, he arrived home well before his time and found Manning there. It was the first time he had seen Manning, but it was evident it wasn't the first time Freda had seen him. He remembered hitting Manning between the eyes and could recall the momentary satisfaction he felt. But his elation was brief for within a second Freda had knocked him onto his back. This last incident seemed to degrade him and the following day when she packed her things and left him, he felt nothing but relief. His relief became boundless when she returned some weeks later and asked him for a divorce. He could go ahead, she had said, and state the facts as they were for she didn't care a damn; she was living openly with Manning and she didn't care who knew it.

He had made up his mind to sell his few bits of furniture and enlist, and he was actually taking the lino up from the kitchen floor one evening when there came a knock upon the front door. He could see himself now, standing looking at the girl on the pavement. She had asked to see Mrs Gascoigne and he had said that she wasn't in. And then she asked if she could come in and wait for she must see her. Not knowing what next to say he had asked her in, and he remembered her surprise at the sight of the half-stripped house. It was when she had asked in a quivering voice if he was expecting his wife back that he had to admit he wasn't. She had nearly passed out then and he had made her a cup of tea. Over it, and with bowed head, she had told him that up to a short time previous she and Manning had been courting and were going to be married, and then he had met Freda.

The girl's idea was simple. She thought if she saw Freda and explained the situation to her she would leave Manning alone. Because she was in such a state, he had given her Freda's address, knowing full well that her journey would bring her nothing but final disappointment – he knew his Freda. Then the next evening he had a visit from Freda. She had stormed in on him. What did he think he was up to? She was getting a divorce whether she married Manning or not, but she was going to marry Manning. Anyway, he said the kid wasn't his. It had come as something of a shock to him to learn that that nice girl was going to have a bairn by Manning.

He had never thought to see the lass again but six weeks later he was passing a fruit shop and there through the window he saw her serving a customer, and he had gone in and bought some oranges and spoken to her. Her sad eyes and the fear in their depths, had touched his heart, and the touch remained on it still.

The divorce took some time in coming through and the child was born to Florrie before he could marry her. Although at first he had felt a natural feeling of resentment towards the baby, it had soon passed, for the child took to him and he to it.

Then there was his mother and the fiddling he had to do to explain the complicated business to her. When on one of his rare visits to her he broke the news that he had been married for over a year and had a son, she nearly went through the ceiling. Oh, he would never forget that day. It was a good job she hadn't demanded to see the marriage lines which showed the ceremony to have taken place but two months earlier. Strangely enough, or perhaps just to be contrary, she took to Florrie from their first meeting.

It was after the war when he was demobbed and trying to get used to his own four-year-old son, who strangely seemed less his own than Arthur, that Freda paid them a visit. It was her second visit, at least to Florrie, for after Frankie was born she had come and made the proposition to take Arthur off her hands. They were living in cramped quarters in Newcastle at the time. He remembered the rooms and the day very clearly for Aunt Lucy was there. It was after Freda made an impassioned plea to Florrie that she should give up Arthur to his rightful father now that she had two children of her own, and the rumpus that ensued, that Aunt Lucy had warned him to put as much space between his family and Freda as possible if he didn't want trouble.

Whether Manning wanted his son or not, John never knew, but definitely Freda did. The twists in human nature were beyond John's comprehension. He had no means of understanding the change that had come about in his former wife, but what he did understand was that she meant business. So when the following week Aunt Lucy came with a proposal, he jumped at it.

At the time, there were plenty of jobs for everybody with big attractive pay packets attached but there was a growing scarcity of houses and people were herded together like cattle. When Aunt Lucy said she could get him a job in the country with a nice self-contained house and garden, it seemed like a gift from God. She had kept the nature of the job until the last and even then she had called it . . . being a sexton. The main work, she said, was looking after the church but they must go and see the house first.

The thought of being a gravedigger had given him the jitters. He had seen all the dead men he wanted to see, but when he had looked at Florrie's face as she walked round the house, that had settled the whole business. He became a gravedigger and as he had served his time as a fitter and worked in the yards all his life, a country village gravedigger would be the last clue of his whereabouts that Freda was likely to follow.

So sixteen years had passed and he had heard nothing about Freda or Manning – whether they were dead or alive – up to this minute. And now here she was again, and where Freda was there also, you could bet your life on it, was trouble.

As if coming out of a trance, John looked at Aunt Lucy. 'Why has she come to live in this part anyway?'

'She says she wants fresh air. She's had enough of the towns.'

'She didn't know we were here?'

'No, I'm sure of that. She seemed surprised to see me. But there is one thing I gleaned in a very short time – she hasn't forgiven you for disappearing.'

'Did you tell her where we lived?'

'No, of course I didn't, lad. But she's no fool; she's only got to keep her eye on me and she knows one day I'll lead her to you. Anyway, she'll put two and two together and ask where John Gascoigne lives and folks for miles round would tell her. A gravedigger's better known by his name than a priest.'

John once again wiped his face round with his hand, then muttered, 'It only needed this.'

'Well now,' said Aunt Lucy brightly. 'It might be a blessing in disguise. For when your mind's got this to tackle, it will make you forget the other thing.'

'You're just like the others, Aunt Lucy, you just think . . .'

'*No, she isn't, John. No she isn't.*'

John's head swayed a moment before he turned roughly round and addressed the figure standing in the middle of the room. 'For God's sake, man, you'll scare the wits out of her. Keep out of this, will you, and mind your own bloody business.'

The soft white hairs on Aunt Lucy's neck rose individually until it felt as prickly as a hedgehog. Her body was rigid and her lips were dry and she had a creepy-crawly sensation all over her skin. When John's hands came on hers she almost jumped out of the chair.

'It's . . . it's all right, Aunt Lucy. Look, do something for me, go on, turn your chair round and look towards the wall. Go on.'

It seemed that Aunt Lucy had great difficulty in taking her eyes off John and she didn't turn her chair round but she slowly swivelled her head in the direction he indicated.

'Can you see anything, Aunt Lucy?' John was breathing as if he had just emerged from deep water.

She gave a tight little shake of her head.

'*It's no good, John. She won't be able to see me.*'

John closed his eyes for a second and when he opened them he saw that Aunt Lucy's were screwed up tight. In desperation he turned towards the Saint and pleaded, 'Look, make her the second one that can see you. Go on . . . I'll put up with anything if you only do that.'

St Christopher shook his head slowly. *I'm sorry, John, but Aunt Lucy, dear, kind creature that she is, never even thinks about me. I'm nothing to her one way or another.*

'John.' It was a weak whisper from Aunt Lucy. 'Lie quiet, lad, and don't distress yourself.'

'My God, Aunt Lucy . . .' John thrashed about the bed in desperation. 'If I can't convince you then there's no hope for the others. I tell you, Aunt Lucy, he's there, standin' not a yard from you, as large as life . . . larger than life. My God, aye.'

'All right . . . all right, lad.' Aunt Lucy was aiming to keep her voice low. 'I do believe you but I can't at the moment say I can see him, that's all, not like you do, you know.'

'Don't go, not for a moment.' John put a detaining hand on her as she made to rise, then turning his head sharply, he addressed the Saint in no weak manner as he said, 'And you leave me alone for five minutes.' When he turned again to Aunt Lucy she had put her head down and he appealed to her, 'Oh, Aunt Lucy, I'm not off me rocker, no matter how things look. I'm neither mad nor barmy, honest I'm not.'

'No, lad; no, lad.' Aunt Lucy patted his hand quickly, her head still down.

'About this other business.'

'I don't think you should let that bother you, lad . . . Not for the moment.'

'If she's in the neighbourhood, Aunt Lucy, and I don't let it bother me, it won't be five minutes afore she's doin' the bothering and, what's more, at Florrie. But there's something troubling me even more than that. You must remember, Aunt Lucy, that me mother doesn't know a thing about Freda. Just you imagine how she'll go on if she finds out I was married afore, an' not only married but divorced. God alive, life won't be worth livin'. She's hard enough to stomach at times now.'

Aunt Lucy had risen to her feet and her voice was trembling as she said, 'I thought of that but above everything else I've thought of Arthur. How's he going to take it if it comes out?'

'Believe me, Aunt Lucy, if this comes out it will get Arthur out of a jam that's goin' to tie him up for life. I bet me bottom dollar that he would welcome it.'

'Welcome the fact that you're not his father, John?'

'Oh.' John dropped his eyes. 'There's that. I wouldn't like him to hear that, not for the world.' He paused and thought a moment, then ended, 'I'll have to see her.'

'Yes, yes, do that, John, but when you're better.'

'Oh, Aunt Lucy.' John moved his head wearily. 'I'm not bad; honest to God, I'm not bad, Aunty.'

'No, John, you're not bad, you just need some rest. Look, I'll go down and get a cup of tea, eh? Oh, and send you another up . . . that one's finished now.' She picked up the cup of cold tea from the table.

'You do that, Aunt Lucy.'

'And I'll come up afore I leave.'

'Yes, Aunt Lucy, yes, come up afore you leave.'

When the door had closed on her, John looked towards the middle of the room. There was no one to be seen but nevertheless he spat one word fearlessly into the emptiness. 'You!' he said.

Aunt Lucy's legs were almost giving way beneath her by the time she reached the kitchen and she made an effort to calm her disturbed feelings as she heard the sound of strange voices coming from the kitchen – there were visitors. Perhaps this was just as well, she thought, because she did not know what she was going to say to Florrie about

John's condition, for although he talked all right, at least to her, he was far from being all right. Her heart was sore with worry over him for she loved him and often thought he should have been her son and would have if it hadn't been for our Mamie. So it was as the mother of a son that she was worrying now.

When she entered the kitchen, she recognised one of the two visitors. One was Katie McNally from next door; she did not know who the other was, but whoever she was, she looked a sour docken.

Florrie turned an agitated face to Aunt Lucy and hesitantly made the introduction. 'This is Mrs Duckworth, Aunt Lucy. She is Joan's mother. You know Joan, Arthur's girl.'

'Pleased to meet you,' said Aunt Lucy.

'How do you do,' said Mrs Duckworth with a cool nod, ignoring Aunt Lucy's outstretched hand. Then turning abruptly to Florrie again she said, 'I'll come back when you haven't got so much company for we must have a talk, and soon.'

'Don't let me disturb you.' Katie waved her hand at Mrs Duckworth. 'I can sit through anything – blather, lies or blackmail.'

Mrs Duckworth cast a glare in Katie's direction that had no need of interpretation, then, going towards the door, not accompanied by Florrie this time, she let herself out.

'If I had me way . . .'

'Well, you haven't got your way, Gran. And if you hadn't put your nose in in the first place she would have had her say and gone, and I wouldn't have the thought of her coming back again.'

'Well, I like that,' said Gran. 'And you don't like the thought of her coming back here again . . . No! Well, let me tell you, after the wedding, this house will be as open to her as a railway station, and if she isn't telling Joan how she should run Arthur, then she'll be telling you how to run . . . him' – Gran pointed her thumb at the ceiling – 'an' your house. If you don't want to see Mrs Duckworth again, you'd better tell Arthur to emigrate or some such.'

'You're right, Gran, you're right.' Katie was laughing. 'After the wedding there's only one room in the house you'll be able to keep her out of, and then only if you put down the sneck. It'll be worse than havin' a lodger.'

Florrie had ceased to pay any heed to either Gran's or Katie's chatter for she was looking towards Aunt Lucy where she had taken a seat just inside the door, and going to her she said softly, 'What is it, my dear, aren't you feeling well?'

Before Aunt Lucy could open her mouth to answer, Gran exclaimed loudly, 'She's seen what we've all seen, and it's turned her over. It would,' she ended scornfully.

'Do you think John has gone up the lum a little bit?' This from Katie who was leaning forward and asking the question of Gran, but it was Florrie who answered, her voice sharp and hard. 'He hasn't gone up the lum, Katie, and I'll thank you not to suggest any such thing.'

She might have reached the terrible conclusion in her own mind but she wasn't going to stand by and hear the neighbours proclaiming it.

'Now, Florrie, I meant no offence, none in the wide world. You know me. My gob would take two battleships but there's no badness in me, nor mean intent. Now you know that, Florrie. I'm as concerned about John as if he was me own, and Broderick said last night—'

'Katie . . . I don't want to hear what Broderick said, not at this moment.' Florrie's voice was not loud but it seemed to ring round the room. 'Aunt Lucy's not well and wants to be quiet.' She guided Aunt Lucy to the couch by the far wall, and easing her onto it said, 'Lie yourself down for half an hour.'

'I'll be going then,' said Katie, edging up from the chair. 'I can see you want to be to yourselves. All I dropped in for was to see if I'd knock you up a meat pie for the morrow's dinner. I'm going to do a bit of baking the night for Broderick to take out the morrow and I thought, with you handicapped running up and down stairs, you might like something to put you over.'

Florrie's voice was now kindly as she turned to her neighbour. 'Thanks, Katie, but I've got it all in for the morrow. Thanks all the same; it was good of you.'

Florrie kept her eyes from Katie's hands as she said this. The very thought of those grimy nails digging into pastry that she would eat caused a little heaving movement in her stomach, but in spite of this she recognised her neighbour's goodness of heart, and she went with her to the door, saying in parting, 'You understand, Katie. I'm sorry I was blunt.'

'Of course I do, lass. If you can't be yourself with me after all these years, then God knows who you could be yourself with . . . What are neighbours for?' She dug Florrie in the ribs with her elbow and, jerking her head back towards the Duckworths' house, she whispered, 'Not to come the la-de-da and play Mrs God Almighty. Some folks would like to be, wouldn't they? Put the Devil in horseback and he'll ride to hell.' Then, her whisper dropping much lower, she continued, 'Between ourselves I don't envy you, Florrie, begod I don't. Havin' your family tied up with them . . . Chapelites are the worst in the world. Do you know what Broderick says? If her shift was . . .'

'Ssh!' said Florrie in a sweat of apprehension. 'Be quiet, Katie. You don't know where she might be . . . if she's round in the garden . . .'

'Aye, cuddy's lugs. All right, I'll be off . . . Keep your pecker up, lass, an' I'm just across the grass should you be wantin' me.'

Katie waddled off down the path, and Florrie hesitated a moment in the shelter of the porch and sent a prayer heavenward for strength to cope with the burdens of the day as they mounted upon her, and not least of them were the good intentions of both Katie and Broderick McNally.

Chapter Four

It was turned eight o'clock the same evening and Aunt Lucy was gone. Gran had retreated much earlier than usual to her room, likely because she could see nothing more of a spectacular nature happening that day. Linda was at the Youth Club and Arthur was out . . . Where Florrie didn't know, but one thing was certain, he would be with Joan, fighting a losing battle against putting the wedding off. Among other things now, she was worried about Arthur for he seemed disturbed and unhappy. She'd had words with Linda too, before she had gone out, on account of the way her face was made up. She had never seen her made up like it before – she could have been twenty-seven instead of seventeen. As she went about the business of setting the table for breakfast, she glanced to where Frankie was lying on the couch, his feet hanging over the head. Frankie was the only one of her family that she had no need to worry over. In spite of his chattering and jabbering, he was a good boy and had stayed in the night to keep her company because he knew she was troubled. He looked comic and uncomfortable lying like that and she didn't know how he could read in such a position.

His feet swung from the head of the couch and his paper fell to the floor in the same second that she turned to the doorway leading into the hall. Standing fully dressed, even to his cap, was John. She hadn't heard him moving overhead nor coming down the stairs. After a moment of staring she went hastily towards him, muttering, 'John, oh, John. What are you up for?'

He silenced her with a lift of his hand, then, closing the door behind him, he said softly, 'I was waiting until me mother came upstairs. I'm going out for a while, Florrie.'

'Out? But the doctor . . .'

'Look, lass, no matter what the doctor says, he's wrong. I'm sick of telling you I'm not bad. I feel like a breath of fresh air and I'm just going for a stroll. Now, is there anything wrong in that?'

Florrie looked him up and down then said quietly, 'But you've got your good suit on, John.'

As if in surprise, John looked at his trouser legs then exclaimed, 'Oh, so I have. Well, I took the first to hand.'

'You're not fit.' Florrie shook her head. 'Don't go out. You'll have me worried to death. You know what happened this morning.'

John now sighed a deep sigh then, patting her arm with a soothing gesture, he said quietly, 'That won't happen again, lass. I can assure you of that.'

'How are you to know?'

'I know all right.'

'Would you like me to come with you, Dad?'

'What?' John turned abruptly towards Frankie. 'Come with me? What for?' Then without waiting for an answer he said, 'No, no, I want nobody with me. I've told you, I'm just going for a bit of a stroll; I just want the fresh air.' He looked from one to the other then, turning away, he walked towards the outer door. Before he opened it, he turned round again and said with weary emphasis, 'Stop fussing, will you? For God's sake, stop fussing. I'm not bad but you'll have me in a damned sanatorium afore you finish if you keep this up, an' I'm telling you.'

When the door had closed on him, Florrie sat down weakly by the table and bowed her head, and Frankie, coming to stand by her side, said,

'He never takes strolls at night. That's funny in itself.' Then he added, 'Look, Mam, do you want me to go after him? I'll not let him see me.'

Florrie's head came up now. 'Yes, yes, you do that, Frankie, but for goodness' sake don't let him catch sight of you.'

The position of private detective appealed to Frankie and he dashed to the cupboard and got his coat and was down at the garden gate just in time to see John disappear around the bottom of the street.

From leaving the street until his father had reached the village green, three people had stopped him. Apparently, Frankie thought, to ask him how he was. One thing Frankie noticed in particular: his dad didn't look as if he was out for a dander for he was striding along seemingly intent on going someplace, and the impression was borne out when he saw him turn up Moor Lane. Where on earth could he be aiming for going up Moor Lane . . . ? The garage? Was he going to the garage? Had he heard about him hiring out the motorbike for learning? Frankie became hot with resentment. Well, it didn't matter what his dad said, he was going to have a motorbike, so there.

Frankie's present notion of ultimate success was to arrive on a motorbike at their front door. You could keep your cars, big, middle and small. Give him a motorbike any time. He reckoned he had achieved a great deal already for, unknown to any member of his family, he had obtained a supplementary driving licence and had had three goes on a hired bike from the garage.

The storm of resentment against his father welled up. He had always been down on him; Frankie never could do anything right for his dad. His dad didn't like him; it was Arthur who had everything in their family. Well, his dad wasn't going to put his spoke into this wheel. He could say what he liked but he wasn't going to stop him having a motorbike.

His teeth were clenched together as he saw his father approach the garage but when John did not stop and continued on up the road, not only did Frankie's jaw relax, but so did the muscles of his whole face, until his expression looked like one wide gape. He wasn't going to the garage then. So where was he off to? There was nothing on the road beyond the garage until you got to Biddleswiddle and that was a good four miles on. Perhaps after all he was just going for a stroll.

As Frankie himself reached the outskirts of the garage he was just in time to step into cover when he saw his father stop, and his bewilderment grew when he realised that John was waiting for a bus. It was half past eight and this was the last bus out of Downfell Hurst. It called at Biddleswiddle, Befumstead and Battonbun before making for Hexham. There was only one bus coming back this way and that wouldn't get in until ten thirty.

Frankie's attention was suddenly taken from his father by Mr Norton coming from the back of the garage, his hands thick with oil. He greeted Frankie cheerily, saying, 'Hullo there. Come for the bike?'

It being Monday, Frankie's resources were low, and it was the condition of his pocket more than his concern for his mother which had kept him at home this evening. But as soon as Mr Norton spoke, Frankie saw the bike as an absolute necessity. He couldn't get on the bus with his dad, and it had now become imperative to find out where 'the old man' was going. 'I'll have to tick it,' he said.

'That's all right. How long do you want it for?'

Frankie hesitated. 'An hour maybe?'

'OK. She's ready in the back.'

Within a few minutes Frankie had the machine wheeled to the side of the garage and at this moment the bus went past and Frankie waited to hear it grind to a stop before he put his head round the side of the building, there to see his dad getting on it.

'Be careful how you go,' warned Mr Norton.

'I'll be careful,' said Frankie.

He let the bus get a good start on him, and pushing the bike out into the road he revved her up. Then joy on top of joy, he was not only soaring through the air, deafened by the noise that was sweeter than music to his ears, he was also a detective . . . a private detective. After a moment or two he had to moderate his flying to keep out of sight of the bus, for should his dad happen to see him the game would be up in more ways than one.

The bus made several stops before reaching Biddleswiddle and when eventually it stopped at the War Memorial in the centre of the village and Frankie saw that his father did not get off, he asked himself once more, 'Where's he going to, then?'

The bus started on its journey again and when it reached the outskirts of the village it turned right and made a detour, going through the new estate. It was at the stop at the very end of the new bungalows that Frankie saw his father alight from the bus, and he was just in time to find a hiding place for himself and his bike behind a builder's hut when he saw his dad walking back down the road in his direction.

Coo! What was he to do now? Without the least resemblance to a detective of any sort he scampered for cover behind some bushes near a heap of gravel. The bushes formed a good vantage point and he watched his father walk to a fork in the road where two bungalows were in the middle of being erected. Then he saw him hesitate, look up and down the road, before taking the right-hand fork which brought him onto a path and back within a few yards of the actual bushes again.

The 'coos' were racing through Frankie's mind now, and when his father passed him almost within arm's length, he began to tremble with a mixture of fear and excitement.

When the sound of John's footsteps had nearly faded, Frankie moved cautiously onto the path and, keeping close to the screen of bushes lining the road, moved slowly forward. He was too near his dad now for comfort and he was cautioning himself not to go any further when he saw him moving up an incline. Only his innate curiosity overcoming his fear drove him along the path to the cover of the last bush, and there in the clearing before him stood a new bungalow. It was built on a slight rise and had a fancy porch over the front door, and on the porch stood his dad ringing the doorbell.

Frankie, his eyes popping and his whole body alerted for a running retreat, watched John ring the bell again and yet again. When he received no answer he saw him turn and gaze about him. At one time he was gazing straight at Frankie as if he had spotted him, and Frankie's legs had the feeling of being turned into jelly.

He was in line with the corner of the house and at the same time as he saw his father move away from the front door and walk over the unmade garden, he saw a woman come round from the back of the house. Then he saw their meeting. His father's face was half turned from him but the woman's face was full to him. He saw the smile that spread over it and heard her voice quite clearly as she exclaimed, 'Why, John, this is a surprise.'

There was a pause before his father spoke then he called her by her Christian name, saying, 'Hullo, Freda.'

To hear his father speaking another woman's name shocked Frankie, but he had no time to realise just how he was feeling for the woman was moving towards the front door and speaking again. 'I didn't expect you so soon. Come in, John, come in.'

When the door closed on the woman and his father, Frankie found he was actually shaking – convulsed by an emotion he had not experienced before. It was anger, and it was rising swiftly to a feeling of hate. He knew all about men having other women . . . married men . . . but these men hadn't wives like his mother. His mother was good and bonnie; his mother was attractive and worth ten . . . twenty . . . a hundred of his father. What she had ever seen in him he didn't know. He had a compelling urge to dash to the house, bang on the front door and yell, 'You dirty old swine, you.' But in spite of his feelings he did not take this step. His father had always had the power to intimidate him and the knowledge he had just gained of him, strangely enough, did not lessen this feeling of intimidation, rather it increased it. His father now appeared as a stronger, subtler character. He was a man cunning enough to be leading a double life.

Frankie was faced with the first real problem of his life. He turned, and without taking cover now, he went down the path to his motorbike. Mounting it he rode slowly in the direction of home. The main question in his mind was, 'What was he going to tell his mother?' He knew it would give him a kick to expose his father, but it would hurt him equally to see his mother upset. The word 'upset' wasn't, he knew, adequate enough to express how she would feel when his dad's capers were made known to her. Yet he couldn't keep this awful knowledge to himself, he would have to tell somebody . . . Their Arthur . . . Yes, Arthur was the one to tell, but where was Arthur? Out with young Duckworth somewhere, getting lessons on how to toe the line.

Whether it was because at that moment he was thinking of his brother, or the sight of him so far away from the usual courting haunts startled him, or again that his driving wasn't proficient enough to stand up to any shocks, Frankie found himself driving straight into a ditch and up the other side. Fortunately, it was shallow and dry, and after a number of wobbles and bumps he pulled the bike to a stop, and shutting her off and leaving her where she was, he made his way at a run the short distance back along the country road to where a lane turned off.

It was as he glanced sideways at the couple going up this lane that he recognised their Arthur. He had his arms round . . . Although Frankie's legs were carrying him swiftly towards the lane, his thoughts came to a dead halt and it was some seconds before his brain clicked in again and said to him, 'That wasn't Joan Duckworth he was with.'

When he reached the bottom of the lane, he saw Arthur in the distance, his arm still about the girl, and his nervous chest heaved. No, not on your life that wasn't Joan Duckworth. This was a night of surprises and no mistake. He found he was angry, even more angry than before, and he bawled, 'Our Arthur.'

If a bullet had hit Arthur in the back of the neck he couldn't have left the ground more sharply, but apparently his wits were about him for as he turned he thrust his companion into the cover of the hedge and after a moment of staring at Frankie's quickly advancing figure, he moved to meet him.

'What do you want here?' Arthur's sharp tone belied the scared look on his face.

'I can ask you the same thing.' For the moment Frankie had forgotten the burden of knowledge that he wanted to share with his brother. 'I know who you've got up there.'

'Look, you mind your own business.'

'It is my business.' It was almost as a revelation Frankie found that Moira McNally was his business. He wanted to hit out at his big brother and say, 'You leave her be, I'm gonna ask her out, I've just been putting it off until I could ride the bike.' This self-knowledge was as startling in its way as the duplicity of his father, and he found, as in his father's case, he was all boiled up inside – real mad – and he spluttered as he cried, 'Isn't one enough for you?'

'Look, Frankie, I'll talk later the night. I'm trying to finish with Joan, but—'

'You're a bit late, aren't you, and the wedding all set? By, you've got a nerve, our Arthur, and you're the one that everybody says – "Oh, Arthur is a nice lad, quietlike." I'll say you're quietlike an' I'll tell you something else, there's not a pinch atween you and me dad.'

'What d'you mean? What you getting at?' Arthur's brows were meeting and his voice was low.

'Just what I say. All this St Christopher business is a cover-up – a cover-up for his women.'

'Have you gone screwy an' all.'

'I shouldn't wonder with the shocks I've had the night.'

They were glaring at each other now.

'What are you talking about? Take it I'm playing a double game, what's that got to do with Dad?'

'For your information he's on the same tack.'

'Dad!' Arthur now put his head back and laughed, but he stopped abruptly as Frankie cried, 'Shut up!'

'You're not serious?'

'No, of course I'm not serious, it's all fun. I've just followed him to Biddleswiddle where he went to a bungalow, one of the new ones, and he met a woman and she called him John, and was over the moon to see him and he called her Freda and he's inside there with her now . . . No I'm not serious.'

'Dad!'

'For God's sake stop saying "Dad" like that as if he was McNally's Blessed Virgin or somethin'. Yes, Dad. And he's carrying on with another woman like you're carrying on with Moira McNally.'

'He's not carrying on with me, Frankie.'

They both turned round in surprise as Moira stepped out from the cover of the hedge.

'Oh, Moira you shouldn't.' It was a weak protest from Arthur, but Frankie's protest wasn't weak for he turned on Moira shouting, 'I suppose you've had an earful of things that don't concern you, sneaking down like that.'

Moira's head was cocked tantalisingly on one side as she said, 'I've heard enough to make it interesting – your dad's got another woman.'

'If you dare say a word a this.' Frankie took a threatening step forward and as Arthur thrust his arm out protectively in front of Moira, she said, 'Who said I was going to say anything. You know, Frankie Gascoigne, you hate me so much you can't see straight, never could.'

Frankie stared at her fascinating face while trying to ignore her fascinating figure. Was she bats, hate her . . . hate her? When he was all churned up inside about her and could kill their Arthur this very minute. Hate her? Why he . . . Frankie couldn't speak the word even to himself. He couldn't explain that his teasing and his jibes over the years had been but the laying of the foundation of love, for he hadn't known himself. All he could do now was hang his head helplessly.

'What was she like, the woman?'

It was some seconds before Frankie answered, and he turned his back on Moira before saying, 'She's older than Mam, all dolled up and painted. Sort of good-looking in a way, I suppose.'

'I'd better go home.' Arthur looked at Moira and when she nodded understandingly he turned to Frankie again asking, 'How did you get here?'

'On a motorbike.'

'A motorbike?'

'Oh, for heaven's sake stop repeating things, our Arthur. I'm learning to drive a motorbike and the only way to learn to drive is to sit on one and let it go.'

'All right, all right,' said Arthur in a big-brother voice. 'You'll soon be like Gran with your tongue.'

'I'm not like Gran, and don't say I am.' This was the second one in the last few days to say he was like Gran. The world seemed a very unkind place to Frankie at this moment.

Arthur said no more and they all walked dolefully down the lane.

'I'll come on the back,' said Arthur when they reached the bike.

'What about her?' Frankie, with a curt point of his head indicated Moira as if she wasn't there.

'I'll walk.'

'Walk?' Frankie was forced to look at her now. 'All the way?'

'I'm used to walking . . . I like walking.'

Frankie turned about and mounted his bike and although his back was towards them he knew that they were holding hands. He heard a few whispered words and then Arthur was sitting behind him. As Frankie drove away he was not thinking of traffic signals, or the rudiments of driving a motorbike, nor yet the astounding side to his father which he had discovered, nor even their Arthur's double dealings, but of Moira, naturally, her hips swaying, walking the four miles into Downfell Hurst.

'Oh, why didn't you follow him?' said Florrie.

'I've told you, Mam. He was on the Biddleswiddle Road and I just slipped into the garage to see Mr Norton. I wasn't a second and when I came out he was gone.'

'And you say the bus didn't pass you. He didn't get on the bus?'

'Oh, Mam, we've been over it again and again.'

Florrie looked round her family. They were all there, including Gran, and she said helplessly, 'But look at the time, it's ten past eleven.'

'He could have called in at the club,' said Arthur weakly.

'You know he doesn't go to the club, Arthur; and anyway he said he was just going for a walk.'

'Well.' Gran was speaking now, flatly and definitely. 'If you ask me, you won't get any further until he comes in, and as he's neither in swaddling clothes nor on crutches, he'll be back . . . That's if,' she added, 'his mind holds out or he doesn't get himself knocked down.'

'Oh, Gran!' It was an exclamation of indignation from Linda.

'All right, miss . . . Oh, Gran. Well can you think of any explanation that's kept your dad out to this time?'

'Ssh! All of you . . . Here he is.' Florrie's wary ears had picked up John's footsteps in the street, and they all listened to the gate clicking and the steady rhythmic tread as he neared the door.

John was brought to a halt immediately as he stepped into the kitchen. Whatever reception he had expected he hadn't imagined his whole family still being up and waiting for him . . . plus Gran. All eyes were fixed hard on him and he looked from one to the other before saying, 'What's this? Why didn't you send the bellman out for me?'

'Oh, John, I've been so worried. Where did you get to?' Florrie came towards him and as he pulled his coat off she took it from his hands.

He did not answer her right away but walked towards the table, throwing his cap onto the couch as he did so. It wasn't until he'd sat down that he said, 'I just went for a walk as I told you and I came back by the cemetery and called in the hut to see to one or two things.'

'In the cemetery in the dead of night?'

John, turning towards Gran, said quite evenly, 'Yes, Mother. I was in the cemetery in the dead of night. I've got nothing on me conscience and nothing to be afraid of.'

Gran's chin was doing its wobbling stunt and when it stopped she remarked, as she moved her gaze from one member of the family to another, 'The bus must have gone out of its wits an' all and gone round by the cemetery where never a bus has been known to go afore.'

John's eyes were narrowed and his face was red as he turned on his mother sharply, 'What d'you mean, the bus?'

Dramatically Gran pointed to the floor. 'That bus ticket fell out of your cap when you took it off.'

Through force of habit John had stuck his bus ticket up under his cap near his ear. For a moment his heart quickened, then he said boldly, 'All right then, I took a bus ride. Is there anything wrong with that? And I took it early on and went as far as Biddleswiddle.' It was no use trying to hide where he had been, the old devil had only to look at the ticket and she could work that out.

'Will you have something to eat?' said Florrie soothingly.

'No, thanks, I'm not hungry.'

'Then a drink of something?'

'No, nothing at all. I think I'll just go up.'

In dead silence they all watched him cross the room and when he had reached the door he turned and said with emphasis, 'Goodnight.' And one after the other they mumbled, 'Goodnight.'

'Well! What d'you make a that? He's been drinkin' or somethin'.' Gran nodded knowingly to each member of the family in turn.

'Aye, it was . . . or something,' thought Frankie. By, he never thought that his dad had it in him to be so two-faced. He was forty-faced, not two, and so bloomin' calm with it. He had the desire now to rush upstairs, push open the bedroom door and shout, 'You twister you.' He could see himself doing it, but as before it got no further than a picture in his mind.

Arthur on the other hand was thinking, 'He's got himself into a jam.' Arthur knew the subtler shades of his father better than Frankie, and he had seen the change in his face when Gran had mentioned the bus.

'Let's get to bed. We'll have no more talking the night.'

One after the other, Florrie bustled her family upstairs and when finally she followed them and went into the bedroom, John was already in bed but his eyes were open. He greeted her immediately in a soft undertone, saying, 'Come here.' And she went to him, sat on the side of the bed and, after looking at him for a moment, she fell against him and he put his arms about her and stroked her hair.

'I'm all right, lass. I wish you'd stop worryin'.'

'Oh, John, I can't. Where did you get to the night?'

It was a while before John replied and then he said, 'I went for a walk and I had a little bit of business to do. I'll tell you about it sometime, but not now. Look at me.' He raised her tear-stained face to his, then smiling on her he said tenderly, 'I love you now the same as I did the first minute I set eyes on you, and the night I've found out that you're the bonniest woman in the world.'

John talking in this way, like when they were first married. Oh, what was the matter? Oh, something was wrong, radically wrong.

Even under ordinary circumstances, Florrie would have been surprised at this stage in her married life that John should say such things to her, but under the present stress, his tenderness and loving phrases only increased her worry, and as she cried herself into her first sleep, John was made aware of this and he sighed a deep sigh.

Well past midnight, John was still awake, for his mind was churning with his problems and as he listened to Florrie's regular breathing he wondered if he should tell her about Freda. Not for the world would he add to her worries, but from what he had seen of Freda tonight, he was going to see a great deal more of her if she had her way, for she had suggested paying a visit to the house.

'Tell Florrie,' she had said. 'And you can invite me to tea like an old friend – and I am an old friend, aren't I, John?' His body went hot under the bedclothes. She had stood near to him when she had said that, and then she had cocked her head to one side and remarked, 'You know, John, I wouldn't have believed it, but you've grown into quite a good-looking man – attractive an' all. But there's one thing you haven't lost and that's your dour expression. You were always dour, weren't you, John? I think that's what I couldn't stand. It got my goat. But now, I don't know, for somehow I think you've developed compensations.' She had poked him in the chest with a heavily ringed finger. She wore a lot of jewellery and it all looked good. The house too was furnished in style. It was more than evident that she was very comfortable, and she had said as much to him.

'George had a selling manner,' she had said. 'But he would never have got anywhere if it hadn't been for me, for, God help him, he never had much brain. I was the brains in our business.' Then she had ended, 'And so you're a gravedigger, John.' She had spaced each word and hammered them home. He felt some of the uncomfortable old days with her wash over him once again.

When he had told her without much diplomacy that he had no intention of inviting her to the house, she had laughed and said, 'Well, it will be the easiest thing in the world for me to find out where the boy's working and make myself known to him.'

Quickly he had corrected her, telling her that Arthur was no longer a boy but a man of twenty-one and about to be married. And he had also informed her of what she had never seemed to understand – that she had no claim whatever on Arthur. She had been quick to take this up and had said she understood well enough her position with regards to Manning's son, but the fact that he was Manning's son was the reason why she wanted to see him, and what's more, she would see him. She had gone on to say that she had had no idea that he himself was anywhere in the neighbourhood when she took this house, but once she did know she admitted that her interest was revived, 'For, moreover,' she had added with a laugh that held a trace of bitterness, 'I don't forget you skedaddled all those years ago. I know that I could have won Florrie over to let me have the boy if you hadn't scooted.'

It had been no use telling her that she could never have won Florrie over; it was never any use telling Freda something that she didn't want to believe. Freda had changed in only two ways, he considered. She had lost most of her looks and she was no longer poor. For the rest, she was as dogmatic and as mean of nature as ever he had known her to be.

John's mind was in such a turmoil that sleep was receding further and further away from him, and it was just as the clock downstairs struck two that he became aware that he was so wide awake that he wanted to get up. He looked at this feeling, as it were, and recognised with a wave of apprehension that it was the forerunner of . . . the state . . . which was how he had become to think of the feeling that always preceded his meetings with the Saint, and he protested loudly within himself. Not at two in the morning and with Florrie lying here, it would scare her out of her wits. He closed his eyes tightly. If he didn't look at him and didn't answer him what could he do? Nothing . . . nothing.

As he lay feeling himself being lifted, reluctantly, onto a plane of well-being, he longed for the days when he hadn't thought one way or the other about how he felt. Never having felt really bad, he had never questioned if he was feeling really well. One thing were certain, he had never experienced this alive feeling until . . . that state had started, and he had to concede that if it wasn't for . . . the state . . . it would be a real fine way to feel. He couldn't describe the feeling to himself other than it was like getting a kick out of something.

'*John.*' When the whisper came to him he refused to look.

'*John.*'

He had only to keep his eyes closed and his mouth shut and he would go.

'*John.*'

101

Oh God above. He turned on his side and right onto the edge of the bed but keeping his eyes still closed he whispered, 'Go away, will you.'

'*I want you to come to the crossroads tomorrow morning around ten.*'

'All right, only go away, for God's sake.'

'What is it John, are you dreaming or something?' Florrie was sitting up leaning over him and he turned to her with a great flounce and muttered as if coming out of a sleep, 'Oh, aye, must have been dreamin'.' Then he said solicitously, 'Don't tell me you haven't been asleep yet, why I thought you were long ago.'

'I can't sleep, John. I'm . . . I'm . . . so . . . so worried about you.'

'Aw, Florrie.'

Like a balloon that had been pricked, the airy feeling was seeping quickly away and he put his arms around her and drew her head onto his shoulder and comforted her as if she was a child. 'There, there,' he said. 'Get yourself off to sleep now, and no more of it.'

'And you, John.'

'Aye, I'll go to sleep an' all, never fear.'

And in a surprisingly short time they were both asleep and John was dreaming, not of St Christopher, but of McNally, and some time towards morning he woke with a wonderful feeling of achievement, for he had just returned home from burying him.

'Joan, I've told you,' said Florrie. 'I don't know where Arthur was last night. If he wasn't with you, then I can't tell you where he went.'

'Well, he wasn't with me and what's more I'm beginning to have my suspicions.' Joan wagged her head then jerked it around towards Gran as that lady said, 'And who wouldn't. Looks fishy if you ask me, eh?'

'Gran, will you stay out of this.'

Gran gave a hee-hee of a laugh as she split a pea pod and squirted the peas with a flick of her thumb into a basin. 'If you don't know where he is now you'll have your work cut out when you get him.'

'Well, I can tell you this much, Mrs Gascoigne.' Joan was now addressing Gran. 'The wedding's all fixed and everything and if he doesn't stop playing about I'll . . .'

'Aye, go on,' said Gran. 'Tell me what you'll do.' Her voice sounded ordinary and enquiring but it didn't hoodwink Joan into thinking that she would receive any sympathy from the old woman.

'I'd go easy, Joan, if I was you.' Florrie's voice was low. 'Arthur's a quiet lad. You might think he's slow but he's stubborn and he's got a will of his own, so I'd go easy.'

'My mother says—'

'I'm not interested in what your mother says, Joan. I'm talking to you and I'm telling you if you want things to go smoothly, go easy on Arthur.'

Florrie felt bound to give this advice but at the same time she was wishing that his absenteeism last night would result in a row of such proportions that the whole thing would be broken up. But she knew this was just wishful thinking; it would take more than that incident to break up the forthcoming marriage. In fact, she couldn't see anything big enough happening to put it off.

'How many of your relations have you invited to the weddin'?' asked Gran, splitting open another pea pod.

'Forty-five,' said Joan pertly.

'Oh.' Gran wagged her head sideways. 'Forty-five, and there's only six of us. Seven,' she added without any acidity in her tone for once, 'with me sister Lucy. It doesn't balance does it?'

'Well, we are—'

'Yes, yes, I know,' put in Florrie sharply now. 'You're paying for it, and I know this too, all this bickering and fighting doesn't say much for your future happiness, and I might as well tell you, I think Arthur's wise

103

to put it off for a while. At least until things settle down and we're all seeing straight again!'

Joan looked from Florrie to Gran then stretching her thin neck upwards she declared flatly, 'Mother was right.' And on that she marched out without adding anything more.

Gran split yet another pea before turning to Florrie and stating in no small voice, 'Summat must be done in that quarter. If that wedding goes through life won't be worth livin'.'

'It's questionable whether it is now, with one thing and another,' said Florrie with unusual tartness.

Gran took the bowl of peas and placed it on the table and her tone was unusually soft as, looking at Florrie's back, she said, 'Try not to worry so, lass.'

'How can I do anything else?' murmured Florrie.

The subject between them now, they both knew, was John, and Gran said, 'Things have a way of panning out.'

'It's all right saying that but in the meantime he's ill and he's getting worse.' Florrie was remembering the incident in the middle of the night, for she knew John hadn't been dreaming, but like herself was wide awake.

'I know what I would do if I had my way.' Gran had returned to her pea-shelling and her voice had returned to normal, and when Florrie demanded almost angrily, 'Well, what would you do?' she just wagged her head as she replied, 'I'll keep it to meself, it's better that way.'

At this moment they both paused and looked upwards, for there came to them the sound of movement in the room above.

'He's up, then,' said Gran. 'What'll happen if the doctor comes?'

'Don't ask me,' answered Florrie wearily. 'He says he's going for a walk as far as the crossroads.' She sighed. 'I can't do anything more. I can't tie him up so I'm not going to say anything or try to stop him, and you, Gran, keep your tongue quiet when he comes down, mind you.'

It was quarter to ten when John left the house and he was glad to be outside. His mother was too quiet and Florrie was too sad to be natural. He had told himself a number of times this morning that he wasn't going to the crossroads. It had even come as a surprise when he had heard himself telling Florrie that he was going to take a dander along there. The crossroads was the last place he wanted to dander to, for within a few yards of it McNally and his gang were working. Yet here he was, going in search of the Devil, as it were.

He took side cuts and turnings out of the village for he did not want people stopping and enquiring how he was, and the nearer he came to the crossroads, the more intense became his feeling of well-being. As this feeling grew, he looked from side to side expecting to encounter the reason for it, but he saw no one.

When he came to the end of the Downfell Hurst road he took up his position near a farm gate and from there he had full view of the intersecting roads. Straight ahead at the other side of the crossroads, the men were at work and he could make out McNally's huge frame shaking under the pressure of the drill. He turned his eyes away, for even in his present highly elated state, McNally still had the power to irritate him.

He hadn't been standing by the gate more than a few minutes before his interest became taken up with the traffic. It was thick at this time of the morning: large, heavy-laden lorries making, he supposed, for Newcastle; farm tractors; vans and private cars of all shapes and sizes; and sprinkled among them, motorcycles and a very occasional pushbike. Within a few yards of passing him, all the traffic was forced to slow down and he found his eyes searching each vehicle. He could not see into the high cabs of the lorries. Anyway, he supposed, they'd have more in common sense than to carry superstitious junk around with them – the men on the big lorries had their work cut out and had to depend on themselves, not on bits of tin.

It was at the very moment this thought presented itself that he saw him again, standing not a yard away, leaning against the oak post of the five-barred gate. John closed his eyes then gulped. The first glimpse of the Saint still had the power to knock him off balance.

'*How many have you counted?*' asked St Christopher.

'None so far,' said John bluntly.

'*Oh, I'm peeved at that.*' The Saint was smiling broadly. '*I reckon that eighty per cent of things on wheels have me as a passenger.*'

'And that's when the trouble starts.'

'*I'm out to prove you wrong, John.*'

'All right, go ahead. I'm ready to be convinced but I know full well that I won't be.'

The roar that the Saint let out almost deafened John; it certainly drowned the noise of the passing traffic. '*That's as good an Irishism as McNally himself could bring out – you're ready to be convinced but you're determined not to be. Well, well. Anyway, that's why we're here this morning, John, and I'm positive that within half an hour I'll have broken through the armour of your prejudice.*'

'You think so?' said John. 'Well, look at that.' He pointed to an open MG tearing past them and drawing up practically within its own length behind a stationary car. The driver, like his car, looked smart, added to which he appeared blasé. In the lapel of his coat he wore a pin and on it a print of the Saint wrought in coloured enamel. It was really too minute for John to see but he knew instinctively that it was a St Christopher pin and he turned to the Saint and said, 'Did you see that? He's got you up and dashing along hell for leather.'

'*No, no, you're wrong there, John. That man's a good driver. He wasn't dashing, he was driving fast.*'

'And you mean to tell me that's good driving? And stopping almost on a hair.'

'*It's because he's a good driver that he could stop almost on a hair, as you term it. And let me tell you something, John.*' The Saint wagged his finger slowly at him. '*It isn't the fast drivers that are the menace on the roads today; no, it's the slow ones, the cautious ones who keep their foot on*' *their brakes. They're always brake drunk, and they brake for anything and everything irrespective of what is behind them. As for that fellow'* – the Saint thumbed the driver who was setting the car roaring off now – *'he's never had an accident and he's been driving for fifteen years now to my knowledge.'*

'It's more by good luck than management, then, and because other folk have given way to him,' commented John.

Again the Saint laughed.

'Well, look at this one coming.' John was shouting excitedly now. 'Weaving about like a butterfly and it's a woman at the wheel . . . It would be. Aye.' He pointed. 'Look at the size of you on that windscreen. You're so big she's got to dodge to see past you.'

'Yes, yes, now you've got me there, John,' said St Christopher sadly. *'She's one of my worst cases. But there's hope for her yet – she only learnt last year.'*

Both the Saint and John watched the woman come to a halt on the extreme left of the road, then, putting out her indicator and without looking either way, turn sharply right, cutting across an oncoming car in the process.

When John looked in triumph at him, the Saint had one great hand shading his eyes, and when he lowered his hand he nodded to John saying, *'All right, all right. I'll admit everything you say about her is true. I have nightmares about that lady.'*

'She'll be one of them somebody'll be burying shortly,' said John with a slightly pompous air. 'She's well ahead in the race to Kingdom Come.'

'I shouldn't be at all surprised,' said the Saint.

'And won't she be on your conscience?' John was aggressive now. 'If she hadn't got you up and wasn't relying on you, wouldn't she be usin' her head?'

'No, she never would, for she has very little in it, John. I am really a form of protection . . . Not for her alone, but for those that she meets. You see, John, my presence in a car has a cautionary effect. People want to go fast but they're slightly afraid so they call on me and say, now I've got you along with me I'll be all right . . . But wait.' He put up his hand like a signal as John was

about to interrupt. '*Let me finish. You must face the fact that people's fear often makes them cautious – so although they go fast they are very much alive to the risks and their driving becomes better, and quite undeservedly they give me the credit for their continued safety.*'

'You've got it all worked out, haven't you?'

'*No, John, no. I'm just stating facts. I just happen to know people. I've been in the traffic business for a long, long time, you know.*'

'You're as clever as McNally with your tongue.' John now sounded surly.

The Saint shook his head and smiled. '*You will connect me with McNally, John, and I don't know whether I like it or not. For I knew a man once who used to get my goat much in the same way McNally gets yours today.*'

John's eyes widened slightly with questioning interest and the Saint nodded and went on. '*It was when I was doing the ferrying job across the river. I'm a big man, as you can see, and I'm strong as any shire horse, but every day there would come one who was the spit of McNally and he would say, "Take me across, Offero." As, you see, I wasn't known as Christopher in those days but by the name Offero. And I would take him across and later in the day he would call me over from the far bank: "Come and get me, Offero." And across there I would go and hump him on my back again, and always he would offer me payment by way of a wooden gourd full of a wine made from herbs that did strange things to a man. Now, I was working for the good of God but being of human nature, I had to eat, and when I wasn't ferrying the good folk on my shoulders, I would till my piece of land. But I had very little time to give to the tilling and the produce from it was small, so the people to whom I did service were kind in their offering a piece of goat flesh or a gourd of milk and such that would keep my strength together. But this man, this man who was your McNally, he offered me nothing but the drink that I had known in the wild days of my youth before I had given myself into the service of our dear Lord, and he would laugh at me and say, "Go on, Offero, drink. It is like honey to the gullet." And each time I sent up a prayer to my Master to give me the strength to refuse and my prayer was answered. But this man would drink from the gourd and he would sing and make jokes at my expense and at times I had to do a lot of praying, John, to stop my hands from swiping him one.'*

John's eyes were wide now, and his mouth was slightly open. That was just how he felt about McNally. He couldn't say that he himself prayed, but he knew that he always had to do something to curb the desire to hit out at McNally. He stared at the Saint. There was something about this fella that was really taking. Under other circumstances he could have found himself liking him.

'You know how I got the better of that man, John?'

John did not answer but shook his head and waited eagerly to hear the Saint's solution to his particular McNally.

'I turned the tables on him by giving him a dose of his own medicine, the medicine he relied on. I started to laugh at him. I not only pulled his leg, I pulled his ear. And do you know, John, he couldn't take it. The leg-pullers of this world can't stand having even their own toes tickled. You play a joke on a practical joker and he's finished. You tease or laugh at a McNally and he doesn't know which end of him's uppermost – he just can't take it. You try, John.'

John could not see himself at this moment ever teasing or laughing at McNally, yet he knew if he could do it he would prove the Saint to be right – oh, if he could only take a rise out of McNally, just one time.

'If you fear to do a thing, John, never put it off, for the next time you've got to make the attempt your fear will be doubled and on and on it will go. I've found that the best way to cure fear is to tackle it; get it by the throat and throttle it like all evil things.'

For a man of peace, the Saint was looking very ferocious – just as if he had fear within his hands and was throttling it to inefficacy at this very moment.

'Look, look, what's up with you, man? It's me, Broderick.'

John flung the hand from his arm and turned round to face Broderick in the flesh. Definitely he was startled; Broderick had been filling his mind and he seemed to have conjured him out of the air. He had been so taken up with the Saint that he hadn't noticed his approach, and forgetting the advice that he had just received, he barked, 'Why do you have to jump on a man like that?'

'Jump on you, John?' Broderick's head went up. 'Why, man, I've been standin' these minutes trying to get your notice. You're not yoursel' again – are you feeling under the weather?'

'I'm feeling neither under nor on top of the weather,' answered John facetiously. 'I'm feeling all right, at least I was up till a minute ago.' He gave Broderick a nod that left no doubt as to the implication of his words, and Broderick, nodding back, said, 'Aye, well. Well now, John, that's more like yourself, but a minute ago you didn't appear yourself. Are you having one of your seeing turns?'

John glared at McNally, denial on his lips, and then something made him turn and look towards the gatepost. The Saint was still standing there, and now he nodded sharply to John and John read the nod as if he had spoken aloud. Then finally, and for all time, the Saint made it impossible for John not to like him, for he winked at him, a large, slow wink that said, 'Go ahead and give him a dose of his own medicine.' John could not refrain from returning the salutation, so he winked back. Then explained his action briefly to Broderick by saying, 'A pal o' mine.'

'In the name of God.' It was merely a mutter from Broderick and then John, giving him his full attention now, said, 'Aye, as you would say, I'm havin' a spell of seein' things, and achieved on the cheap an' all, mind. I haven't even to spend one and two on a pint.'

Broderick's expression now was so similar to the one that the Saint had predicted that John felt as if he had been injected with a dose of glee, and he laughed as he said, 'Would you like me to tell you about it, Broderick?' For the first time during their long acquaintance he had called his neighbour by his Christian name.

'Well, not now, John.' McNally had forced a smile to his face. 'Me break time's finished, but I'd gladly listen the night. That all right with you?'

'Aye, that's all right. The night will do me fine.'

McNally was laughing again and refusing to be other than master of the situation. He went on, 'I don't know which of the two of you appeals to me most, John, the one that won't open his gob not even if he's prodded in the pants with a pin, or this other new one. This talking one; this Brodericking one. But anyway, whichever one you are, you're always a great source of entertainment to me, John.'

'I'm glad of that,' John nodded at him genially. He could not do otherwise for a kind of impish geniality seemed to be oozing out of his pores like sweat. 'And I hope you're here for a long time yet to get amusement out of me. It's to be hoped anyway that the dream I had of you last night doesn't work out.'

'You dreamt of me, John?'

'I did,' John nodded his head heavily. 'And if it comes true I'll have the sad task of shovelling the dirt on you.'

'Now, John . . .' cautioned Broderick, his face without the vestige of a smile. 'Stop your jokin' about things like that, and it the thirteenth by the same token. There's things that shouldn't be joked about. Even I know that an' I'm a one for me jokes.'

'I'm not jokin' at all, McNally, honest Injun. I dreamt about you last night, and it was the first time in me life I've done it.'

'Aye, all right, I'll take it you did, John. I won't doubt your word, but I'm not for hearing it if it's all the same to you. Anyway, I must get back to work.'

'Don't worry,' put in John with raised hands. 'I wasn't goin' to tell you. Black-robed priests and the polis are not in my line of discussion. I had enough of them anyway in me dream. They brought me out in a sweat.'

'Name of God.' McNally had turned away but was now facing John again. 'And was I there among the priests and the polismen?'

'Now I'm not goin' to tell you. Go on, get back to your work.'

Broderick had moved closer. 'Just this, John, did you see a hospital in it – in the dream?'

'No; no hospital.'

Broderick drew in a deep breath and then almost choked as John ended, 'Only an ambulance.'

'You saw an ambulance?' It was a whisper from Broderick.

'Aye.' John nodded and waited. He waited in the most pleasurable state he had experienced in his life. So this is how it felt to pull another man's leg; this is how it felt to take a rise out of somebody. McNally had had a lot of this pleasure at his expense but, considered John definitely, that was finished. If St Christopher had brought him a deal of worry, he had done him one good turn at least; he had taught him how to deal with McNally.

John did not remember at this moment that he had received similar advice from Arthur and also from Florrie. Perhaps their advice had been ineffective because it was unaccompanied by illustrations, whereas the Saint was very good with his illustrations; so good he could bring the actual picture alive before your eyes.

After a moment of watching McNally striding back to his work, John turned to the Saint again, and he saw at once that his face was one large conquering beam – a replica of his own, in fact.

'*You did that very well indeed, John. You're to be congratulated on your first lesson.*'

John squared his shoulders and looked down at his bulging chest as he said, 'Well, if that's all there is to it I can't see why I haven't done it afore.'

'*Nor can I, John. But just to return to cars for a moment – or vans in this instance – will you look at this one heading up the road. Look at him nipping out and passing that car. And what for? They'll both have to wait at the crossroads and to my mind he shouldn't have taken the chance of passing.*'

'Nor to mine, either,' said John gruffly. 'But see who it is? It's Duckworth.' He turned and looked at the Saint and asked pointedly, 'Has he got you up?'

'*Duckworth? Oh no, Duckworth wouldn't have me up, John. He's the kind of fellow who wouldn't have the good God himself up. Duckworth doesn't need any assistance from anyone; he's a tower of strength within himself. At least so he believes.*'

'Aye, there you've got it.' John nodded at the Saint. 'So he believes. All these chapel-going wallahs think they're temporary Lord Gods Almighty, and Duckworth there, he's about the brightest of the bunch – do you know his daughter's gonna marry my son?'

The Saint nodded solemnly. '*That'll be a sad day, John.*'

'Aye, it will, that. I suppose you know an' all that he's got his eyes in another quarter.'

'*Arthur? Yes, I've observed that, John.*'

'What d'you think of her?' John was giving his whole attention to the Saint now. They were both leaning on the top of the gate, their backs turned to the traffic on the road. In fact, the traffic seemed to be forgotten entirely. It could have been a subject that had never arisen, so deeply did they both become engrossed in the subject of Moira McNally.

Florrie thought that she could not cope with one more thing this morning when Mr Duckworth dashed in through the back door without even knocking. His eyes were wide and his mouth was open to speak when he saw the doctor and the Reverend Collins standing in the kitchen, and it was to them he spoke rather than to her when he blurted out, 'He's at the crossroads, waving his arms about and talkin' to himself. I've never seen anything like it. He didn't know me. He pointed at me but he didn't know me. I saw McNally further along the road and he said he had been there carrying on for the last hour or more. Something must be done about it.'

Florrie did not speak; she looked at the doctor picking up his bag from the chair and he was looking at the minister. And when, feeling that she was about to collapse, she murmured, 'I'll go an' fetch him', it was Gran's clipped tones that cut off both the doctor's and the Reverend Collins' reply as she said, 'You stay put. Let the doctor handle this. You'll have enough to do when he comes back.'

'I . . . That's right, Mrs Gas . . . Gascoigne,' said the Reverend, stuttering in his agitation. 'The doctor and I will go and see to him.'

The doctor did not add anything to this but went briskly towards the door followed by Mr Duckworth. But the Reverend Collins paused, and coming back to Florrie, he said, 'I feel terrible about this, Mrs Gascoigne. I hold myself responsible for what has happened to your husband.'

The concern on the Reverend's face could not help but get past Florrie's own anxiety and she answered comfortingly, 'You mustn't do that, sir. These things happen. You mustn't blame yourself.'

'But I do. Lashing out like that, determined that our side should win, striving for applause and self-aggrandisement – these have their penalties and I can assure you, Mrs Gascoigne, that it isn't only your husband who is suffering at this moment.'

Gran let out a long drawn sigh that brought the minister's eyes to her and he coughed and said, 'Yes, well, I'd better be going. The doctor's waiting. Don't worry, we'll see to him.' And with one last look, not at Florrie but at Gran, the minister's long gangling legs took him from the room.

After the door had closed, Gran, sitting down in her usual place by the table, breathed deeply before saying, 'Well, it's an ill wind that blows no apples over the fence. This could be a way out, for one of the family anyway.'

'What do you mean?' asked Florrie wearily.

'Arthur and the Duckworths. If John's off his nut, I'll bet you a shilling they won't have any of us.'

'Gran!' Now Florrie's voice was high and angry. 'It's as Linda says, you're without feeling. You haven't got a spark of feeling for John; there's not a drop of mother love in you. You're a bad old woman.'

Gran did not immediately answer Florrie for her chin was at its wagging again, and when she did, her eyes were lowered to the table and she said quietly, 'You're wrong you know; like all the rest, you're wrong. But if you can't see through me ways then I guess nobody can.' And, getting up from the table and keeping her head turned from Florrie's face, she shambled out of the kitchen.

Florrie sat down. On top of all her other troubles, she had to have a feeling of guilt over Gran now. Gran was a dab hand at turning the tables. Oh, where was all this going to end? She looked around her kitchen; her lovely kitchen. If John lost his job they'd have to leave this house. Her thoughts began to leap hither and thither; she didn't like that doctor, he was too sharp, too abrupt. She wished old Dr Sanderson was back. These young ones didn't have any patience with men like John. They didn't understand that people could be just as uppity and off-hand as they were themselves and could have minds of their own an' all . . . And Mr Duckworth bouncing in like that, as if John had committed a crime or something; who did he think he was?

At that instant, the squeaking of brakes brought her out of her chair and to the kitchen window, and she could scarcely believe her eyes to see not only the doctor's car at the gate again but Duckworth's van as well. She saw the doctor and minister alight from the car and waited to see John but there was no sight of him. Then she watched the minister and the doctor go to Duckworth's van, beside which Henry Duckworth was now standing, waving his arms and pointing to himself.

There was always a slight dusting of flour on Mr Duckworth's clothes, as there was on Arthur's, but as Florrie screwed her eyes up to see through the sun, she saw that there was not just a sprinkle of flour on Mr Duckworth, but he seemed to be enveloped in it. And then she realised it couldn't be flour, for it was much too dark. It looked a greyish-coloured

115

powder. The apprehension in her chest linked up John with this powder, but then she thought, he could have had nothing to do with Duckworth looking like that.

As Mr Duckworth disappeared up the path and into his house the doctor and the minister made their way towards her. Trembling she went to the door to open it for them.

'Is he here?'

'You mean John?'

'Yes, yes, of course I mean . . . John,' the doctor snapped as he went past Florrie and into the kitchen without being asked.

'No, he's not,' she said to his back.

The minister, following the doctor, added soothingly, 'We could hardly expect him back so soon. We were in the car you know.'

'The way he was running he could have beaten any car.' The doctor was snapping at the minister now.

'What's happened?' asked Florrie in a weak voice, as she looked from one to the other.

The doctor turned to her now and said, quietly but definitely, 'Your husband must have attention, Mrs Gascoigne. He's just knocked Mr Duckworth into a heap of cement. It's a good job it wasn't wet, but it was very distressing to your neighbour.'

'It . . . it wasn't entirely his fault, not altogether, do you think?' the minister had one hand on his chest and was rubbing the back of it with the knuckles of his other hand.

'He hit the man, didn't he?'

'Yes. Yes, he did, but then Mr Duckworth had taken hold of his arm, you must remember that, doctor, and he did it in rather a rough manner.'

'Well, if we're going to knock down everyone who takes hold of our arms things are coming to a pretty pass, aren't they?'

'There's a law about laying hands on people and if Duckworth laid his hands on John then he had every right to knock them off.' They all turned and looked at Gran where she stood in the scullery doorway.

'Duckworth's too big for his boots. He'd like to run this village – he thinks he does. If my son doesn't want to be touched by him, then he was in his rights to push him off . . . Right?' The last word was in the form of a demanding question.

'Your son,' said the doctor quietly, but in a special firm tone that he kept for old ladies such as Gran, 'your son pushed Mr Duckworth a little harder than was necessary; he did it with his fist under Mr Duckworth's chin.'

Florrie lowered her head, gripped her hands together and groaned as Grandma asked, 'Where'd this come about?'

It was the minister who answered Gran, moving towards her as he said placatingly, 'Mr Gascoigne was talking to your neighbour.' The minister nodded his head at the wall that he thought divided the house from the McNallys. 'You know, Mr McNally—'

'You could hardly call it talking; I would have said he was upbraiding Mr McNally . . . Anyway' – the doctor turned to Florrie again – 'as soon as he returns, telephone my house and I'll come over and see him.'

'What are you going to do to him?' Florrie's eyes were dry and burning but the quiver of tears was in her voice, and the doctor, a little more kindly now, said, 'Well, the first thing I must do, Mrs Gascoigne, is see that he has a sedative that will keep him in bed, and if that doesn't do much good, then I'm afraid we must get him to a hospital, where he'll have some attention and his head X-rayed.'

'There's more'n him wants their heads examined.'

The doctor turned his startled, indignant gaze on Gran. Age to him was no licence for this kind of talk, nor did he treat her with the respect due to an elderly woman, for his parting shot as he went to the door was, 'You're right there, Mrs Gascoigne.' And this statement left Gran in no doubt to whom he referred.

'Can I drop you anywhere?'

The doctor was calling from the front door and the Reverend called back, 'No, thanks. I'll be staying a little while, but if I can look in on you sometime this evening.'

'Very well.'

Now that the doctor was gone, Florrie turned to the minister and asked quickly, 'What will they do to him?'

The minister took her hand and pressed her into a chair before saying, 'They'll just examine his head.' Following this statement, the minister cast a wary glance in the direction of Gran, then he coughed and went on. 'You see, the ball might have fractured some . . . some small thing that is causing your husband to have a form of hallucination.'

'But, Mr Collins, it's so real to him, and he only sees the one person, this saint. He's not getting religious mania, is he?'

The vicar smiled then shook his head and said, 'No, Mrs Gascoigne, I don't think you need fear that. Your husband is not a religious man, not in the sense you are meaning. You see, at the moment the ball hit him he must have been thinking about the Saint in connection with the emblems people carry about with them in cars and such like. St Christopher has reached a popularity in this age that no other saint has acquired, and it's a very strange thing for there is so little known about him, and what is known we read mostly in the legends written around the thirteenth century. But he has always been the guide of travellers and, as you know, there has never been so much travelling in the world since it was made as there is today. So I suppose one can understand his being made use of. But I'm afraid,' the vicar shook his head sadly, 'there is little sanctity attached to the worship of this saint; it has grown into rather a cult, like the material worship of a film star.'

'Well, there's one thing we can be thankful for: if he's seein' saints he's seein' a male one.'

If this remark of Gran's had been intended to terminate the Reverend's visit, it succeeded, for he gave a little tickling cough and rose to his feet.

Then, bending towards Florrie and patting her shoulder, he said, 'Don't worry, I'll make it my business to find him. I've left my bike near the green, but if he should return before lunch would you mind phoning the vicarage when you phone the doctor to let me know?'

Florrie merely nodded – she was weary and beyond words.

'If you want my advice,' commented Gran to the minister's departing back, 'you'll leave him be. He'll find his own road home. If you leave him be he'll likely come to, but if you set a manhunt on him, the end of that'll be there'll be more of you lying on your backs.'

The minister could find nothing to say to this and he left, closing the door quietly behind him. Florrie did not chastise Gran because for once she wholeheartedly agreed with her.

It was half past five and all the family, with the exception of John, were gathered in the kitchen. But they were not sitting down to tea as was usual at this time – even the table wasn't laid. Florrie's face was the colour of lint and her voice had a flat, hopeless sound as she said, 'If he doesn't turn up within the next half hour, I'm going to the police.'

'We should look again, Mam,' said Linda tearfully.

'We've looked everywhere,' said Florrie. 'Everywhere . . .'

At this point Arthur and Frankie exchanged a quick glance. There was the house in Biddleswiddle and ten to one, thought Frankie, that's where he was, so it was he who said to his mother, 'Look, Mam, leave it until around nine.'

'Nine!' exclaimed Florrie. 'Nine?' Her voice was almost a squeak. 'I'll be stark staring mad by nine o'clock if he's not in.'

'Look, here's Moira. She's just come home but she's coming in here.'

As Linda spoke they all moved towards the window. Moira could be the bearer of news for she worked for Dr Spencer at his house in Befumstead, and if anyone could have any inside information it would be her. By the time they had crowded into the scullery, Moira had reached the back door, and it was Florrie she singled out and addressed directly. 'You'll never believe what Uncle's doing, Aunt Florrie.'

Florrie swallowed hard then asked, 'You've seen him?'

'Yes.' Moira's voice was high. 'I've just been talkin' to him.'

'You have?'

Moira nodded at Florrie again. 'He's in the cemetery at work.' Her eyes now flashed round the family and she showed a mouthful of white, even teeth as she laughed. 'All this hullabaloo, looking for him everywhere, and there he is at work as calm as you like. I was riding down by the cemetery wall and I thought I made him out in the distance so I got off me bike and went in, and there he was, cleaning up the graves like he does every day, and the paths on the east side were all new-mown. He must have been there all the time. Oh, I did laugh.'

'What did he say?' Florrie's voice was scarcely audible.

'Nothing much.'

'Did he say anything?' Again Florrie was speaking.

'Well, I asked him to buy a raffle ticket.' Moira patted her pocket. 'It's the big raffle, you know. For the hospitals. Dr Spencer's helping to run it. They're smashing prizes given by big firms. Look.'

As Moira brought the book of tickets from her pocket, Florrie said impatiently, 'I don't want to know about raffle tickets at the moment.' She nearly added 'Have some sense, girl', but she checked herself and went on, 'Listen, Moira, tell me; what did he say? How did he talk?'

'Oh, he talked all right. Just as ever he did, only a bit more so, and he bought three tickets. He even laughed when I pointed out what the prizes were.'

'Three?' said Gran. 'Well, if anything's needed to prove he's not himself, that's it.'

Arthur had moved nearer to Moira and he looked down into her face as he asked, 'How long had he been there, do you know?'

'From what I could make out, I think he's been there since this morning.' Moira was returning Arthur's gaze intently, seemingly oblivious of the lookers-on.

'And never a bite.' Florrie turned into the kitchen on this and quietly and automatically began to set the table. But in the middle of it, she rounded on her family and, addressing them as a whole, she said, 'Mind, no questions, just act as if nothing has happened.'

'I don't see how we're going to do that, Mam,' said Arthur quietly. 'For as soon as he puts his nose in the door, they'll be on us.' He indicated the Duckworths.

'Well, we'll deal with that business when it arises, only don't ask him any questions. Say nothing, all of you.' As Florrie finished, she let her eyes linger on Gran. Gran replied to the look by saying, 'If you all said as little as me there'd be less trouble.'

On this there came a natural reaction from Frankie in the form of a loud 'Coo!' and Florrie turned on him sharply. 'Stop it! Let's have none of that.'

Frankie stopped it and they all sat down, but not at the table.

When only a few minutes later, the door opened and John walked into the kitchen, Florrie closed her eyes and held her breath a moment before managing to bring out the usual greeting of 'Hullo'. She felt a little flicker of relief when he did not answer her as he went to hang up his coat. But when, after having deposited the coat in the cupboard, he turned and confronted his family and said in a tone of enquiry, 'Well?' the feeling of relief fled.

Slowly John advanced towards the table and, taking his place at it, asked, 'Doesn't anybody want to eat?'

When, without a word, they were all seated, John let his eyes travel around them, then as rationally as a judge he said, 'If a man lays hands on you roughly the natural reaction is to strike out. I did that this mornin' with Duckworth and I'll do it again with anybody who attempts the same thing, and I'm neither drunk nor daft. What's more, I've been at work all day, while there's no doubt they've been scouring the lanes for me.'

Once again John looked from one to the other, but not a word did any one of them say. At that moment there came the click of the back gate and the sound of quick heavy steps on the path, and John raised his hand to indicate that he would deal with the visitor. Rising slowly from the table, and under the fascinated gaze of his family, he went to the kitchen window and, throwing it wide, he looked out at the bristling form of his neighbour. Before that indignant visitor could say anything, he said quite calmly, 'I'm about to have me tea, Duckworth, if you've got a mind to come round later, well and good.'

'I'll see you now, Gascoigne . . . This minute. There's business I want to settle with you and another member of your family.'

'Very well then, you come back later and we'll settle all you want.'

'We'll settle it now.'

As John saw Duckworth make a move nearer to his door, he cried, 'Go on, you put a foot across me step, Duckworth, and I'll repeat the dose I gave you this mornin', and mind you I mean it. I'll see you in me own time, or not at all, get that.'

'John, John, stop it. Come away in.'

John withdrew his head and, speaking calmly again, said, 'Aye, I'll come away in.' Whereupon he closed the window and returned to the table. As he sat down, the voice of Mr Duckworth could still be heard shouting as he retreated from the garden, and John, looking round his family, asked, 'Which one of us do you think needs to see the doctor now, eh?'

Still nobody spoke, not even Gran. For this John Gascoigne was a very unknown quantity.

The tea was eaten in a strange, unnatural silence, and when it was over and John rose from the table and seated himself in the easy chair with the paper, Florrie gave a warning shake of her head to the rest of the family that told them to go about their business and take no notice;

and this the majority of them did. Arthur and Frankie going upstairs to change, Linda helping to clear the table, but Gran . . . Gran did none of the things she usually did at this time of the evening but she continued to sit at the table and tap it with her forefinger from time to time while she stared unblinkingly at her son.

John was not unaware of his mother's fixed gaze, and after a time he became fidgety under it. He had a strong urge to take himself upstairs to bed, for he was feeling very tired. There was no elation about him now, and though he often felt tired after a day's work, tonight there was a heavy weariness about him as if he had been working for days without sleep. It was just as he had decided he was going to bed that there came a rap on the back door and for a moment some of the feeling of weariness fled. Duckworth back? As he met Florrie's apprehensive glance he rose from the chair saying, 'Don't worry, I'll deal with him, and there'll be no rows.' And again he repeated, 'Don't worry.' But as he went to open the back door some higher sense told him he would not find Duckworth there and when he saw Broderick he was not surprised.

'Oh, hullo there, John. I thought I'd look round to see how you were farin'?'

'I'm farin' perfectly well, thank you,' said John stiffly, but quietly, for the weary feeling was heavy on him and he found to his dismay he would not be able to deal with Broderick as he had done this morning.

'And how's our friend and neighbour?' Broderick was leaning towards John, his big arms outstretched to each side of the door, and his head wagging with suppressed laughter. 'I thought I would have died,' Broderick whispered hoarsely. 'I've never seen anything so funny in me life. The dignified Duckworth, spluttering in that heap of cement – the only thing I prayed for at that moment was rain. They've never stopped talking about it on the road the whole day.'

'I'm glad they got a laugh,' said John flatly.

'Laugh!' repeated Broderick. 'Turner, you know Dick Turner? Well, he said to me that he never thought you had it in you and I said to him, "Ha ha." I said, "You don't know the depths of John Gascoigne with or without saints." But I admitted, John, that if seeing saints gives a man courage such as yours I'd see saints the morrow meself.'

'Perhaps I could arrange something for you.'

The roar that Broderick let out rang down the back gardens and it brought Florrie from her waiting position in the kitchen to John's side, and she spoke to him as if Broderick was not there. 'Are you comin' to get your wash?' she said.

'Aye.' John turned about and, taking the loophole she had given him for escape, left her standing confronting Broderick, and Broderick, bending his great length down to her, whispered, 'He's himself, Florrie, as ever was. Begod, it's strange, isn't it? If you had seen him up at the crossroads this mornin', you wouldn't have believed your eyes. But it's glad I am . . .'

'Yes, yes, I know you are, Broderick. And now I've got things to see to and if you'll excuse me . . .'

'Yes, yes, I understand and if there's anything I can do, or my Katie, you've only got to come next door, you know that. We're not like those stink-pits.' He thumbed in the direction of the Duckworths. 'Y'know something I heard?' His voice dropped lower. 'He's for putting the wedding off all on account of this mornin'. Mind you,' he winked at Florrie, 'not that it wouldn't be pleasing some parties and them not a long spit from either of us.'

'Well, that'll be for the Duckworths and Arthur to decide,' said Florrie stiffly. 'Now if you'll . . .'

Broderick backed two or three steps, holding up his hand as if in blessing. 'All right, all right, Florrie, I'm off. But remember what I told you – rely on me if you want help. I'm just next door.'

When Florrie closed the back door, she stood for a moment staring at it. Yes, he was just next door and she knew it, for in some way she laid the blame for John's condition on Broderick's shoulders. Over the years they had lived near to each other he had never stopped pulling John's leg and it must have become unbearable. She got fed up listening to it herself sometimes.

When she returned to the kitchen John was not there, but Gran was still at the table tapping away with her fingers. She looked at her daughter-in-law and said, 'I've a good mind to do it.'

'Do what?' asked Florrie without much interest.

'Nothing,' said Gran enigmatically. Whereupon Florrie sighed, and turned to where Arthur stood at the far side of the kitchen dressed for out, but it was Linda who put the question she was thinking at that moment to him. 'Are you going to see Joan tonight?' she said.

'Yes.' Arthur avoided the eyes upon him.

'You'd better be prepared for high jinks then,' warned Linda.

'I'm prepared all right,' said Arthur.

'She'll likely be the one to call the whole thing off now.'

Before Arthur could answer his sister, Gran put in, 'Then we'll all be pleased, won't we?' She asked the question of him and he turned to her and, giving her a straight look, said, 'Aye, Gran, we'll all be pleased.' Then, going to Florrie, he murmured quietly, 'In any case, Mam, I won't be late and Frankie's staying in . . . Don't worry.'

Florrie just nodded in answer and she remained quiet until Linda, putting the last of the dishes away, said, as if talking to herself, 'I don't like that Dr Spencer. He seems bent on getting at Dad, rushing around the lanes in his car trying to pick him up. Pat says young doctors are . . .' The name had slipped out and with it Linda's voice trailed to a guilty stop, giving herself away.

Slowly, Florrie turned to her daughter. 'When did you see Pat? You've been at the shop all day and him at work.'

Cornered, Linda blinked, then said, 'Well, I ran across him at lunchtime and he told me he had seen Moira out with the Spencer children and she had told him.'

'Your path crosses Pat McNally's quite a bit these days, so it seems.' Gran was staring at Linda, and now Florrie, remembering the way Linda had been getting herself up lately, cried, 'Linda, you're not . . .'

'No, Mam, I'm not.' Linda flounced round from the cupboard. 'Surely I can speak to Pat. I just met him and I spoke that's all.'

'Yes, yes.' Florrie's voice sounded apologetic but as she turned away and went upstairs, she was crying to herself, 'No, no, not Linda and Pat and him thirty and divorced into the bargain . . . I've got enough to put up with, not this now.'

When she opened the bedroom door and saw that John was not only in bed but asleep, really asleep for he was snoring gently, she turned quickly and went into the lavatory and there, locking herself in, she pressed her face into her apron and gave way to a bout of weeping. After having her cry-out she went into the bathroom and washed her face, then, composing herself, she returned downstairs. She had a number of jobs she should do but she had no inclination to tackle any of them, so she sat in John's chair and closed her eyes and for Gran's benefit pretended she was dozing.

Perhaps she did doze for when Gran's voice said, 'D'you hear that?' she sat up with a start. Gran's eyes were directed towards the ceiling and when Florrie listened she could hear unmistakably now the low murmur of John's voice. Her hand went to her throat and she forced herself up from her chair and out of the room. When she reached the landing, Frankie was standing at his door and he whispered, 'He's been on like that for some time.'

Florrie said nothing, but moved slowly to the bedroom door, Frankie close behind her, and when she pushed the door open, there was John. He was sitting on the side of the bed in his shirt, his hand outstretched to someone and he was speaking very airily as he said, 'It's a bargain then, shake on it. You do that for me and I'll do as you ask. I'll get one as soon as I can. It'll take some time but I'll do it. There, how's that?'

Florrie watched John's hand pumping up and down in a vigorous handshake and she saw his head go back and heard him laugh with a gaiety that was foreign to him. Then, still laughing, he said, 'By gum, that'll be the day; that'll shake 'em, eh?'

A chill passed over her body. She had a weird, turbulent feeling in the vicinity of her stomach and for a moment she felt she was going to see what John was seeing – that there was someone besides themselves in the room. A sweat was breaking out on her, and she felt sick. When she found herself sliding down by the door, she knew she was going to faint, and the last thing she heard was the loud frightened voice of Frankie shouting, 'Gran! Gran!'

It was the following morning and Arthur and Frankie were downstairs getting themselves ready for work without the assistance of their mother who, after the business of last night, was having a lie-in.

Arthur's face was particularly gloomy, for besides worrying over his dad and now his mother, the situation with Joan had taken a retrograde step – at least, so it appeared to him. For she had not disdainfully thrown the ring at him last night because his father had hit her father. No, on the advice of her mother, she was overlooking the whole business and she was forgiving his father and himself and the whole family for their very odd behaviour of late. Last night when Mr Duckworth had come roaring to their door he'd had great hope that this would split the affair between him and Joan like a blow from an axe, but all it had done was to bind him more firmly.

Arthur put the bacon in the frying pan with the skin on, for he couldn't be bothered to cut it off like his mother did. Anyway, he concluded, he didn't want any bacon. When a ring came on the front door he said, 'That's the postman; see to it, will you?'

Frankie put down the knife with which he was cutting the bread and went heavily to the front door. He too was worried and about many things. About his dad, for he was sure going balmy; and then there was the woman; and now his mum; also his motorbike. And, added to it all, the niggling, secret worry surrounding this feeling for Moira McNally.

There was only one letter on the mat and he picked it up and glanced at it casually. Then, his eyes screwing up, he muttered the address to himself – 'Mr John Gascoigne, Twenty-four Dudley Street, Downfell Hurst . . .' Mr John Gascoigne . . . all the letters that came here were addressed to Mr and Mrs Gascoigne. Aunt Lucy always wrote like that and Mam's cousin in York addressed her envelope in the same way. Those were the only two people who ever wrote to Mam and Dad. He was still looking at the envelope when he reached the kitchen and without lifting his eyes from it, he said to Arthur, 'Here a minute.'

Arthur, looking over his shoulder, asked shortly, 'What is it?'

'A letter addressed to Dad. You know something . . .' Frankie paused. 'It's from that woman. Look.' His voice became excited; he was playing detective again. 'It's got the Hexham postmark on it. See. I bet you a bob it's from her.'

Arthur was now looking at the envelope in Frankie's hand. 'Aye, well, if it is, what can we do about it?' he said.

'I know what I'm going to do about it.' Frankie went to the stove, where the kettle was steaming.

'Here!' Arthur pulled at his arm. 'You're not going to open it.'

'Why not?'

'Well, because . . .' Arthur paused. 'It isn't your letter. It doesn't concern you.'

'Doesn't it? Me dad carrying on with another woman and him up the pole into the bargain. Me mam conking out like she did last night and scaring the wits out of me, and you say it's not my business . . . our business . . . It's the business of everybody in this house to know what he's up to. Because after what I saw last night it won't be long afore he's in the loony bin.'

Arthur said no more but stood helplessly by as Frankie steamed open the envelope. In many ways, he recognised that Frankie was more forceful than himself. He watched him unfold two sheets of paper, and in growing surprise he saw his face slowly drop into an amazed gape. Then, the letter in his hand, he watched Frankie drop into a chair. 'God's truth.' It was so like a McNally ejaculation that Arthur could have smiled, but this was not the moment for smiling. He pulled the letter roughly from Frankie's hand, and now he too read it. It went:

> Dear John,
>
> After you left the other night, I felt pretty sore. I was determined to come over and confront Florrie for I didn't see, and by the way I still don't see, that I'm being unreasonable. I told you I could come over as an old friend, and over a cup of tea, perhaps, I could have met the boy and spoken to him. I don't expect you to understand this for you don't know what it's like to be deprived of a child. Anyway, I did make my way to Downfell Hurst today with the purpose of seeing Florrie and then something happened. I had just got off the bus and was going to enquire the way to your house from the man at the garage when I heard one man say to another, young Gascoigne's gone tearing round there to have a look at that bike again, so I stood to one side and waited, and then I saw him and I recognised him immediately, John. There was no mistaking him. He was in a tearing hurry or I would have spoken to him on some pretext or another. Now the situation is that since I have seen him I want to get to know him more than ever. It's such a simple thing

that I'm asking. He needn't know anything whatever
about it if you and Florrie act sensibly.

    If I don't hear from you I'll make it my business
to pay you a call, say Saturday.

The letter ended briefly with the name Freda, and the abruptness gave to
the last line an ominous foreboding suggestion.

    When Arthur lifted his eyes from the letter it was to see Frankie
looking lead-coloured and rather sick, and his glibness seemed to have
deserted him, for when he spoke he spluttered, 'You . . . you . . . see . . .
see what this means? That woman is . . . is me mother.'

    Yes, Arthur saw, and he was shaken; shaken to the core by the fact that
his father could have given another woman a child and this child could be
Frankie. Frankie turned on him, words pouring from him now, although
he still looked dazed. 'I knew it. I've known all along. I'm different from
the rest of you; always have been. I'm always wanting to talk and none of
you do, except Dad now, and he's off his nut.'

    Now Frankie beat a fist into the palm of his hand and he stretched
his meagre thin height to mannish proportions. He was a man; he was a
man who had found out his origins. He stalked about the kitchen. It did
not seem big enough for his striding, which took him into the scullery
and back again. But his reactions were very genuine when he stopped
once again and confronted Arthur, saying quietly now, 'Y'know he's never
liked me.'

    'That's daft,' said Arthur, not really knowing what to say. 'You're
talking through the top of your hat.'

    'He's never liked me, I tell you. If he's ever done any talking it's been
to you. Has he ever told me anything?'

    'Well, there's been nothing to tell.'

    'Nothing to tell? Huh! That's rich. But I didn't mean about this. I
mean has he ever talked to me about anything – games or anything else
– like he has to you? No, you've got to admit it, and it's funny.' Frankie

turned his head sideways and seemed to be looking back over the past as he said, more to himself than to Arthur, 'I was talking to me mother about something like this once, and I said I wasn't like any of you and you know what, she started to cry and she said I was like Gran . . . Gran!' He turned quickly to Arthur again, his voice a whisper now. 'Look, our Arthur,' he was beginning when . . .

'Haven't you got your breakfast yet?'

They almost left the floor as they turned to confront Florrie as she entered the kitchen noiselessly in her slippers. It was Arthur who murmured hurriedly, 'We're just getting it, Mam.' Then he added, 'How d'you feel?'

'I'm feeling all right.' She looked at Frankie and the letter in his hand and asked without much interest, 'You've had a letter, Frankie?'

'Aye . . . Yes.' He brought the 'yes' out on a gasp as if he had been holding his breath. Then, as he folded the letter quickly up and put it back in the envelope, he said, 'Yes, yes, I've had a letter.'

Frankie stared at this woman and as he stared he experienced an indescribable feeling – a kind of vast emptiness. She wasn't his mother. He had lived with her all these years, and she was the only one in the house who he could talk to or who really wanted to listen to him, for she always listened to him, and had always been nice to him, and she wasn't his mother. She had done it out of kindness. His father, like most of the men in the war, had got himself into a fix with some girl and his mother had taken him . . . But she wasn't his mother, this woman was no relation to him. He watched Florrie turn swiftly from him, saying, 'Oh, the bacon, it smells burned to a cinder.' She lifted the pan, exclaiming, 'Oh, look at that. Oh, look at that.'

'I'm sorry, Mam.' Arthur too was looking at the pan now and he added, 'Anyway I didn't want any bacon.'

'But Frankie will.'

'No,' put in Frankie in a voice that had a falsetto note. 'No, I don't want any. I don't want any breakfast at all.'

Florrie looked from one to the other and thought she understood, and not feeling up to the business of coping with pressing them to eat, she just said, 'Oh, very well then.'

It wasn't unusual for the brothers to leave the house together and when fifteen minutes later they were in the street, Arthur muttered under his breath, 'That letter, how are you going to get it to Dad now?'

'I can't,' said Frankie flatly. 'And, anyway, who's to say it arrived? It might have been lost in the post . . . and . . .' He paused before going on, 'And if she doesn't get a reply she'll come on Saturday and there'll be a showdown.'

'Showdown,' repeated Arthur. 'Don't you think there's enough showdowns in the house without creating more?'

'That's their trouble and this is mine and I've got to know more about it.'

Arthur looked hard at Frankie; he was taking this badly. Of course, he could understand it was a bit of a blow and, moreover, the thought came to him, they weren't really brothers, only half-brothers. It was as Frankie said, he was different; he had always been different. He felt very sorry for Frankie and felt he had been dealt a dirty deal, but nevertheless he could in no way condemn his dad. These things happened, only it was a bit startling when they happened in your own family.

So much had happened in his own family lately. For him it dated from the time he found he was going to marry Joan Duckworth. The thought of his own troubles outweighed those of Frankie's and when they came to Duckworth's shop he left him with just a brief, 'So long.'

Frankie went slowly on his way, burdened with the knowledge that had turned his particular world upside down. So much so that he passed the garage without sparing a moment to dash round the back to have a look at his particular motorbike. All he did was to allow his mind to dwell for a moment on the bike as a joy that had taken place in the far off days of his careless youth.

Chapter Five

It was right in the middle of his tea that Broderick got the urge to go and see John. He laid his knife and fork down and stared at his plate still heaped high with food, and he said to himself, 'Away, there's enough time after I've had me bite.' But as he continued eating, the urge continued to grow and he looked to where Katie was moving back and forth in the paint-skinned rocking chair and he brought her out of her wee doze when he cried sharply, 'Have you heard tell of what John's been up to the day?'

'Eh?' said Katie with a start. 'Oh, John. No. I've been round twice, y'know. Florrie's very close since this thing's come on John. I only know he went to his work the day, but I did see the doctor and that walking corpse of a minister drop in this afternoon.'

'So you don't know if he's had any more delusions?'

'No, I haven't heard a thing. But when I saw him go out, he looked sensible enough to me. But, there, you can never tell, now, can you?'

'He might look sensible enough but he's far from it as far as I can gather.' They both turned to where their eldest son was adjusting his tie in front of the fly-specked mirror hanging above the mantelpiece.

'Are you after hearing somethin'?' asked Katie, looking with admiring eyes at the brawn that went to make Pat.

'A little,' said Pat over his shoulder. Then he turned to his mother. 'You didn't know Aunt Florrie fainted away last night, did you?'

Katie was sitting up. 'No, begod! I didn't.'

'Well, she did. She went up to the bedroom and there was John leading off to whoever he sees and it made her pass out. Then he was on again this morning afore he went to work. Laughing this time, he was.'

'How did you find all this out and me not knowing a thing?' Katie's eyes were almost lost behind the fat of her cheeks as she peered enquiringly up into the handsome face.

Pat turned to the mirror again and said casually, 'Oh, I was just havin' a few words with young Linda.'

'Oh, you were?' Katie looked none too pleased, and when she glanced at her husband and saw that his attention was fast held, apparently, by the remainder of his meal, his ostrich attitude spoke volumes to her. 'Mother of God.' She pushed herself to the edge of the rocking chair and bawled at Pat. 'You're not seein' that youngster, because if you are, mind, there'll be hell let loose next door.'

Pat, pulling his coat on, looked down at his mother and his face took on a hardness that completely wiped away the jocular expression that was an inheritance from both his parents, as he said, 'This time, Ma, let me do me own pickin' will you . . . Or else . . .'

The 'or else' brought Broderick's head up and he cried harshly, 'No threats, Pat. No threats. Away with you now and run your own life as best you can and do your own choosin' as you say, but no threats to your mother, now, no threats.'

As Pat and his father exchanged glances, the hardness seeped from the younger man's face as he turned and grinned at his mother and nodding his head at her said, 'So long, I'll be seein' you.'

'So long,' said Katie pleasantly in return, but the door had no sooner closed on him than she was standing over Broderick demanding, 'Is there anything in this, d'you think?'

Broderick chewed hard on a piece of steak and swallowed it in a gulp before he answered, 'If I'm not blind, there is. But I warn you, Katie' – he pointed his fork up within a fraction of her nose – 'let it run its course. They know nothing about it next door, so don't you set the house on fire afore they strike the match, for, as you say, hell will be let loose soon enough. Yet I'm thinking, and have been for a while . . .' Broderick smiled to himself. 'There would be no better time than the present to spring this news for there's so much on their plate they mightn't take the notice of it they would do at a more peaceful moment.'

Katie straightened herself up and her eyes darted here and there before she said, more to herself than to her husband, 'Begod! If this isn't a set up and him just been ladled out of one boiling pot – and then only by the hand of God.'

'And I'll tell you something else while we're on.' Broderick was giving her his full attention now. 'If we're not soon connected with the Gascoignes in one way, we will be in another unless I'm very much mistaken. Did you know that our Moira and Arthur are courtin' on the sly?'

'God and His Holy Mother. What are you saying, Brod!' Katie had her hands clasped as if in supplicating prayer. 'Arthur's to be married, the day's fixed an' all.'

'Aye, but I can bet you me pay packet this week that it won't be to Miss Duckworth he'll be getting hitched. Not if I know me daughter.'

'God bless us this night,' cried Katie. 'There's trouble comin' upon us.'

'Well,' said Broderick with a laugh, 'sit down in your chair now and enjoy it, for I'm going to have me wash and then I'm going next door to have a word with John. I've a hankering somehow to have a word with him the night.'

So Katie sat down to enjoy her troubles and Broderick had his wash and put on a clean muffler before going next door to take a rise out of

John – for that's how he explained this urge that had come upon him to see his neighbour. He was badly in need of a laugh, he told himself . . .

When Broderick knocked on his neighbour's back door and it was opened by Gran, who informed him without any preamble that John wasn't in, that he had already had his tea and gone out again and she didn't know when he'd be back, he experienced a decidedly flat feeling.

'And where was he makin' for, Gran?'

'The cemetery,' said Gran briefly.

'But he's just come back from there – he was at his work the day, wasn't he?'

'Well, that's where he's gone,' said Gran. 'He said afore he went out he had one or two things he wanted to finish and he was going back there to do them. Very explicit he was about it an' all.'

'Aw, well,' said Broderick, disappointment in his voice. 'I just wanted to ask how he was.'

'I guessed you did,' said Gran, and the tone of this remark brought forth Broderick's bellow.

'I cannot see meself going up to the cemetery, Gran.'

'Not walkin',' commented Gran caustically.

'Aw. Aw, now, Gran, don't joke along these lines. Y'know I'm superstitious about things like that; cemeteries and such.'

'You'll go up the road one day.'

'Aye, aye, likely, of course, when the time comes.' After nodding to Gran, Broderick retreated back down the path. The conversation had taken a turn he did not relish, for like all superstitious people he could not bear to discuss death, especially his own.

So Broderick made his way to the club as he usually did in the evenings, and there he met his workmate, Dick Turner, and Dick's first words to him were, 'Well, what's the latest gravedigger doings, Broderick?'

'Devil a thing I have to report,' said Broderick, calling the barman to him with a lift of his chin. 'The only thing I know is that he's still seeing the Saint and him not paying a penny for the privilege . . . And mind you, aye, that's not my crack – he said it to me himself and I thought it was rich, at least for him to come out with, and here we are throwing away our hard-earned money and seeing nothin' for it larger than life . . . except the wife, that is.'

This quip raised a laugh among the nearby company as Broderick intended it should, and it made him feel more like himself again. But as he plunged his lips into the foaming froth of his first pint, he once again experienced the strong urge to see John. The urge grew with each successive drink until he had to chide himself with such remarks as, 'Oh, to hell. What's up with me anyway? I'll see him soon enough, afore I turn in.'

It was a good hour and a half before closing time when the strange urge, getting the upper hand of Broderick, forced him to his feet in the middle of a conversation, and as much to the surprise of himself as to his mates he heard himself saying, 'Well, I'll be gettin' along, fellas. I've things to do.'

As Broderick made his way to the door he was followed by a loud protest of which he took not the slightest heed until he was standing alone in the bar yard, and there he asked himself a question: 'What's come over you an' all?' When he received no answer he moved on, thinking, 'You've lost a good hour's drinking time. What's so important in taking a rise out of him?' Still he could not give himself an answer.

When he reached the street he did not turn in at his own gate but made his way straight to the Gascoigne's back door again, and it was Florrie this time who opened it to him.

'Aw, hullo there, Florrie. I just looked in again to see how John was.'

Florrie lowered her eyes for a moment before replying, 'He's not in, Broderick.'

'No?' Broderick's face and voice showed his surprise and also his disappointment. 'Well, where has he got to till this time? Don't tell me he's still up.' He jerked his head to indicate the cemetery.

Florrie's voice was very low as she answered, 'Yes, he's still there. He's working.'

'Well now, workin' at this hour.' Broderick leant towards Florrie and asked in a whisper, 'Is he more of himself the day?'

When Florrie lowered her eyes again but made no reply, Broderick said, 'Aw, now, I wouldn't worry meself unduly, he'll come round, it's only a spasm he's havin'. Look, it's really early yet, I left the club afore me time the night, I think I'll just take a dander up the road and meet him.' As Florrie's head jerked up at this and she put out a hand of protest, he added jocularly, 'And it was Gran who said to me the night I'd never go up on me feet.' He laughed loudly now. 'Gran's the one full of jests. She's as good as meself at them, only on a different tack, aye.'

Florrie had had to wait until Broderick finished and now she said quite firmly, 'I wouldn't go and meet him if I was you, Broderick.'

'And why not? John and me's on the best of terms. I pull his leg but he likes it. Aw, he doesn't say much and he keeps up a grim front, at least he had up until this week, but he'd miss me and me leg-pullin', I can tell you that, Florrie. And for me own part I can state that if I hadn't John to joke with me life would be empty indeed . . . Now I'm away and you'll see us comin' back arm in arm the best of pals, so don't you fret.'

Florrie could say no more; she always felt helpless against Broderick's garrulousness and reasoning. She watched him walk jauntily to the bottom gate before turning and closing the door. She felt bound to voice her feelings when she entered the kitchen. 'I believe he gets a kick out of tormenting John . . . You know what I think?' She looked from Gran to Aunt Lucy, who had braved another visit. 'I think it's him – Broderick – who's turned John's mind; not that cricket ball at all.'

'Aye, well.' Gran's nondescript nose twitched. 'You may be right, but I wouldn't say that. If it hadn't been one thing, 'twould have been another. It was ready to be turned in any case. He's been simmering darkly underneath for years. He's my son and I should know.'

Gran cast a taunting glance at her sister but Aunt Lucy was apparently oblivious to it for she made no remark whatever but went to the window and from there watched Broderick's swaying gait as he walked towards the bottom of the street. She was about to comment that it was odd he hadn't looked in at his own house if he had just come from the club, when she saw John and quietly said, 'Here he comes.'

'John?' exclaimed Florrie, hurrying to her side.

And yes, there he was. As Broderick disappeared round the bottom of the street, John was entering it from the top end. This wasn't the way he came when returning from work. Where had he been? Florrie shook her head, and at that moment Gran startled her by remarking almost in her ear, 'T'other one will have his walk for nowt, strike me.'

'Come away from the window,' said Florrie hastily. 'In case he sees us.'

When John entered the kitchen it was to see Gran sitting in her usual chair, Florrie setting the table and Aunt Lucy sitting on the couch, and it was to her he spoke first saying, 'Why, hullo there, Aunt Lucy.'

'Hullo, John, how are you the day?'

'Fine.' John let out a long breath then repeated, 'Fine. Never better, Aunt Lucy.'

'Good evenin'. It's been a nice day.' Gran's voice speaking the greeting to herself was heavy with temper and sarcasm. Her son had spoken to their Lucy but had never a word for her.

When John turned and looked at his mother she was not only taken aback but made a little apprehensive, for she noticed something akin to a twinkle in his eye, and when he said to her in a voice that was almost jocular, 'Now if I had said . . . "It's been a nice day" to you, Mother, your answer would have been "Well, you've had your share of it", wouldn't it?' Her mouth fell agape and for a moment she could not find a word to say in reply. Then, almost spluttering her indignation, she cried, 'It would only be me due and common decency to give me a chance.'

Florrie, not wanting a row to start between the two of them, and not having seen the merriment in John's face as he quipped his mother, made an effort to turn the conversation away from her and took the first thought that came to hand, which, if she had taken the time to consider, she would not have voiced. 'Broderick called twice the night to see how you were,' she said as she passed him.

'Aye, I thought he would.'

This remark brought Florrie up short and she looked at her husband and repeated, 'You thought he would . . . Twice?'

'Aye, twice, maybe three times. You told him I was at the cemetery?'

She nodded then said, 'Yes, yes, I told him.'

'And he's gone up there now?'

'Just a few minutes afore you came in.' Florrie watched a smile almost split John's face. She could not remember seeing all his teeth at one time before.

Looking at his watch John said now, 'I think I'll sit down for five minutes.'

The women glanced at each other as John took his seat at the table, and Florrie said, 'I was going to cook you something.'

He replied, 'I want nothing but a bit of cheese and bread and a cup of tea.' Then he nodded at his watch and repeated, 'Five minutes, ten at the outside.'

'What's going to happen in five minutes?' asked Gran grimly.

'I don't rightly know, Mother; you'll just have to wait and see.'

John's next question, which was put with a startling eagerness, almost caused Florrie to drop the teapot. 'Has the doctor been the day?' he said.

'Yes,' said Florrie briefly.

'And is he comin' back the morrow?' His voice was still eager.

Florrie moved to the table, placed the teapot on the stand and looked at John very, very hard, and he returned her stare as he said, 'Well, lass, is he?'

'I expect so.' Now her tone was curt.

'Well, that's a good thing,' said John. 'For he's likely to have another patient. In fact, McNally and me could be in the same bed, both with the same complaint.' He turned to Aunt Lucy on this and laughed. 'That would be funny, Aunt Lucy, eh?'

Aunt Lucy managed a smile in reply but did not speak.

Florrie now found she was trembling and that she was experiencing much the same feeling as she had done last night before she fainted. But tonight she was determined she was not going to faint, so placing her hands before her flat on the table, she forced herself to look into John's smiling face and demanded, 'John, pay attention to me. Stop that grinning and tell me, what have you concocted up for Broderick?'

John blinked and seemed to recall himself from some pleasant place, then he pressed himself back from her in mock indignation and drew his chin into his collar and pointed to himself as he said, 'Me? Concoct anything for Broderick? Me? Why, lass, the shoe's on the other foot and always has been. Broderick's the arch concoctor, you should know that by now.'

'He's gone up to the cemetery because he thought you were there.'

'Well, what's that got to do with me?'

'You knew he would go up.'

'Aye, perhaps I did.' Slowly John rose from the table and drew his chair towards the sink. Putting one foot on the seat of the chair, he rested his elbows on the draining board and leant forward so he could have full view of the bottom of the road.

The three women in the room behind him looked at each other and then at his back.

The minutes passed slowly and Florrie forced herself to pour out some more tea and hand it to Gran and Aunt Lucy. It was when Gran had reached the dregs of her cup, which she indicated with a loud straining noise through her teeth, that John's foot came off the chair, knocking it flying, and leaning further forward he shouted, 'Here he comes.'

As if they had been shot to the window Florrie, Gran and Aunt Lucy crowded round him, and there before their astonished gaze came Broderick McNally racing down the street, coatless and hatless, his mouth agape and his arms flailing the air as they speeded him nearer home. But it was not up his own path he turned; as earlier, he made straight for John's house and John, knowing what was coming, turned calmly to Florrie and said, 'Open the door or else he'll come through it.'

Florrie did not immediately obey her husband for she was staring at him, her eyes full of fear. She was becoming afraid of this man, afraid of her John, her quiet tongue-tied, reticent John, for he was no longer quiet and tongue-tied or reticent; he was a man who was not himself but had become possessed, of this she was sure. She was surprised when she found herself at the door and she had just opened it when Broderick fell into her arms.

'Florrie, God Almighty . . . John . . . What has come upon me this night? John, where is he? Oh, my God, Florrie, is it mad I'm goin'?' He was almost gibbering.

'Come in and calm yourself.' Florrie's voice was steady – more steady than she was feeling – and when, almost supporting Broderick, she led him into the kitchen she felt a moment of anger against her husband for she saw that John was surveying Broderick quizzically and getting a great kick out of what he saw. In fact, she guessed he was laughing loudly inside.

Broderick staggered straight for John and clutching his arm between his great hands he cried, 'Mother of God, John, the things I've seen the night. But it is you who'll understand. I saw him, John. I saw him with me own eyes, and it's not me that's mad, is it? And he spoke to me, John. He spoke to me. I heard him with these ears.' Broderick released one hand and actually belted himself on the side of the head.

'Sit down and get a hold of yourself, man, and tell me about it.' John's voice was cool and distant.

Broderick, as if half blind, groped at the chair that Florrie held for him, and when he had sat down he found himself in line with Gran's eyes and Gran spoke. 'If this is one large mickey you're takin', Broderick McNally, you'll pay for it. Mark my words you will, for them that sows such fun weeps sorrow.'

'Glory be to God.' Broderick closed his eyes and moved his head from one shoulder to the other. He repeated, 'Glory be to God, then would I be in the state I'm in taking the mickey out of anybody? I tell you, Gran, I've witnessed something this night that has galloped me towards me grave, of that I'm sure.'

As Gran spoke Florrie motioned to Aunt Lucy and when Aunt Lucy, her eyes popping out of her head, came to her side, Florrie whispered, 'Go and get Katie, quick.' Then going to the cupboard she took out a bottle and pouring out a generous measure into a glass she went to Broderick where he was now sitting with his head bowed and his hands hanging between his knees. Tapping him on the shoulder she said, 'Here, drink this, Broderick.'

He lifted his eyes sideways to the glass and his hand went half out to it before waving it aside saying, 'No, Florrie, no. There are one or two things that could have caused the night's business. Either I had too much when I went up there looking for John, or I've gone completely out of me senses, an' I would like, Florrie, if you don't mind, I would like to think it's the first of the two.'

'Don't be silly,' said Florrie harshly. 'Drink it.' She pushed it towards his mouth, and obeying her with the docility of a child, he drank the whisky. As she took the empty glass from his hand, she glanced at her husband and at this moment there was little love in her look. She had blamed Broderick for having unbalanced him but she had done that only on guesswork. But now she knew without a doubt that John was responsible for the state that Broderick was in, and for him to have the power to reduce her vibrant neighbour to this jellyfish condition spoke to Florrie of something beyond the known and brought back that eerie feeling of last night.

Broderick gave a mighty shiver – whether from fear or the effects of the spirit it was hard to tell. Then putting his hand out feelingly to John, he whispered, 'Tell me, John, tell me. This man that you see. Is he a towering fella with a head on him as big as a barrel?'

John's eyes were lowered and he was some time in replying. 'I wouldn't say as big as a barrel. At times I've thought he looks uncommonly like yourself.'

'Like me?' Broderick's voice sounded as if it was corkscrewing itself into the distance for it faded away on a thin squeak. 'Like me?' he repeated. 'The thing I saw – the fella I saw – for he was a fella, like flesh and blood, he was twice me size if not more.'

'Tell me how it came about?' said John quietly. He was looking at Broderick now.

Broderick glanced at Florrie and then to Gran before bringing his eyes back to John and then he said in a hoarse whisper, 'I can't rightly tell you, John. It was as if I was drawn to the cemetery the night. I felt – you might not believe it – I felt that it was yourself I wanted to see. I'll go and see John and have a laugh with him, I said. Cheer him up, I told meself. I left the club an hour or so afore me time. It was like an urge on me, John, like an urge—'

At that moment the sound of Katie's voice could be heard coming up the garden path, and Broderick put his hand to his head and turned to the door as she bounced into the room. When she stopped dead at the sight of him, he said to her, 'Don't start, woman, don't start.'

'Holy Mother of God, what's taken you? Where's your coat in all this?' Katie moved nearer to him. 'Look at your shirt, and it on clean just the night. Is it palatic you are?'

'Be quiet, woman.' Broderick closed his eyes. 'I may be palatic drunk or I may be mad, it's one or t'other. I'm trying to find out by telling John what happened. Be quiet.'

'God Almighty, look at your face – it's the colour of ash and your hair's on end. What's struck you, man?'

'Sit you down, woman, afore I knock you down.' There was the shadow of the old Broderick in this command and Katie sat down saying, 'Jesus, Mary and Joseph, what's come over him?'

Broderick, treating his wife as if she wasn't there, now turned his attention once again to John who had not moved during the altercation. 'As I was saying, John, I felt drawn there right up to the gates. It was as if a hand was out towards me, tugging me, and when I got there I looked about for you but couldn't see a hair of your head and then I went on up to your hut. And, y'know another strange thing, John? I've never been as far as your hut in all me born days, but there I was going straight to it as if I took the path every mornin' of me life. I have no use for cemeteries, John, I don't mind telling you. Time enough, I've always said to meself, to go into the cemetery when you've got to, but there I was going quite gaily in search of you and not a tremor in me. And as I said, I got to your hut only to find it was locked. Then I got a sort of feeling that you were around in the bushes to the left, and I went round and through the gap but there was nothing to be seen but the great manure heap you've made, and as there was no way out of the place but by the way I'd come in I turned meself about, John, and it was then I saw him.'

'Jesus, Mary and Joseph!'

Broderick turned and looked at Katie where she sat blessing herself as she mumbled the words, and he nodded to her and said, 'Them's the very words I used. I closed me eyes tighter than they've ever been closed afore and I said to meself "Jesus, Mary and Joseph", but when I opened them he was still there. And, John . . .' Broderick's two hands now went out in pathetic appeal to John. 'John, he spoke to me and he called me by me name. "Hullo, Broderick," he said.' Broderick covered his eyes and bowed his head at the memory and, on this, Katie closed her eyes and putting her head back appealed to heaven, wailing like a banshee now. 'Holy Mother of God, lift the blight off him.'

'And what then?' It was John speaking for the first time, and Broderick, opening his eyes once again, went on, his voice low and trembling. 'He moved towards me, John, talkin' all the time, and I backed, step with his step, I backed. The sweat was squirting from every pore in me body like a fountain, and I knew what it was to feel faint for the first time in me life. Round your manure heap we went, me backing one step and he taking one step forward all the time. And him talking the while, never stoppin'.'

'What did he say?'

'I can't rightly recollect, John, for me wits were goin', but he did talk of you of that I'm sure, and us being neighbours and me pulling your leg. He knew everything, John, everything. But I was backing, John, all the while I was backing and I backed, John, until I felt I was near the opening and then I turned ready to flee . . . but, begod, there he was, standin' filling the gap again. John, I tell you, the hairs on me body stood up one by one. I felt me senses goin', but even so it occurred to me to make a dash right through him for he could not be real.'

Again Broderick closed his eyes but only for a second this time, and now he was leaning forward nearer to John, and his voice sunk to a faint whisper as he said, 'But then he touched me, John, he put out his great hand, and, John, before God, if I had to meet me Maker this very minute' – Broderick made the sign of the cross – 'that was the hand of no ghost for it was warm and heavy on me arm. I only felt it for a split second but I felt it, an' I screamed so loud that the dead must have kicked in their coffins. And the next thing I knew I was tearing back over the muck heap and goin' hell for leather through the shrubbery. That's where I lost me coat and me hat.' He cast a quick glance in Katie's direction, as he gave this information, but Katie had her eyes closed. 'I don't know if it was all the claws of the fiends of hell that tore them off me or it was the branches or what, I only know that when I got through that thicket me shirt was in ribbons as you see it now, and I was coatless and hatless and as near mad as I'll ever be in me life without bein' tied up. And, John, I never stopped until I reached this room . . . Aw, don't John, don't.' Broderick was on his feet now, his hand raised as he towered above John. 'For God's sake, don't laugh at me. You can't laugh at me in this predicament after what I've been through this night.'

Broderick stood gazing down on John's bowed head and shaking shoulders, and now his voice was full of reproach as he cried, 'You've no Christian spirit in you, John, to laugh at me and me in this state. I've been devilled. What's more, I've seen what you yourself have seen, John, so you should understand a man.'

Now John raised his face to Broderick and it was wet with tears of laughter, and he muttered, 'In that case, then, you have nothing to worry about.'

'In the name of God, John, I've everything to worry about, the state I've been in all evening wasn't me natural state. I had an urge on me, and it wasn't natural.'

'No, of course it wasn't.' John got to his feet, then added casually, 'But you'll always have it just afore you see him.'

'Just afore I see him,' repeated Broderick in an awestruck whisper.

'Aye,' repeated John. 'Just afore you see him. It's called . . .' He scratched his head. 'Now what is it called? He told me the name this morning. Now what was it?' Again he scratched his head, then went on, 'It's slipped me mind at the moment but—' He stopped abruptly and turning in the direction of the clothes cupboard where not one of the occupants of the room was standing, he smiled and said, 'Oh, there you are. What did you say it was?'

'*The dimension of awareness, John,*' replied the Saint, smiling back broadly at him.

'That's it. It's rather a mouthful to remember. Thanks again.' He turned now and confronted the awestruck company, but addressing

147

himself particularly to Broderick, he said, 'He says it's called the dimension of awareness.'

'He's not . . .' It was a weak protest from Broderick.

John nodded and said, 'Yes. Yes, he is.'

'Oh, my God. Aw . . . aw . . . aw.' It was a sickly wailing groan, not from Broderick but Katie as her fat bulk slithered to the floor in a dead faint.

Aunt Lucy, shaking with her fear, was about to beat a hasty retreat to the scullery, there to be sick, when Florrie's cry of, 'John Gascoigne, stop this! Stop it at once, I say!' brought her with head bent to Katie's side, and when a few minutes later Gran liberally splashed cold water over Katie's face, half drenching her, she did not protest for she felt that she needed water or something even stronger to get her over this experience.

'Oh, my God, what's come upon us this night?' Broderick groaned when, with the assistance of Florrie and Aunt Lucy, he helped Katie onto a chair.

His mutterings were joined by his wife's pleas to the Almighty for enlightenment when a few minutes later he helped her to her feet and guided her out of the seething room.

During all this, John stood aside doing nothing and saying nothing. Gran too stood aside and waited. She waited until Florrie and Aunt Lucy, following Broderick and Katie with solicitous help, had left the room empty but for herself and her son, then turning on him she cried breathlessly, 'I don't know what you're up to, me lad, but it's got to stop. I believed that you were seeing spooks, but nothing on this earth will convince me that Broderick McNally is seeing them an' all, and the same one into the bargain. Lightning never strikes in the same place twice. Now, I don't know what your game is, and I don't know why you started it, but I'm going to tell you this much, that Dr Spencer is not for playing games, and if I can read anybody aright, he doesn't like you, and he's made up his mind that he's going to put you some place where if you haven't seen spooks afore you go in, you certainly will afore you come out. Your fun and games will land you in the asylum, John Gascoigne, do you realise that? And what's more, if she has any more worries you'll have Florrie along with you and you'll be to blame for it, mind you that.'

John was looking at his mother and there was no laughter in his face now and no trace of amusement in his voice as he said, 'You've always had the idea you know everything. You're always bloody well right. Well, you might be in this an' all, but if I go into the asylum, I won't go alone and it won't be Florrie that'll go with me, it'll be McNally. But they won't get me into any asylum. They've got to prove I'm mad first.'

'They'll get you there and prove it after. From what I heard Spencer say the day, there's ways and means of doing just that.'

'Just let them try it on.' John was now bristling, and he stalked past her and out of the room crying again, 'Let them try it on, that's all.'

Gran, left alone in the kitchen, nodded her head slowly to herself. There was one thing she was positive about: if she didn't take things into her own hands soon the trouble that was on this house now would be like a flea bite to what would come upon them in the future . . . It was worth a try, anyway. Anything was better than an asylum.

Chapter Six

By dinner time the following day it was all over the village and into the outskirts that Big McNally had had the wits scared out of him last night and had reached home on the verge of collapse. Where and how? were the questions. Oh, somebody had got themselves rigged up as a spook in the cemetery and when McNally was passing that way with a full load on, the thing sprang out on him and started to jabber. By the time he reached home, he hadn't a stitch on his back and scared some woman stiff in the street with his nakedness.

The story had lost nothing when it reached Dr Spencer's house surgery in Befumstead at three o'clock in the afternoon. It came by way of a patient from Downfell Hurst. Now added to it was the claim that the ghost himself had been none other than John Gascoigne, and he had galloped all the way home from the cemetery after he had startled McNally, flapping his arms like wings. It was said that he was still laughing at twelve o'clock last night and had the street raised.

The doctor restrained himself from comment to his patient but once the surgery was clear, he made his way to his wife to tell her that if she wanted to be dropped at her friend Trixie's she'd better get a move on. As he gathered his belongings together, he explained to her the need for his haste. It was that damned gravedigger. If something wasn't soon done with that chap, serious trouble would ensue, for he had now reached the stage where he was taking a delight in frightening people. The next stage would be one step further when he would be hitting them on the head with something. He would call on old Fowler; Fowler would speed things up. The quicker they got the fellow under control the better for all concerned. If Fowler was available, he might come along with him and if they could catch the chap at some of his tricks, all the better. The thing was to catch him off-guard for he was as cunning as a fox and could talk quite sensibly when he liked.

From a slit of a room off the hall which was known by the name of the nursery, Moira McNally had been listening to all the doctor had said, and no sooner had the front door closed on him and his wife than she whipped their dozing son from his cot and in spite of his whimpering protests dressed him, and, taking him in her arms, she left the house just as she was without hat or coat. By a stroke of luck, she caught the three thirty to Downfell Hurst, but she did not go right into the village. Alighting two stops before the garage, she climbed over a gate, after depositing Andrew through the bottom bars into the field beyond. Then picking him up again, she hurried across a series of fields and over a number of stiles, until she came to the top of the hill where the tail end of the cemetery sprawled. Gratefully she saw that the little-used gate was open for her arms were breaking with the weight of the child, and she was puffing loudly when she came to John's hut. The door was open but she saw he wasn't there and it was only after some minutes of further searching that she found him . . . and in the very place that her da had described to her last night. There was the great manure heap with the thick bushes all around it and there was Uncle John spreading grass cuttings evenly over the sides of the heap.

'Uncle John.'

John turned sharply and looked at where Moira stood in the gap in the hedge and his brows drew together questioningly as he emitted tersely, 'Aye, what is it?'

'I've got to talk to you.'

151

After straightening himself, John stared at her blankly before saying, 'I'm in no mood for listenin' at the minute.' He turned his head away. 'And what's more, I know what you're going to say, and my answer is, he's to be married . . . It's all settled, as you well know.'

'It isn't about that.' Her voice was rough. 'An' you've got to listen to me.'

Slowly he turned to her again. He saw that her face was red and sweating, even her hair looked wet, and the child in her arms had been crying for its face was all stained. He dusted one hand against the other and asked, 'What's brought you here, then?'

Moira cast a swift glance around her, looking for some place to sit, and seeing nothing in the nature of a seat she said, 'I've got to sit down or I'll drop. I've run all the way from Thomson's Cut.'

He hesitated for a long moment before going to the bushes and pulling out a box and when he stood it on its end, Moira sat down with the child on her knee. Looking up at him, she started without any preamble. 'I had to come and tell you that I heard Dr Spencer say what he was going to do.'

'Well, what is he going to do?'

She noticed he wasn't laughing at all today, not even smiling. Her da said he had nearly burst last night. He looked now as she had always remembered him: a bit grim. Hesitantly she began to tell him what the doctor's intentions were.

As he listened to her, John began to have a strange quaking in the pit of his stomach and the sweat began to break out around his neck and on the palms of his hands. It was all right telling himself that they couldn't do it, but there were occasions when men like Dr Spencer did do things. They might be wrong but the law was on their side, and after a man was marked for life with the stigma of an asylum, they could be sorry for making a mistake, but nothing then could lift the brand from the man for by that time it would have reached his innards. The quaking in John's stomach increased, and as it did so he realised he'd had a slight quaking there all day. From the time he had got up this morning, he had felt a bit flat and he recognised this as his normal feeling. But not the quaking; no, that was different . . . new.

'They'll likely come up here,' said Moira. 'You've got to get away and hide for a time.'

He made no angry response to this outrageous suggestion yet his mind was rebellious. Hide? It was ridiculous . . . Hide! Him! The quaking now took on a voice. He supposed she was right but where could he hide . . . ? Freda's? No, by God, he wasn't going to Freda's, she would get a laugh out of this all right and it would be louder than McNally's ever was. Freda had a streak of spite in her that was as broad as her body. No, he wouldn't go to Freda's whatever happened. Then where?

Moira seemed to read his thoughts for she said at this moment, 'You'd be safer any place than here. This is where they'll come first since they know you came straight back to work yesterday.'

John found he was looking at the young girl before him with just the slightest trace of suspicion. She was McNally's daughter, wasn't she, so why was she doing this and after what happened last night an' all? And he asked her point blank, 'What are you doing this for me for?'

Moira's eyes slipped downward before she said, 'Well, I've always known you, Uncle John, and then you see . . .' Her great brown eyes came up to his and explained in a flash how Arthur had become enthralled by her without the assistance of her bust. 'You see,' she said. 'I happen to like you.'

Added to the sweat there now came a pink heat to John's face.

'And what's more,' went on Moira, 'from how me da described him last night, I believe you do see the Saint.' She now cast a swift, half-frightened glance around the enclosure. 'Me da wasn't bottled. I know when me da's bottled. I know him inside out because you see . . .' She gave John a half-apologetic smile. 'You see, we're alike. We love to

153

laugh and joke and pull people's legs but there's another side to us, so that's how I know me da.'

As John listened to her talking he was overwhelmed with a sense of shame, and no one had had the power to create this feeling in him before. But at the same time, he was aware of a feeling of injustice that he should be made to feel like this. For anything he had done to McNally, McNally had richly deserved, aye, by God he had.

The child had started to cry again, and Moira got to her feet and began to walk up and down as she held him across her shoulder. She patted his back as she walked, and as she walked she talked haltingly as if delivering her thoughts as they came to her. 'I know what you could do.'

John did not move from where he was but his eyes followed her and as if appealing to an elder he asked, 'What?'

'Well, first of all there's one thing certain, you've got to get away out of here and I think you'd better do it now.' She walked a while and was quiet as if considering. Then she said, 'You could go up to the Holly Wood near Thomson's Cut and stay there for a bit and after I get off I'll come back and see you. I'm off at five thirty the night and by that time I'll have thought of something.'

It did not seem much of a way out to John but he found that he was obeying her, for the quaking in his stomach seemed to be increasing with each second. Gathering up his tools, he hurried out of the enclosures and went round to the hut and put them away, then he locked the door and put the key in his pocket. Without a word now, and without feeling the incongruity of the situation in the least, for his position had taken on a desperate note, he followed Moira to the top gate of the cemetery and across the fields to Thomson's Cut. When they reached the wood, and before she left him in the prickly seclusion of its depths, she said with motherly concern, 'Don't worry, Uncle John, just stay put and I'll bring you something to eat if I can nip anything from the pantry.' Then she added, 'It'll be all right, you'll see.'

He looked at her for a time before turning away and the thought in his mind at this moment was, 'How could you heartily dislike somebody one day and like them the next . . . ?'

In the hour or so he waited for Moira's return, he had no visit from St Christopher, no airy feeling. He felt very much the old John Gascoigne, and as such he asked himself what had befallen him; how had this come about; and was there anything he could do about it? As far as he could see, no. He couldn't undo what had happened this past week and in spite of his present flat, normal feeling he couldn't be sure but that at any moment he'd be feeling on top of the world again; and what then? Well, as he only too well knew, then things happened, and while they were happening he was a different man and didn't give a damn for anybody. The whole thing was out of his control . . . Aye it was, there was nowt he could do about it. Nowt. And that being so he was open to the control of Dr Spencer. John started to shiver, and try as he might, he couldn't stop.

'I appreciate the reason why you are trying to shield your neighbour, Mr McNally,' said the doctor. 'And under the circumstances it is very commendable of you, for from what I hear you haven't always been on the best of terms.'

'They're liars whoever said that.'

'Well, they might be, and am I to think you're a liar too? For I cannot, and simply will not, believe – it's against all reason to expect me to believe – your story of what happened last night.'

Broderick shook his head and then turned it to one side and looked to where his workmate, under the pressure of digging, had one ear cocked to the conversation. He turned it to the other side to where behind the doctor's car stood another car, that of Mr Fowler, Justice of the Peace. He stretched his arms wide to both sides and said, 'All right then, doctor, have it your own way. I didn't see anythin', but one thing I'll ask you to reconsider and that is the putting of the blame of what I experienced up in the cemetery on the shoulders of John Gascoigne. The man was in his own house when it happened. There were three members of his family who watched me going out of one end of the street as he came in by the other, and so they'll tell you. And when I returned, there he was sitting quietly at home.'

'That doesn't do away with the idea,' said the doctor quickly, 'that he could have rigged something up.'

'He would have had to do a helluva lot of rigging to make anything the size of the man I saw. I tell you he was the biggest creature that walks the earth.'

'Then you're sure in your own mind it wasn't a ghost you saw.'

'I am; he was as solid as yourself.' Broderick thrust out a finger that did not speak of either awe or respect for the doctor.

'Are you of the opinion, then, that the man or thing you saw is the same as that which the gravedigger sees?'

'I am,' said Broderick flatly.

The doctor sighed, and his voice had an edge to it as he said, 'I have two theories about what happened last night. One is that John Gascoigne got himself rigged up to scare you, and if he can scare a man of your stature and cause you to run hell for leather home, as you said, minus half your clothes, just think what effect he'll have on a less strong character should he decide to scare somebody else. My second theory is that you're trying, out of the goodness of your heart, to help your neighbour now that he's in a jam. Therefore, being a joker' – the doctor gave Broderick a small understanding smile – 'you put on the whole show, and very realistic you must have made it. Your intention was merely to prove that your neighbour wasn't going off his head, so you pretended you had seen the same thing that he had.'

'God Almighty,' exclaimed Broderick, closing his eyes. When he opened them he asked the doctor quietly, 'Do you believe in your Maker?'

Definitely the doctor was embarrassed by the question and his voice was curt as he replied, 'I'm not going to discuss theology at this point.'

'So you don't believe.' Broderick's voice was still quiet and his head swung up and down as if on wires as he went on, 'Good enough, if you don't believe in a God then there's little hope of you believing in the Devil. But, mind, I'm not tryin' to convince you that it was the Devil I saw; this man was no Devil. If I hadn't been so plumb down scared and taken off me guard I would have said he was of good countenance, and what's more—'

'Doctor.'

The call came from a white-haired man who was leaning out of the window of the second car. His voice sounded weary and he looked weary, and both were a perfect indication of his feelings. Mr Fowler was a moderate man, but he had always been allergic to wild goose chases, witch hunts and spirit banishers, and he was of the strong opinion now that this was a mixture of all three. Enthusiastic young doctors, like enthusiastic young priests, were menaces to be found in no other vocation or profession. So had been his experience, and it was proving right again. He had not much time for this young man – give him old Sanderson every time. You knew where you stood with Sanderson. This one had got him out today to help certify a man he had known for years, if only at a distance, and he could not at the moment call to mind anyone less likely to be fey than the gravedigger.

On the odd occasions he had met him, the man had been very respectful, he remembered. Besides which, he was most stolid of appearance. That he of all people was seeing things, saints into the bargain, he couldn't take in. And he had said as much to this young enthusiast but he had had an answer to that. 'Saints,' Dr Spencer said, 'were the first things a gravedigger would be likely to see. The whole graveyard was dotted with tombstones and flying angels. The connection was so evident it didn't need any explaining.'

Mr Fowler had felt rebuked at his lack of insight into the business of hallucinations. But now he was losing patience. They had been to the man's house, they had been to the cemetery, they had travelled the lanes and here they were, at a roadworks, and if Spencer hadn't the sense to see that he might as well beat his head against a stone wall as try to get reason out of an Irishman, and such an Irishman, it was time that he himself saw a member of his own profession.

'Doctor,' he called again. This time it was a command, and when, with seeming reluctance, Dr Spencer left his companion, Mr Fowler withdrew his head, put his hand on the wheel and started up his car, saying briefly, 'I'm wasting no more time on this, doctor. Pin down the man and I'll come and see him.' He looked at his watch. 'I was due at a committee meeting fifteen minutes ago.' He let the throttle out and, backing his car to avoid the doctor's, he turned it smartly in the middle of the road and drove off, leaving Dr Spencer to comment among other things, 'Pig-headed old blockhead . . . committee.'

'Look I've told you, Joan, I can't get out the night.' Arthur was standing under the back porch looking at his very angry legitimate fiancée. He was speaking in a whisper. 'Why don't you go to the club?'

'Go to the club and have all of them saying "Where's Arthur?" And you needn't think it's because of your company I'm keeping on, it's because I want to have something out with you.'

Arthur forced himself not to take his eyes off her as he said, 'Well, whatever it is it'll have to wait for I can't leave the house the night. There's me mother there nearly demented because me dad isn't in yet and he can't be found.'

Joan moved her hand impatiently and blinked a number of times before she muttered, 'I took a stand against my father the other night about your dad, but now I think he's right; he ought to be put away or seen to after last night's business and—'

'Shut up, you.'

'Don't you speak like that to me, Arthur Gascoigne.'

'I'll more than speak to you if you talk like that about Dad.' Arthur was still speaking in a whisper but he had moved closer to Joan, threateningly close, and he added, 'He had nothing to do with last night's business. As for your father, if he doesn't mind his own business he'd better look out.'

Joan's wide, astonished stare brought home to Arthur just what he was saying. In a flash he saw his job being wrenched away from him, then came the dubiously comforting thought that if he got rid of Joan then the job would automatically go with her anyway.

'Dad'll be pleased to hear this.'

'Well, go and tell him.'

'I will.'

'Righto.' Not waiting for her to depart on her mission, Arthur turned round and going into the scullery slammed the door, there to be brought to a halt at the sight of Gran putting a dirty towel into the empty copper. As he watched her replacing the lid he wondered how long it had taken her to do that. She'd likely been listening in as usual. But to his surprise she made no reference to what she had heard. Instead, she beckoned him to her and said under her breath, 'Here a minute. What's up with Frankie?'

Arthur stared down into his grandmother's face. She was like a witch, he thought, and in more ways than one. She seemed to get wind of everything, but then Frankie's behaviour at teatime had been a bit odd. It was only because his mother was so worried that she hadn't noticed it. Perhaps she had noticed it but hadn't remarked on it having enough on her mind.

'Do you think he's going to do a bolt?'

'A bolt? Our Frankie?' This had not occurred to Arthur.

'Asking for his best shirt, an' putting it on and it still damp from the ironin' and goin' out dolled up like a dog's dinner. 'Twouldn't surprise me if he didn't come back either.'

'Don't be silly, Gran.' Arthur walked past her and into the kitchen, but when he came to think of it, it was odd – Frankie getting dressed up like that. He wouldn't get dressed up to go on the motorbike. The next thought brought Arthur to a stop; he'd likely got dolled up to go and see that woman – his mother. Arthur looked quickly to where Florrie stood at the sink, her gaze fixed out through the kitchen window. Surely he wouldn't go and do that, would he? But Frankie was a funny lad, jumpy . . . nervy, he considered. It was a wonder he hadn't suspected something about his origin before now, for he was as different from himself and Linda as chalk from cheese.

It was at this point that Florrie swung round from the window and looked towards Gran where she was entering the kitchen and her voice sounded desperate as she said, 'I've just got to go out and look. I must. I can't stand this waiting any longer and it nearly dark.'

'If it's nearly dark you might as well pipe jigs to a mile store as go looking for him now. As I said in the first place, stay put and he'll walk in on us. But if one or t'other of you go scratching round the lanes looking for him, you won't know where to lay hands on anybody and I've got a strong feeling there might be need of many hands one of these nights when he brings himself home.'

'Oh, Gran.' Florrie held her head and turned to the window again. 'You say the most awful things.'

'What's awful about that?' Gran's chin was out. 'I'm merely making a plain statement of things I see comin'. The difference atween me and the rest of you is that I can see things.'

'That's where Dad's got it from then.' This cynical quip came from Linda where she sat tensely on the sofa, a book on her lap but making no pretence of reading it.

'I'll have no more cracks like that, miss, or I'll wrap me hand around your lug.' Gran's voice was high and obviously she was angry.

Florrie turned from the window again and said, 'Let's have a row – that's all we want, a row now.'

'Well, I ask you, Florrie, was that called for?'

'The things you say, Gran,' cried Linda, 'are never called for, you cannot take your own medicine.'

'That's enough, Linda.' Florrie looked at her daughter. She too, like the rest of her family, seemed to have altered in the last few days. She knew she didn't care for her gran but she had never come out in the open and said such things to her before. What had come over the house, and all of them? In less than a week, there was John off his head, for he surely was – of this she was firmly convinced although she wouldn't admit it to the others; Arthur in a fix and unhappy; Linda trying to alter herself overnight to look double her age; and lastly Frankie. The change in Frankie had come about only today. He had seemed a bit odd this morning before he went out but his attitude tonight was positively strange. And the way he kept looking at her when he thought she wasn't aware of it. Then him putting on his good suit and shirt and, the strangest thing of all, he had scarcely opened his mouth to her from when he came in to when he went out. This was most unusual. She recollected now he had only spoken to any of them in reply. But Frankie wasn't the kind to wait for replies; Frankie was the questioning kind – he always spoke first. Was he being affected by what was happening to his dad? Oh. She shook her head, she didn't know.

The time moved slowly. Gran had taken a seat in sulky silence. Linda was once again pretending to read, and Florrie stood at the window until the light went completely and she could see nothing but

161

the radius illuminated by the street lamps and the lights behind the curtains in the house opposite.

It was sometime later when Arthur came to her and said gently, 'Come and sit down. I've made a cup of cocoa.'

'No. No.' She almost jumped round. 'I'm going to look; I must. Where's my hat?'

She had just pulled her hat and coat from the cupboard when the knock came on the back door, and before any of them could go to answer it, they heard it open and steps in the scullery and there was Moira standing in the doorway looking at them.

'What is it?' asked Florrie quietly, staring fixedly at her.

'Nothing.' Moira shook her head then said, 'Well, I mean there's nothing to worry about.' She looked at Florrie's hat and added, 'You needn't go out, Aunt Florrie.'

'You've seen him?'

'Yes.' Moira nodded again. 'He's all right, there's nothing to worry about,' she repeated. She moved further into the kitchen now then asked, 'Has Dr Spencer been back the night?'

'Yes,' said Florrie impatiently. 'He was here about eight, but where's John? Where did you see him?'

Moira did not answer Florrie but went to the table, and there she stood and addressed her remarks to Gran as she said, 'I used to like Dr Spencer but not now. He's got a bee in his bonnet bigger than any . . .' She paused and did not go on to make mention of the comparable bee in John's bonnet, but added, 'He seems bent on causing trouble, making mountains out of molehills, I think.'

'Look, Moira, stop beating around the bush.' Florrie swung Moira roughly by the arm towards her, which was a very unusual action for her to make. But Moira showed no resentment, she just looked her full in the face and said, 'Mind, Aunt Florrie, if I tell you where Uncle is you've got to promise to leave things be and that goes for all of you.' She cast a swift glance round the rest of the company. 'He's all right and he's settled down and he's quite content to be there, for he seems now to realise the danger he's in. He didn't believe afore that the doctor meant just what he said, that he'd have him taken away. In fact, put away would be a better name for it. But Uncle sees this now and he says to tell you that he's all right and to leave him be.'

Florrie groped at the top button of her blouse and undid it, then buttoned it up again before she asked in a distraught voice, 'Where is he, Moira? Tell me child, where is he?'

Moira dropped her eyes from Florrie's face then looked quickly in Arthur's direction before she said, 'He's in my room. At this minute he's asleep in my bed.'

'Your room,' whispered Florrie.

'Your room.' It was a grunt from Gran and although you couldn't hear Arthur repeating 'your room' his lips framed the words, and it was apparent that they all would not have been more astonished had Moira said that John was at this moment perched on the top of Penshaw Monument.

The eyes on Moira brought a wave of colour to her face and she said defiantly, 'It's the only place I could think of. Me ma and me da were for it from the minute I mentioned it. Me da was all for it for the doctor went at him like a sergeant major this afternoon trying to trip him into saying it was Uncle John who got dressed up last night and went to the cemetery with the sole idea of scaring the wits out of him, and he had brought Mr Fowler along with him – I mean the doctor – and you know what he is? He's a Justice of the Peace.' Moira paused for breath and Florrie unbuttoned and buttoned her blouse once again. Then she sat down and, still looking at Moira, she said lamely, 'But . . . but John to go into . . . into your house.'

'Our house is all right, Aunty.' There was a note of rebuff in Moira's voice.

'Oh, lass, I'm not meaning that, nothing like that, of course your house is all right, but you know John and your da have never hit it off.'

'Perhaps not. That was because Da's a joker and Uncle John couldn't take it, but now that they're landed in the same boat, sort of, and seeing the same things, it might work out . . . It's as if they've got something in common like.'

'And how long does he intend to stay in your room, may I ask?' This question, of course, came from Gran. Moira, turning to her, said, 'I don't know, Gran, but he can stay there as long as ever he wants. I don't mind sleeping in the kitchen, and our house is the one place they won't look for him. Anyway, I think he should bide there until the doctor cools down, or Dr Sanderson gets back from his holiday, or until . . . until he gets better a bit.'

'That could be a very long time. He mightn't come out until he's ready for his pension, because knowing my son, if he wants to see things, he'll see things, just to be contrary.'

'Oh, listen to her. There you go again, Gran.'

'Be quiet, Linda.' Florrie almost bawled at her daughter, and in the uneasy quiet that followed she turned to Moira and taking hold of her hand, said, 'Tell me how all this came about, lass, how did you get him there?'

Again Moira's eyes flicked to Arthur who was staring at her, his love now patent for all to see, and as her fluent tongue became hesitant over her part in the affair that had brought John to the house next door just a short while ago, Arthur made a vow he would marry Moira McNally or nobody. The Duckworths could take him up for breach of promise if they liked, but he would tell them he was finished.

When Moira ended her tale, Florrie stared at her for a time then she stood up and bending forward she touched her on the cheek and whispered, 'You're a good girl, Moira. A good girl.'

Moira did not laugh or say anything flippant, but with her head cast down she turned about and bidding them all goodnight with a muttered 'Be seeing you', she went quietly out of the kitchen.

A temporary silence fell on the kitchen and Gran, leaning one hand against the mantelpiece and with the other hugging her waist, proclaimed loudly, 'Now I've heard everything, there's no need to go to the pictures and see the cowboys dodging the posse, and what do we want a television for?' Her chin worked. 'John skulking in that chit's room, aye, I've heard everything now.'

'Then you can go to bed then, can't you?' Linda flounced by her grandmother and with a hurried peck at her mother's cheek, she said goodnight under the hail of Gran's tongue.

'That one needs takin' in hand, if you don't want more trouble.' Gran's jaw was out to its limit.

'Look, Mam,' Arthur interrupted at this point. 'You get off to bed and,' he added as if on an afterthought, 'and you an' all Gran, and I'll stay up and wait for Frankie.'

For a moment Florrie considered this proposal in silence and then she said quietly, 'There's no point in doing anything else, is there?' She flicked her eyes in the direction of the McNallys before walking slowly out of the kitchen. Then from the hall her voice came back wearily saying, 'You coming, Gran?' And Gran, her chin still working, reluctantly obeyed.

Arthur was now left alone and he spent the time waiting for Frankie's return not thinking of his father's plight, but of the girl who, to him, appeared so clever – almost brilliant – and kind. Aye, she was kind. It was her kindness that had got to him, not her figure, as his dad had suggested, and now he loved her so much that his whole being was burning to proclaim it to the wide world; which meant simply the Duckworths.

It was nearly an hour later when Frankie came in and his condition had not improved, for apart from a quick look round the kitchen he made no reference to the emptiness of it. It was Arthur, for a change, who did the talking. Briefly he explained the situation to date and not until he had finished his story did Frankie make any comment, and it couldn't have been more brief. 'So now what?' he asked flatly.

'Well . . .' Arthur, slightly nonplussed by Frankie's lack of interest, pondered a moment. 'Your guess is as good as mine. Moira seems to think that Spencer's got a personal spite in for Dad – why, God alone knows. I don't see that Dad's done anything to him.'

'No, I can't see that he has either. It's me that's entitled to the personal spite; it's me that he's done things to.'

'Oh, come off it,' said Arthur impatiently, getting to his feet. 'Don't go all dramatic about that business; you're the same as ever you were. Because you know about it now that can't alter you or things.'

'That's all you know,' returned Frankie harshly. 'I watched her the night and I couldn't take it in that she was me mother, yet all the time I knew that she was and it made me feel awful. She's painted up like a prossy.'

'So that's where you've been?' Arthur was uneasy. 'You've been talking to her?'

'No. No, I haven't.' Frankie turned his back on his brother.

'D'you mean to say you've just been watching her then?'

'Whatever I've been doin' is me own business.'

'If she sees you, or somebody else sees you, at that game there'll be some explaining to do, and we've got enough trouble here. Don't you realise that that doctor's trying to run Dad into the asylum?'

'And I should cry, shouldn't I?'

Arthur was momentarily speechless at Frankie's callousness but he checked the quick retort that jumped into his mouth as he watched him shambling listlessly across the room towards the hall. He could be magnanimous because he was in love . . . and added to that his mam was his mam. By, yes, taking this thing seriously, it must be awful to find out that your mam wasn't your mam.

Chapter Seven

What, asked John of himself, for the countless time, was he doing here anyway? Sitting in this little glamourfied, half-clean bedroom, which was permeated with the smell of cabbage and the stife of fat from the kitchen below. To allow himself to be aimlessly cooped up in here seemed to him more evidence of unbalance than the visitations of the Saint.

It was over forty hours now since he had had any visits from him; the longest spell since their first meeting. But he did not delude himself for a moment that he had seen the last of the Saint. And it was this very fact that kept him here in McNally's house . . . Of all the houses in the world, it had to be McNally's that was sheltering him in his trouble. Yet, he had to admit to himself, however reluctantly, they were kind; they were all very kind. That was the remarkable thing about it, that they should be so kind and understanding – even McNally himself. But his particular kindness, John thought, had likely come about because of the eye-opener he had got up in the cemetery. Anyway, whatever had caused his change of front didn't much matter, for John found that he couldn't take to him any more than he had ever done, and if he wanted proof of his own absolute normality this was it.

The door opened and Katie entered into his thinking. She had a cup of tea in one hand and a plate of cake in the other.

'I've brought you a drop of tea and a piece of me spiced loaf. Are you comfortable, John?'

John had lost count of the cups of tea she had brought him since early morning, and if he saw any more food he would be sick. As to the question, was he comfortable, she had asked it on each of her visits. As she put the plate and cup of tea in his hands she said, 'That'll put you over till teatime; it isn't far off, and you'll feel brighter when Brod comes in and has a chat with you, eh?'

All John could do was move his head in a downward direction.

At that moment the sound of the garden gate clicking brought Katie from her hovering position over him to the window, and as she peered down below the slit of the curtains, she exclaimed loudly, 'Mother of God, it's Moira and she has the child with her. Well now' – she turned to John eagerly – 'she's likely the bearer of news. I'll away down and relieve her of the child and she can come up and have a word with you. I bet it's something to do with that devil of a doctor.'

She hurried out, her slippers flapping, and within a few minutes Moira's high heels came tapping rapidly up the stairs and John was on his feet when she came into the room.

'Hullo,' she said.

John nodded, then added to it, 'Hullo, Moira.' He liked this girl.

'I just thought I'd slip home and tell you a bit of good news. She sent me out for the child's constitutional.' She pulled a long face. 'It's good news. After surgery closes for the night, the doctor's off to Newcastle. He's staying there until the morrow because he's the big noise in this hospital's raffle. It's not being drawn till three so he shouldn't be back until the morrow evening at the earliest. And he won't be on duty on Sunday unless he's called out, and by Monday morning he might have . . . well . . .'

Moira could not bring herself to lie blatantly and say that the doctor would have forgotten about this business because she knew he had got his back up about it – he had even questioned her this morning. It must have just dawned on him that she lived next door to Uncle John.

He had put his questions in a jocular, quizzing way but she was up to him and had played dumb.

John pulled at his collar. 'It would be all right to go in, then?

'I wouldn't until after tea, Uncle. He's still out on his round, but once his surgery's over at seven, it'll be OK.'

He nodded and sat down. As long as he hadn't to stay another night here, he could put up with a few more hours.

'Drink your tea,' she said.

He drank it obediently and handed the empty cup back to her, quietly saying, 'Thanks, lass.' Then giving her a little smile, he added, 'For everything.'

'That's all right, Uncle. I'll be seein' you.'

He nodded his farewell and when she had gone he sat thinking about her. She was a nice lass, he had to admit that now, and she would have been fine for Arthur. It was a pity he was in this fix and there wasn't much that could be done about it. If what he himself had done to Duckworth hadn't broken the thing off then nothing would . . . except . . . He moved his head from side to side and dropped his hands between his knees. That would involve Florrie, and Florrie had had enough on her plate this week without adding any more to it. Of course, there was the possibility that Freda might blow the gaff; but Freda was a cat and mouse worker and by the time she had made up her mind to do it, it would be of little use to Arthur. No, he could see no way out of this any more than he could out of his own trouble. It was all a matter of time.

It was as he sat thinking this that his steady normal feeling began to slip, or, as he tried to explain it to himself, he seemed to step up out of it before the airiness enveloped him completely. He protested loudly inside himself, 'No, no, not here.' But he might as well have spat against the wind for all the effect his protests had on the rising ecstatic feeling. He closed his eyes again and told himself there was one thing he must do; he must speak in the lowest of whispers for he did not want Katie passing out in his arms.

'*Don't try to shut me out, John, it's no use.*'

169

As John slowly opened his eyes there was a look of surprise in them, for the voice he had heard held no laughing depth and immediately he saw that the face of the Saint was not one broad beam as he had come to expect, instead his whole countenance was constrained.

'*You're not the only one who's in trouble.*'

This remark caused John to draw his brows questioningly together but he did not speak.

'*This is what comes of showing favouritism and not carrying out my duties according to rules.*'

'What are you talking about?' John remembered to keep his voice just the semblance of a whisper.

'*My stupidity in allowing myself to be guided by you.*'

'Me?' This was a little louder.

'*Yes, John, you. I should never have shown myself to McNally. For you see there was no point; there was nothing to gain by it. I had nothing to convince him of. But because of the bargain I made with you in a moment of weakness, I did it, and got myself into hot water . . . A lot of hot water.*'

John wanted to laugh and say, it would take quite a drop to cover you, but instead he whispered, 'I'm sorry.' And he realised he was sorry. 'He won't be seein' you again, then?'

'*No, most certainly not, John.*'

'That's a pity, a real pity. You know . . .' John rubbed his hand across his mouth. 'I never had such a laugh in all me life. You did a good job that night but I'm sorry you got it in the neck over it.'

'But you'd like me to do it again.'

John gave a low chuckle. 'Aye, I would, no use sayin' one thing and thinkin' another.'

'*I'm sorry to have to disappoint you. And for my part, as I told you before, I think your choice was wrong. If you had asked me to have a word with your doctor friend you wouldn't be sitting here now.*'

'Oh, him. 'Twould take the Devil in Hell to convince that one.'

'*Well, I don't think I would have proved a bad substitute.*' The Saint smiled for the first time then went on. '*Now about our bargain, John.*'

'Aye, the bargain.' John sighed. 'Well, since you kept your part, I'd like to keep mine, but in me sober moments I can't see how I'll ever do it, not for a few years anyway. And what's more, I've been thinking. Even when I get it, it's not going to convince me . . . For, mind you' – he pointed his finger at the Saint – 'I still believe what I said about you.'

'*That's a pity, John, for it only makes my task the longer. You're a stubborn man, you know. Now, if you could just try and see things my way, well then, we could part company and that would be that; but if you won't then you're stuck with me . . . And me with you.*'

When John was not actually confronted by this being he was the last person in the world he wished to see, but once in his presence he had the desire to stay there and so he heard himself saying, 'Well, that's all right with me.'

'*I'm causing you a heap of trouble, John.*'

'Oh, I'll weather that,' said John airily. And in his present frame of mind he was firmly convinced that he could weather it.

'*That doctor's got it in for you.*'

'Yes, I know that, but it'll take more than him to get on top of me.'

'*I'd be careful, John. I've met men of his kidney before today, mostly in the priesthood – they have to prove themselves right, no matter who dies.*'

'You think he'll try to put me away?'

'*I think he means business and I'd be wary of him . . . Oh, look out.*'

John's attention swung to the doorway and there he saw standing not only Katie, but Florrie.

'Come out of it, John, come out of it.' Katie was advancing on him and not a trace of fear to be seen on her face. Katie had fainted because she thought Broderick was seeing things, but as Broderick was seemingly himself on the morning following the incident, she had come to the same conclusion that the doctor had worked out. Broderick had been engaging in a leg-pull to take the rise out of John, and the more he tried to convince her otherwise the more firmly she was fixed in her own opinion. Her Brod seeing things, and him as sober as a judge. She must have been off her head herself to go and faint like that, but he had done it all to the life with his shirt torn to ribbons and his hair standin' on end into the bargain, that she could be forgiven for being taken in. But John seeing things was a different kettle of fish. He was seeing them, all right. He was in a bad way, and she was sorry to the heart for him.

'Leave me be.' John pushed Katie's hands off him and turned to Florrie where she was standing gazing fixedly at him, fear in her eyes, and he said to her in a sort of appeal, 'Don't look at me like that, lass.' When she did not answer he turned to the bed and sat on it with a flop. He felt deflated now and entirely himself.

When Florrie still said no word, Katie put in on a high note, 'Aw, she's worried about you, John, and small wonder, ye know, at that. Come and sit yourself down, Florrie.' She pulled a chair to the bed. 'I'll take meself off downstairs for I'm up to me eyes with things to do as usual, and Brod himself will be in on me at any minute.'

Tactfully, if reluctantly, Katie left them and Florrie, taking the seat near John, looked at him helplessly as he sat with his head bowed as if in shame.

When John felt like himself he had no wish to talk, but now he forced himself to some sort of explanation that would enlighten Florrie as to his state of mind, even if it did not succeed in alleviating her worry. 'I keep telling you I'm not barmy, Florrie.' His voice was a mumble. 'But I can understand full well that you should think I am . . . It's like this, you see; I can be all right one moment, and then I get a sort of feeling . . . I can't rightly describe it . . . It's a sort of airy, happy, don't-care-a-damn feeling. You know me.' He flicked his eyes to her. 'I've never been the jolly, laughin' kind, that's why I can't stand . . .' His voice dropped even lower as he thumbed the floor. 'Well, when I get this feeling, it seems as if I'm being turned into the man I've always longed to be. A kind of happy, easy-going fellow, bubbling inside with chatter and laughter. I've met such men and I suppose I've envied them. These past few days, as I've said, I get this sort of feeling and then . . .' His head sank to his chest and his voice was very low as he admitted, 'He comes. But Florrie' – he raised his eyes quickly to her again – 'he's as real as you are. I can't explain it. I have no means of telling you just how real he is. I was frightened at the sight of him at first. Scared out of me wits, but now, although I don't want to see him, believe me I don't, Florrie, but when he does come I'm sort of glad he's there. Oh' – he moved his body from side to side in his perplexity – 'I just can't explain and make you see.' Now his hand went out and covered her knee. 'I know I've got you worried, lass. I'm worried meself.'

'What's to be done, John?' Florrie's lips were trembling but her eyes were dry. 'You can't go on . . .'

'I don't rightly know, lass. I've got a feeling it might work itself away if I was left alone. But that doctor . . .'

'He's been again, John. A few minutes ago.'

'He has?' John's eyes widened the slightest. 'What did he say?'

Florrie lowered her eyes as she whispered, 'He's positive the business the other night with Broderick was all your doing. He demanded to know where you were and when I told him I didn't know, he said . . .' Florrie paused and John put in, 'Aye, aye, go on; you might as well tell me.'

It was some seconds before Florrie continued and then John could only just catch her words. 'He said the next thing we'll be hearing is of women being scared out of their wits by a man jumping out on them from dark corners. He said . . . he said that's the pattern it would take.'

'My God.' John got to his feet and began to pace the narrow width of the room and Florrie, still not looking at him, murmured, 'He's positive I know where you are and he said that he was coming in tomorrow evening and if he didn't see you then he was goin' to the police, and I had to tell you.'

'A . . . aw.'

It was a long drawn out groan from John, and as Florrie went hastily to him and put her arms about him, he placed his hand over his eyes.

'There, there,' she soothed him. 'Don't take on like that. Oh, don't. Just see him the morrow night. Do that, please, John, for my sake, and do what he asks. Go to hospital – you can go voluntarily. Nobody is going to make you or force you or push you; you can go on your own as long as he knows you're going, and you won't see him there. There'll be other doctors, men who will understand. It was the cricket ball – you should have had yourself seen to last Saturday when it happened. You've never been like this in your life afore. Oh, my dear.' She led him to the bed and sat down by his side and he rested against her as if he was weary and when she asked, 'Will you?' He answered after a while, 'I'll see, lass. I'll see.'

Then Florrie, stroking his head, said, 'I've been thinking afore I came round. He cannot force his way upstairs, and give him his due he didn't try it on, so you'll be just as well in your own room as you would be here. I think you would have been just as well there all along.' Florrie's voice was hardly audible now. 'Not that I don't think it was good of Moira to be so helpful. She's been good, real good.'

Slowly John straightened himself and rose from the bed saying, 'You're right. I'm acting like a scared rabbit. I'm going into me own house and if he comes again I'll see him whether I'm upstairs or downstairs . . . Let's be going.'

He went to the door, then paused with his hand on the knob and, turning, he put his other hand on her shoulder and said below his breath, 'I'm longing for a sight of your kitchen again, lass, after having a taste of this.' His eyes did a circular movement around the room. Then, as if each word had to be dragged out, he said haltingly, 'You're . . . you're a wonderful wife . . . lass.'

After a moment of eye holding eye, Florrie leant towards him and she kissed him; it was a shy kiss, as if they had been parted for years and the man before her was a stranger whom she had to get to know again. Then with her head bent she passed before him and down the stairs.

Chapter Eight

'Aunt Lucy,' said Florrie. 'It's me that's going to go off me head. I'm going stark staring mad.'

'Oh, lass, what's happened now?' Aunt Lucy was smoothing down her hair after taking off her hat.

'About everything that could,' said Florrie.

'Oh dear, oh dear . . . By the way . . .' Aunt Lucy looked around and her voice was a thin little whisper as she asked, 'Where's she?'

There was no need for Florrie to enquire who Aunt Lucy was referring to and she answered with a sigh, 'Upstairs lying down.'

'Has she been on again?'

'Does she ever stop? But it's not about her I'm worried.'

'John?'

'Yes, and more now.'

'Is he out?'

'Oh no,' said Florrie. She jerked her head upwards. 'He's in his room.'

'Has he had any more of them . . . ?' Aunt Lucy left the question unfinished, and Florrie said helplessly. 'Yes, first thing this morning.'

'Laughing again?'

'No, not this time. He was sort of arguing and shouting . . . Well, not shouting but talking loud, something about a bargain and saying that nobody was going to convince him. I couldn't make head nor tail of it although he kept on and on about the same thing. I stayed on the landing until he quietened, then I was just on my way downstairs when he came tearing out of the room, galloped down the stairs and out into the back garden. Before I could stop him, he was yelling to Linda all the time to come back. She had just set out on her way to work. I thought it was all part of his turn, but when Linda came back into the kitchen and I looked at her face, I knew there was something else wrong.'

'Wrong? With Linda?' Aunt Lucy's eyes were stretched wide.

'Yes, Linda.' Florrie shook her head slowly. 'He said to her, "Give me that note", and she didn't deny she had a note but she wouldn't give it to him and I kept saying, "What's all this about? Who's the note from?" And then he turned on me like a wild man. "It's from Pat McNally," he said. "I saw him slip it to her over the railings and what's more he . . ."' Florrie paused then went on. 'He wouldn't say what he had seen Pat do. Aunt Lucy, I was simply amazed; Linda's just a child and Pat McNally, he's thirty and you know . . . Well, he's been divorced an' all, and what's more he's a Catholic. Everything that could be is against him but he's changed my Linda; I couldn't recognise her this morning. She likes her dad; she's very fond of him, but she stood up to him, more than I could have done, and told him that she was going to marry him and she wasn't going to wait until she was twenty-one either, no matter what he said or did.'

'Dear, dear, dear, dear,' said Aunt Lucy.

'And that's not all, Aunt Lucy. I could have sunk through the floor the next minute when John said, "My God, it isn't enough that Arthur's courtin' young Moira on the sly, you've got to go and get yourself mixed up with a man near twice your age, and another McNally at that."'

'Arthur . . . but the wedding, Florrie.'

'Yes, Aunt Lucy, the wedding. That's what's been the matter with Arthur and Joan for weeks now and I didn't see it. It was going on under me nose and I didn't see it. What's come over us all, Aunt Lucy? This used to be a happy house. Quiet, but happy together. But now, everybody seems to have gone off their heads. There's no need for John to go away – this is an asylum in itself.'

'Aw, lass, don't say things like that.'

'How can I help it? Every one of my family is in trouble.'

'Not Frankie, Florrie; Frankie's all right.'

'There's something wrong with Frankie an' all, Aunt Lucy. What it is I can't make out. But he's not speaking to me and his reactions are odd – not as they used to be – for when I tackled our Arthur at dinner time and he admitted carrying on with Moira, but said it wasn't carrying on, it was serious, Frankie didn't say a word, not one word. And that's not Frankie, Aunt Lucy. He never even batted an eyelid when Arthur said he had told Mr Duckworth that he was finished and what he could do with his job. Even after dinner when I had him on my own and I told him about Linda and Pat McNally all his comment was, "Well, well, you'd better build a covered way atween the two houses." Now I know Frankie, Aunt Lucy, and the things that have happened here today would in the usual way have kept his tongue wagging for a week.'

'Is it a girl with him?'

'No, I don't think so. But then what do I know about any of them?' Florrie put out her hands in appeal. 'They're my family and I should know all their doings. But what happens? They're carrying on under me nose and I can't see it.'

'Don't blame yourself, lass – you've been so worried about John and he's still your main worry, don't forget.'

'I'm not likely to forget that, Aunt Lucy.'

'And once he's better, everything else will fall into place, you'll see. Have you had the Duckworths here since Arthur told them?'

'No, but there's plenty of time. Joan's away in Hexham the day; we'll know as soon as she's back – they'll be down on us, never fear.'

It was more than an hour later when a rap on the front door knocker turned Florrie's eye towards Aunt Lucy, and she said, 'They're making it formal. I bet that's them, the Duckworths.'

'It couldn't be the doctor?' asked Aunt Lucy apprehensively.

'No,' said Florrie. 'He's away the day; I know that for sure.'

Bracing herself, Florrie went to the front door, opened it and she received her third severe shock of the day.

'Hullo, Florrie. I don't suppose you remember me?'

Florrie's mouth hung open and her eyebrows stretched up into points.

'Well, I guess I am a bit of a shock. It's a long time, y'know . . . Aren't you going to ask me in?'

Florrie took a deep draught of air before bringing out, 'Yes – yes, come in.'

As Florrie closed the door behind her visitor, the hall became full of scent, and it felt like she was squeezing past it as she made her way in front of Freda and into the kitchen.

'God Almighty!' said Aunt Lucy.

'No, only me.'

Following this facetious comment Freda, after looking around her to take stock of the room, said, 'Well, here we are, all together like the folks a Shields.' Freda turned a lazy glance in Florrie's direction and remarked, 'Aunt Lucy doesn't change much, does she? Not like us.' She made a high sound that was meant to be a laugh.

Florrie did not answer, not even by moving a muscle of her face. She was staring in fixed amazement at Freda and asking herself had the world gone mad, that everything should be happening to her this week and particularly the day. What did this one want, after all these years? What could she want? She remembered something almost forgotten. The real reason why they had come to this very village.

As Florrie put her hand to her head, Freda laughed outright. 'Oh, come now, Florrie, don't say I'm as big a shock as all that. Have I changed so much?' She blinked her mascaraed eyes then asked in a jocular tone, 'Isn't anybody going to ask me to have a seat?'

Still without speaking Florrie pushed forward a chair for her, and as she sat down, Aunt Lucy said harshly, 'What do you want, Freda?'

'Nothing, nothing at all, but I thought I'd just look in and pay a friendly visit as I'm a neighbour of Florrie's now. Quite the right thing to do, isn't it?'

'A neighbour?' Florrie repeated the word on a gasp of astonishment, and Freda said, 'Well, not next door, but I'm in the next village. Hasn't Aunt Lucy told you?'

Florrie looked towards Aunt Lucy in amazement and when Aunt Lucy turned her gaze away, Freda nodded in mock annoyance at her, saying, 'You're a cute one, aren't you? Always the old schemer.'

As Aunt Lucy blinked and let her eyes rove round the room looking for something to fix them on, Florrie tried to pull her scattered wits together. She had met this woman three times in all, and there was only one thing changed about her and that was her face. Her manner was just the same: airy, sarky and a little frightening in a subtle way. She was after something or she wouldn't be here.

Freda was looking at her now. 'You don't know that George is dead, but I'm sure you'll be sorry to hear it.' She paused. 'Funny, isn't it, how the youngish ones are taken and the old ones' – she glanced in Aunt Lucy's direction – 'refuse to let go.'

So George was dead. The father of her first child was dead. Florrie felt neither pity nor remorse, but what she did feel was a jealousy of this woman before her; this painted woman who had stolen her first love from her. Yet why should she, she asked herself, for look at her, she looked a trollop.

The garden gate clicking at this moment brought her to the window as if she had been shot there and she made an effort to hide her relief as she saw it was only Linda who was coming up the path. For a moment she had forgotten that the boys wouldn't be in until later this evening, but just in case, she must get rid of her as soon as possible.

'Who is it?' It was Aunt Lucy speaking.

'It's only Linda.'

There came a laugh from Freda. 'Don't worry about John coming in and finding me here. He knows I'm around, he's been along to see me.'

'What? John's been to see you?'

'There seems to be lots of things you don't know, Florrie . . .'

'Be quiet,' Florrie snapped at her as the back door opened, and when Linda came into the room she found she couldn't handle the situation or think of any way of introducing Freda. It was Aunt Lucy who did this, saying to Linda, 'This is Mrs Manning.' Then she added reluctantly, 'An old friend of mine.'

Freda rose and extended her hand to Linda, saying, 'By, haven't you grown, you were only a baby the last time I saw you. Well, well. And aren't we good-looking too? Who do you take after?'

Linda found herself tongue-tied before this smart woman, for so Freda appeared to her, and it crossed her mind, 'Fancy Aunt Lucy ever having a friend like this.' She was glad they had a visitor for now Mam couldn't start on her – at least not right away. Linda found she was blushing at the compliment, and in embarrassment she turned to her mother and said, 'Tea not ready yet?' She didn't really want any tea, she told herself she was too unhappy to eat. What was more, she had had no intention of speaking to her mother, for earlier on they had parted on anything but cordial terms. But it was the only thing she could think of to say for the woman was staring at her.

'It's on its way.' Florrie went slowly to a drawer and took out the tablecloth and Aunt Lucy got to her feet and went to the dresser and began to collect the crockery. While they were doing this, Freda addressed herself solely to Linda. She talked about clothes and at one point, after asking who was her favourite TV star, she showed her astonishment with a loud 'No' when she discovered that they did not possess a television.

Florrie, catching Aunt Lucy's eye, asked silently, 'What am I to do?' But Aunt Lucy could give her no help, she could only shake her head as if she herself was utterly bewildered.

Aunt Lucy's head had scarcely stopped moving when it jerked upwards on the sound of Gran's door closing overhead. Florrie did not look up but she took the bread knife and began to slice at the loaf rapidly. She did not turn round as Gran entered the room, saying, 'Who was that at the front door . . . Oh!'

Gran had the answer before her and she stared at it. Her eyes narrowed. Who was this piece? She had never seen anybody like her in this house afore. She looked towards Florrie where she was slowly turning from the cupboard.

'This is a friend of mine, Gran, a Mrs Manning. This is my husband's mother.' As Florrie made a compulsory introduction, she was aware of Linda's puzzled gaze fixed on her and she could feel the question . . . Whose friend is she? I thought she was Aunt Lucy's.

Gran noticed that Florrie had used the word husband and not John to this friend of hers so when the woman stood up and said, 'Pleased to meet you, John's mother, well now', Gran's eyes narrowed still further and it was with evident reluctance that she allowed her hand to be taken by the flabby ring-bedecked white one.

Gran said nothing to the greeting. She did not say anything until she had sat down opposite the visitor and then she asked quietly, 'How is it I've never seen you afore, if you're a friend of Florrie's?'

'Well now, Mrs Gascoigne, I can easily explain that. You see we've lived at opposite ends of the country.' Freda's voice had risen, it always did when she spoke to the old, and Gran raised her hand and flapped it in her direction, saying loudly, 'There's no need for you to bellow, I'm not deaf, I've all me faculties left, hearin' included.'

Obviously Freda was a little taken aback by this virile attitude in one who looked so old and frail and she muttered the usual apology of her type: 'Sorry, I'm sure.'

'What did you say your name was?'

'Mrs Manning, Freda Manning.' Freda's voice was stiff and her manner weighed down with dignity now.

Gran nodded, her eyes still screwed up, then she commented to no one in particular, 'Never heard your name mentioned in this house afore. Funny . . .' She turned to Florrie who was back at her breadboard. 'Never heard you mention your friend afore, Florrie.'

Laying the knife down with a deliberate movement, Florrie turned and looked straight at Gran. 'You've only been with us four years, Gran, and I didn't think you'd be interested.'

Gran's chin moved out. 'Four years is a long time and there's nothin' much that I didn't know afore that I haven't learnt in four years.'

'Does it matter? Is it so important?' Florrie's voice was rising and Gran, turning her gaze full on the guest, said in an off-hand tone, 'Well, no, I don't suppose it is, not all that.'

Gran's words and tone were plainly meant to carry offence but Freda told herself that she wasn't going to be riled by an old bitch like this. But she could understand quite plainly now why John had kept the knowledge of their marriage from his mother. By, yes. If they had met in those days, they would have torn each other's eyes out. She was beginning to enjoy herself – the whole situation appealed to her and she was looking forward with a rising excitement to the climax. She approached it now by asking of Florrie, 'How are the boys?'

For a second Florrie's hand became still on the board, and when she continued her slicing she said, 'They're very well.'

'Where are you from?' This straight question could come from no other than Gran, and Freda, smiling fixedly at her, said, 'Oh, quite near now. I was just telling Florrie I've had a bungalow built in Biddleswiddle.'

There followed a silence that was heavy, then Gran shattered it by asking, 'Which of them did you know first, John or Florrie, here?'

'Oh, our Mamie, what a question to ask.'

'Who's speaking to you, Lucy Travers? It's a simple enough question. You mind your own business.'

Freda flicked her eyes downward, gave a little hick of a laugh, then looking at Gran with her head cocked on one side, she exclaimed, 'Well, since you ask, it was John . . . Satisfied?'

'No, I ain't since . . . since you ask.'

'Why are you keeping on, Gran? Give over, behave will you.' Florrie stood now with a plate of bread in her hand, glaring at Gran.

'There ain't no harm in asking a question, is there, if she's a friend of John's . . . and yours.' She paused before the 'and' then asked, 'Does she know the state he's in?' Before Florrie could answer one way or the other, Gran turned her head to Freda and stated, 'He's goin' off his head.'

'Stop it, Gran, do you hear, stop it. I'll have no more of it.' It looked for a moment as if Florrie might deposit the plate of bread and butter on Gran's head.

'Who's going off his head?' asked Freda with eyebrows raised. 'You don't mean John, surely? He'd be the last to go off his head.'

'John isn't well, that's all. He had a blow and it's made him a bit off colour.' Florrie put the plate on the table none too gently.

'Oh,' said Freda looking puzzled. The 'oh' was repeated by Gran under her breath. 'Oh,' she said looking down at her gnarled hands. She didn't like this one. She didn't like this woman who was painted up like a street whore, and when she didn't like people she wanted to get at them, and what was more there was something fishy here. Why hadn't she heard her name mentioned in the house? And not in all her born days could she imagine Florrie having a friend such as her. And hadn't the one just admitted that it was John she knew first. Gran shook her head at this. Stretch her imagination as she would, she couldn't see her son ever having the gumption to even speak to a piece like this one. Aye, there was something so fishy here she could smell it. But she would get to the bottom on it, aye, she would that.

'Oh, John!'

On this trembling exclamation, Gran's eyes swung up to see Florrie hurrying to the doorway where stood her son, his face the colour of lead and the shape of his mouth lost, so tightly was his jaw compressed.

John was not looking at Florrie, he was looking beyond her and he put her gently aside when she stood dead in front of him. He had been feeling himself for some time now and had decided that he would come downstairs so that if the doctor fellow did arrive after tea he would find his mistake out. He would find him calm and casual. But the sight of Freda sitting in his kitchen there was bolting through him such a wave of anger that it was all he could do not to rush at her, take her by the scruff of the neck and fling her out of the door.

'Hullo there, John.' Freda was on her feet and walking towards him. 'Long time no see.' She accompanied this phrase with a slight wink.

John, on the very point of speaking, caught the look in his mother's eyes. They were tight fastened on him, speculative and probing, and they gave him warning that he must watch his step for if she found out about this business he would never live it down until the day she died. So all he allowed himself to say was 'Hullo', and this was something akin to a growl.

Aye, aye. Gran gave herself another small nod. What had she said? She was right. He had looked startled out of his wits. Before long she would be learning things or her name wasn't Mamie Gascoigne.

'Tea's nearly ready.' Florrie made a gallant effort to ease the situation and she spoke to Linda who was sitting staring, as if fascinated, at Freda, saying, 'Will you put the cakes out while I mash the tea?' As she walked from the table amid the tense silence that had fallen on the room, her thoughts yelled at her. What if she talks? Florrie saw her house disintegrating about her. Suddenly her thinking stopped and she turned her eyes towards the kitchen window. When she saw them coming towards the gate – both Arthur and Frankie – the teapot nearly slipped from her hands to the floor.

Why were they here at this time? Arthur had gone off to Battonbun to play in the return match. In the usual way he would not have been in before eight this evening at the earliest, and Frankie's last mumbled words had been, 'I don't know when I'll be in.' Which meant, or usually did, that he wouldn't be returning to tea either and she could expect him when she saw him. And now, here they were. Instead of her mind getting into a mad flurry, it became quiet. She felt cold, even numb. Things were galloping beyond her control.

She placed the teapot on the stand, then looking at John and addressing him slowly and distinctly, she said, 'The boys are coming.'

On this John rose steadily to his feet and walked towards the window, but before reaching it he stopped and turning to look at Freda he said quietly, 'My sons will be in in a minute, I would like you to meet them.'

His sons, oh, there was summat funny here. Gran's chin was moving steadily, steadily outwards. His sons . . . Now that was an odd way to say that the lads were coming in and to supposedly an old friend of his and Florrie's. His sons. Gran's eyes became smaller as her face screwed up with her thinking.

It was Arthur who came into the kitchen first and he took the situation in immediately. It was just as Frankie had said it would happen. He hadn't believed him, but, by God, he had been right. He stared at the visitor, and as he stared he had a sudden feeling of pity for Frankie. Lord, she was flashy and caked with paint. Frankie's description had been correct: mutton aping to be lamb. And what mutton. He looked towards his dad to find out that he was looking at him, staring at him. He had a sort of lost, hurt look about him, yet at the same time he was bristling. He looked as if Uncle Brod had been at him – that kind of look. He felt Frankie standing by his side now and his pity mounted. Then his dad spoke.

'This is a friend of mine and your mother's . . . Mrs Manning.'

John was looking at Arthur but it was Frankie who answered, staring straight at his father as he did so.

'Oh, you can come off it,' he said. 'I know who she is all right. There's no need to beat about the bush any longer.'

To say that everyone in the room was startled was to put it mildly. They all directed their gaze upon Frankie, but Frankie was looking only at his father and his thin face looked pinched and hard.

'She's me mother and I know all about it, and you can stop your playactin'.'

An absolute stunned silence followed this statement and the expressions on all the faces in the kitchen were wide and agape. All that is, except Gran's, and hers was screwed up almost to a button now.

185

'What's up with you, boy? Don't be silly.' Florrie's voice sounded like a squeak as she moved quickly towards him and when she stood in front of him shutting out the figure of John, Frankie turned his head to one side and muttered, 'It's no use you talkin'.'

'Look at me, boy. I'm your mother.'

Frankie, still with his head turned from her, muttered, 'It's no use, I tell you.'

Now Florrie turned her wild distracted gaze towards Freda, and Freda was smiling. The situation was to her liking. She stood twisting one of the large rings on her fingers as she looked at Frankie and she cocked her head archly to one side as she said, 'I wish what you were saying was true, Arthur. I would give one hand and one foot to make it true.'

Frankie dragged his gaze towards her and his eyes were questioningly narrowed as he said quietly, 'I'm not Arthur, I'm Frankie.'

The smile slid from Freda's face as she cast a swift glance between Frankie and Arthur, then giving a hicking laugh she said, 'Oh well, I thought . . .' The laugh was repeated. 'My, my, so you're not Arthur . . .' Turning slowly now she looked at Arthur and in a matter of seconds she watched him turn two tones paler.

As if a miracle had taken place, the weight of anxiety and disgrace, as Frankie thought of it, had been lifted from him and transferred to Arthur. Frankie looked at his brother. Arthur had insisted that the whole business was nothing to worry about, but look at him now. He looked the colour of a sheet and he was backing towards the wall as if trying to get away from this thing that had come upon him.

'What's all this about anyway?' It was John's voice, harsh and loud, demanding an explanation.

'He thought I was his mother, fancy that.' Freda was addressing herself to John. 'I wonder how that's come about.'

'I'm . . . Arthur Gascoigne . . . Are you me mother?' Arthur, with the support of the wall behind him and his eyes popping from his head, was staring at Freda, and Freda looking back at him and, about to speak, was interrupted by a cry from Florrie. 'No, she's not your mother, Arthur. I'm your mother.'

'Are you me mother?' Arthur was still appealing to Freda and ignoring Florrie, who was standing at his side now.

'Well, what do you think?' Freda was acting entirely to pattern.

At this point there came the sound of what might have been a knock on the door, but nobody took any notice of it for John's voice burst on them in a great bellow, crying, 'Stop this bloody nonsense.' With a push to right and left, he thrust Frankie to one side and Freda to the other and stood dead opposite Arthur and, in a tone hardly less quiet, he said, pointing to Florrie, 'That's your mother there. She's your mother, but . . .' He paused. 'I'm not your father . . . There now' – he swung round to Freda – 'I hope you're happy.'

'You can't blame me.'

'Can't blame you! Why the hell are you here?'

'I told you in my letter I would come if you didn't show up.'

'Your letter?'

'I opened the letter.'

They were all looking at Frankie again.

'You opened a letter addressed to me?' John's voice was a low growl.

'Aye, I did, because I knew you were going and seeing her,' Frankie said boldly, jerking his head towards Freda.

John drew his hand across his mouth, then cast a swift glance towards Florrie and she held it for a moment, questioningly, until he drew it away towards Arthur again. Arthur looked sick, very sick, and John said, 'I'm sorry for this, lad, it need never have happened, but since it has you'd better know the lot.' He turned about and moved towards the table, but purposely kept the breadth of it between him and his mother. Then, taking a seat, he drummed his fingers on the table edge a moment before saying, 'I was married afore and this' – he gave a little jerk of his head towards Freda – 'was me first wife.'

There wasn't a sound in the kitchen yet the whole room seemed to be vibrating.

Then Arthur's voice, very low, broke in asking, 'And what about me?'

John raised his eyes to him as he said firmly, 'Your mother was married afore an' all.'

'No, I wasn't.'

Florrie was facing her son now, and speaking to him alone. 'I was to be married but this woman' – Florrie turned an accusing eye on Freda – 'who was at the time John's wife, took him away from me. They went off together and when John's divorce came through he married me. And there you have it. I'm your mother, all right, but Dad isn't your father. Your father was George Manning and because of that this woman wanted you when you were a baby. She pestered me to have you. That's why we came to this village, to get away from her. Aunt Lucy got your dad the job of sexton.' Florrie was now looking towards Freda and, talking more at her than to her, she said, 'And why she wanted to come back at this stage for what I don't know. Only to cause trouble. And you've done that, haven't you?' She now addressed Freda pointedly. 'And I hope it's made you happy.'

It is true to say that no two reactions to this disclosure of any of those in the room were alike. With Frankie, his relief was unbounded. He felt he'd had a reprieve of some sort from a life shadowed by the stigma of shame. That it should have been passed on to Arthur, he was sorry, but then, hadn't Arthur said the past was past and one shouldn't worry about it. Well, how was he going to take his own advice now? He looked towards Arthur.

Arthur's mind was in a state of chaos, but it was running one clear thought. Of the two he'd rather have it this way. Yes, he knew he would much rather have it that John wasn't his father than that Freda was his mother. Yet he just couldn't take it in because all his life he had identified his ways with those of this man, thinking, 'I take after Dad.' He knew he was quiet inside like his dad; he had principles, he knew, like his dad, or the man he thought of as Dad; whereas Frankie, who was really Dad's son, wasn't a bit like him. He now began to doubt that it could possibly be. Everything pointed to Frankie being the odd man out. But then he was the elder, he couldn't get away from that, and this fact did away with the idea of any loophole. He felt lost somehow, a bit sick and lost; he didn't think he'd ever feel right again, not really. And what would Moira say? Well, not anything like what Joan would say, of that he was sure. If he still needed something to scare off the Duckworths, this was it at least, he thought dolefully.

Linda's reaction was one of wide amazement and indignation. Her dad had been divorced and yet he had gone on in that frantic way about Pat being divorced. After all, Pat's wife was dead, she wasn't still at large like he was. She was shocked that her dad had ever looked at another woman, and amazed too that he could have been married to a woman like this one. Smart and all that . . . And her mother, her mother had had another man. Well! She looked at her mother with new eyes. And she had had Arthur before she was married . . . Eeh! Who would have believed it? Arthur wasn't really her brother now, only a half-brother. Would he hate her mam for it? She looked again at Florrie.

Florrie's reactions were off, they even appeared so to herself for they were mostly made up of relief – as if a weight she had been carrying for years had suddenly jolted from her back. She was looking at Arthur appealingly, but Arthur would not meet her eyes. But this did not worry her unduly – later on when they were together she would talk to him and explain. Arthur would understand, whereas Frankie never would have. And yet Frankie was theirs, wholly theirs, hers and John's. Her mind came back to John and she asked herself: would this business affect him one way or another? Would it shock him into sensibility or push him over the brink?

John was sitting at the table, still drumming his fingers on its edge; his head was lowered but he knew that some time, and soon, he would have to raise his eyes and meet those of his mother. She was standing, he knew, looking at him, side by side with Aunt Lucy, and again, as he had done as a child, he wished from the bottom of his heart that Aunt Lucy was his mother. Aunt Lucy always understood – there had never been any need to keep things from her.

Aunt Lucy's reactions were ones of deep sadness. That the exposure should have come at this time of their lives saddened and worried her; worried her not so much because of the effect on Arthur, but on her own sister. She was very, very conscious of Mamie's presence at this moment, and an old sore had been opened in her heart, for the story that had been disclosed was very like her own. She had been sweet on a lad and he on her. Then Mamie had come home on holiday from her place and she had never returned to it, for from the moment she saw Robbie she was determined to have him, and no snake charmer used more fascination and guile than she did. Poor Robbie could not withstand her and they were married in a hurry; Mamie saw to that. But before six months were up, Robbie came to her, almost with tears in his eyes, and begged her forgiveness and admitted that he would never have a chance in his life to make a bigger mistake than he had done in marrying Mamie. Poor Robbie, he couldn't play any underhand games, he was too open, and for the remainder of his days he suffered for it. And now she knew that their Mamie was looking at her as if she could kill her.

And Aunt Lucy was right. Gran had the desire to knock Lucy to the floor. To think that all these years she had known about this whole affair and had never let on. She had always hated their Lucy, for she was soft and simpering and mealy-mouthed . . . without guts. She hadn't had the guts to fight to keep her lad, and when she herself pulled him from between her teeth, she hadn't lifted a finger to prevent her, nor yet said a word. Then Robbie . . . she had taunted him for years with Lucy's name, and although he wouldn't admit openly to wanting her, she knew all right where his thoughts were, and it had nearly driven her mad at times. The pain of those days returned into Gran's withered chest. In one way, Lucy had lost Robbie to her, but in one way only – that was legally. In every other way she had him until the day he died, and not only him but his son. That had to be the bitterest pill of all to stomach, for from the time that the bairn could crawl he had shown an open preference for Lucy's arms. From her own he would wriggle and struggle, but once he could get onto Lucy's lap he would be quiet and fall asleep.

The sight of him in those days within Lucy's arms had the power to drive her almost insane, for she was determined that if she didn't have the love of her man, she was going to have it of her bairn. But, in spite of this determination, the more she fought the more it slipped away from her. John became like his father – silent, withdrawn, never answering back. That was the maddening part of living with them. Neither of them would answer back. Only in the last four years under John's roof had he given her any retort and she had at this late stage taken a delight in taunting him into speech.

Gran was well aware of the traits in her own character; she knew that she must have the upper hand – she must rile, she must order, she had never been able to bear the thought of anything happening within the circle of her family without her knowledge. And she had always prided herself that nothing escaped her . . . Nothing escaped her? It was farcical, while all the time that solemn, dark-browed, close-lipped son of his father had been carrying on to get himself linked up with a piece like the one that was standing there in the middle of the room now. Not only to marry her, but to divorce her into the bargain . . . and she not to know a thing about it.

The boiling indignation within Gran rose to anger and the anger to wrath. She became ablaze with a fury against her son, and her sister, but mostly, at this moment, her son. At her back was the dresser, and on it Gran knew was a roll of newspaper, and inside the newspaper was a sheet of greaseproof paper, and inside that was some hard icing sugar that she had been pounding with the rolling pin that morning.

Gran could never bear to throw anything away, and she had made it her business to roll out the hard sugar and sieve it again for Florrie to use, and there was the unfinished job behind her. Gran did not think of the icing sugar or the job. Her mind leapt straight to the utensil she had used for the grinding – the rolling pin. She was oblivious of Freda's tongue rattling quickly on now, or of the startled jump that Lucy gave as she swung round to the dresser and tore open the paper. The rolling pin in her hand, she swung round to the table again and paused for only a split second as she looked into the startled eyes of her son as he made to rise from the table. Then, with the strength born of her angry passion – for her frail body alone could not have managed it – she brought the rolling pin crashing down on John's forehead in exactly the same place where the ball had hit him a week ago.

John let out a loud wailing cry as his hands flew to his head, and as he was off balance when the blow was struck he fell to the floor, and even before he had touched it, pandemonium had broken loose.

Gran, the handle of the rolling pin still clenched in her bony fist, stood absolutely still while everybody, with the exception of Freda, rained abuse on her as they assisted John to his feet and bore him towards the couch.

'You're a wicked, wicked woman. You'll get out of this house, you will.' This, naturally, was from Florrie.

'I hate you, Gran, I hate you. It's you that's mad. Look at the blood. Look what you've done. Oh, I do hate you.' This, of course, was from Linda.

'Get a bowl, get some water.'

Frankie and Arthur, running to obey this order of Florrie's, collided and Frankie, having his feelings back for his restored parent, yelled at Gran, 'You'll look funny if he conks it.'

'Oh . . . my . . . God.' Each word expressed pain as John groaned them slowly out, and on the sound of them, Aunt Lucy was roused to turn on her sister. 'Oh, you are wicked, our Mamie. Wicked, wicked.'

'You shut up your mouth else I'll give you a test of this an' all. I've been wantin' to do it for years. Anyway . . .' Gran paused to consider for only a second. 'Take that you two-faced deceiving old bitch.' Her hand, not the one that held the rolling pin but the other, swung up and brought itself right across Lucy's face to knock her staggering back against the dresser.

With Aunt Lucy's pained cry came the voice of Freda saying sharply, 'You want to hold your hand a bit, old lady, or they'll lock you up.'

Gran turned on Freda a cold, terrifying stare. 'You speakin' to me?'

'You know right well I am.' Freda was indignant.

'I just wanted to make sure. Now . . .' Gran advanced slowly, the rolling pin still in her hand. 'Get goin' missus, out of this house afore I swipe you one an' all, and not with me hand.' Gran raised the rolling pin higher.

'You just touch me and you'll see what you'll get, old as you are.'

'Don't tempt me.' Gran still came on and Freda decided not to tempt her, but backed towards the door which led to the scullery, calling as she went, 'Florrie, Florrie.'

'She's busy as you see – they're all busy . . . The door's on your left.' Gran's voice almost lifted the latch for Freda. The door was open and Freda was under the porch as she barked, 'You're a wicked old wife. You should be put away.'

'Get goin',' said Gran. Now Gran was on the porch and her sharp eyes went to the gate at the bottom of the garden there to see Mr Duckworth and Joan making a hasty exit. What had they been after she wondered? Well, they'd had an earful she'd like to bet, and if they had heard all she'd heard, the wedding would certainly be off . . . and good luck to it.

'No wonder John could never stand you.'

'Get!'

The rolling pin jerking menacingly aloft emphasised Gran's command and it definitely assisted Freda on her way out. Although, at the gate, after throwing one deadly look back at Gran, she managed to save her face from the peering neighbours by assuming a casual, even dignified, front, and sailed down the street as if the affair going on in number 12 had nothing whatsoever to do with her.

Back in the scullery, Gran closed the door and stood listening to the hubbub coming from the kitchen. She was trembling all over her old body; even her bones seemed to be jangling. Slowly, she moved towards the room and from the doorway she observed that everybody was busy. Florrie and Frankie were attending to John's head, while Linda and Arthur were consoling Aunt Lucy. Determined to keep herself steady until she could reach a chair and sit down, Gran traversed half the kitchen. In doing this she had to pass close to Florrie and Florrie rounded on her, crying, 'You'll pay for this, Gran. I'll never forgive you for this. Never.'

Gran said nothing, but walked on towards the table and the chair, but just as she had her hand on the back of the chair and was about to sit down the sound of grinding brakes brought her attention to the window, and there she saw one after the other two cars come to a halt. She stood upright a few seconds longer in order to see who alighted, then she sat down – or rather slid down – onto her chair. And after she had managed to stop her chin wobbling sufficiently to get her words out, she said with staccato briefness, and to no one in particular, 'He's come at the right time for once, an' the magistrate with him, an' we only want St Christopher now.'

'What?' Florrie sprang to the window, then looking up from it to John's bleeding and discoloured forehead she exclaimed on a quick sigh, 'Well, this is the only time I can say I've been pleased to see him. Open the door to the doctor, Linda.'

The doctor and Mr Fowler were not alone; with them, of all people, was Moira McNally. Why this should be no one asked and Moira offered no explanation, but like the two men, she stood gazing across the room to where John sat leaning back in the armchair, his face grey and streaming with the blood still running from the cut.

'What's happened now?' It was the crisp tone of Dr Spencer, and Florrie, casting a swift glance in Gran's direction, said stiffly, 'He's . . . he's had a blow, doctor.'

The doctor was standing in front of John. 'Had a blow? Good Lord, another, and on the same place. How did he get this?'

When no one spoke he glanced around the room and when his eyes met Gran's defiant glare he said to himself, 'Nonsense, she could never do this.' He turned to John again and bending over him he touched the flesh round the cut, and under his touch John winced and the doctor asked hurriedly, 'Hurt?'

'Hurt?' John's eyes flicked up at him. 'What do you think? That cricket bat wasn't made of paste.'

The doctor's eyes narrowed and he glanced up at Florrie and towards Mr Fowler who was standing on the other side of John's chair, then he said quietly, 'You were hit with a cricket ball.'

'Aye, aye. Parson's boundary, it came straight at me.' John groaned again and put his hand up towards the rising mound but the doctor drew it away.

'I'll have to put a stitch in this.' He turned to Moira. 'Get me my bag from the car, Moira, will you?' When Moira ran to do his bidding the doctor, glancing quickly at Florrie, said to John, 'Well, how did you manage to get home all this way from the field like this?'

John went to shake his head but the action was too painful and he pressed his hand over his ear, then muttered, 'Wife brought me, I think . . . I don't know. I feel a bit dazed – my head feels as if it's going to bust. Wait till I see the Reverend.'

The doctor turned from John and taking Florrie by the arm led her past the staring family and into the hall and there he whispered, 'Tell me as briefly as possible how he came by this blow.'

Florrie had her eyes cast down as she said, 'It was Gran. Some family business came up this afternoon, something that John did years ago. His first wife came here.' Florrie raised her eyes to the doctor and saw that his eyebrows were moving upwards. 'You see, he had never told his mother that he had been married afore – and divorced – and when she found out . . . well, she hit him with the rolling pin.'

For the first time in their acquaintance, Florrie saw the shadow of a smile flick across the doctor's face but it was quickly gone and he said in a low tone, 'Well, she's likely done him a good turn. She's wiped out the past week for evidently this blow has returned him to normality. Although I can't be sure, mind, and for your sake I can only say that I am pleased, for my visit tonight was two-fold . . .' He paused, drew in his breath, then said, 'You know who Mr Fowler is, don't you? He is a Justice of the Peace, I brought him to see your husband, but I'd also come with a startling piece of news, something to soften the blow if your husband had to go away for a short time. Although you might not have thought it much compensation.'

At this moment Moira came to the hall door saying, 'I brought the bag, doctor.'

He nodded to her. 'All right, Moira.'

'Can I tell them now?' Moira's eyes were large and bright and her face was one wide beam, and it could not but bring a real smile to the doctor's face as he said, 'Yes, Moira, go on.' Then touching Florrie, who stood dazed, lightly on the arm, he turned her about towards the kitchen again saying, 'You'd better come and hear this and perhaps you'll still look on it as compensation for all the harassing I've given you this week. For you see, I was the one who had to go and pick his ticket . . . Most strange, really strange.'

'His ticket?' Florrie looked back at the doctor in perplexity as she went before him into the kitchen.

'Uncle John.' Moira was bending over John, her hand on his shoulder, and without raising his head he said in his usual gruff manner, 'Aye, what is it?'

'You remember the ticket you bought off me for the raffle, Uncle John?'

'Raffle?' He raised his eyes painfully to her. 'When did I get any tickets off you for a raffle?' John spoke as if this was the last thing on earth he would have done.

'Wednesday, Uncle John.'

'You must be mistaken, lass.' John's voice was weary and impatient.

'But you did, Uncle.' Moira's smile was slipping and she looked wildly round the room before returning her gaze to John and saying, 'Try to think; think where you put them. Your name's on the counterfoil but you've got to have the ticket to show.'

Not being able to put his hand on the front of his head, John placed it on the back and, screwing up his eyes against the pain, he said, 'Look, lass, I'm in no mood to talk about raffle tickets, can't you see that.'

'But you've won a car, Uncle John.'

John's hand came off the back of his head, his eyes widened and he stared up into Moira's face and said very slowly, 'A car, in a raffle . . . Me?'

Moira nodded happily again.

'But I can't even remember buying any tickets for a raffle, a car raffle.'

'It was the hospital's raffle, remember? And first prize was a car. The Ridley firm were giving it, and you've won it, Uncle John, out of all the thousands and thousands, you've won it. And who d'you think picked your ticket?' She pushed him playfully in the arm. 'You'll never guess.' She flicked her glance full of amusement over her shoulder. 'The doctor himself.'

'Oh, aye.' John moved his eyes towards the doctor. 'You picked me ticket in a raffle, sir?'

'Yes, I'm afraid so, Mr Gascoigne, and I must be honest and admit I wasn't very happy at the time about it, but now, well . . . the way things have turned out I can only be very pleased for you.'

'But me with a car? What can I do with a car?' Painfully John looked from one to another and for the first time in days there was laughter in the kitchen. It came from Frankie; it came from Linda; it came from Moira; it came from Mr Fowler; and although he was still suffering from shock, Arthur's laugh too joined the rest. Only Aunt Lucy, Gran and Florrie did not laugh. Florrie was too dazed, too relieved to let her feelings run freely yet. Aunt Lucy was too hurt, not by the actual blow that Mamie had given her, but the fact that her sister had struck her. And Gran. Gran did not laugh for she knew that her name would be mud in this house henceforth. She had hit Aunt Lucy, who was the apple of everybody's eye, but most of all she had struck her son a great blow that had split his head open. Nobody would say it was the best turn she could have done him. She had thought to herself the other day, 'If he got a hair of the dog that bit him, so to speak, and another knock there, it might pull him to his senses.' But she hadn't been able to get up enough courage to do it in cold blood, and she didn't think she would ever have been able to do it if she hadn't been provoked beyond her endurance.

But would she be thanked for it? Most certainly not. But what did she care? Let them get on with it. Look at them running round like scalded cats looking for the ticket. She hoped they would never find it. But Frankie's voice at that moment, yelling from upstairs, told her that it had been found, and when he came dashing into the kitchen and held the three tickets out to John, Gran thought, 'He can't remember a damn thing about them. He hasn't a thought in his head of what's happened since the cricket ball hit him.' And again she said to herself, 'And they'll give me no thanks for it.'

'Well, we'd better get this head seen to.' The doctor's voice rose above the hubbub, but John's voice came back at him saying, 'Just a minute, doctor, have you got her here?'

'Yes, she's outside. Mr Fowler brought her along for you.'

'Could I see it, sir?' John was pushing himself to the edge of his chair.

'She's your car, Mr Gascoigne.' Mr Fowler was smiling blandly. He was amused; he had not been so amused for years. Spencer had been wild when he knew it was the gravedigger who had won the car. Then he had made himself look upon it as a solace for the family while its owner was under restraint – after he had put him under restraint. And here to come upon a scene like that of a farce. It was as good as any farce he had ever seen. As for the old lady there, he was pleased and thankful she was no relation of his. A real old war horse, that one.

'Here, then, let me put a temporary bandage round your head and then you can go out and have a look.'

The doctor got busy and in a few minutes, the bandage in place, John rose to his feet with the help of Florrie and Arthur, but no sooner had they got out of the door than they were confronted by Broderick and Katie, who had been listening in with ears strained to the commotion and had picked up a great deal of it. Now they wanted to be right in on this last fantastic bit of news, for Moira, on her way to collect the doctor's bag, had dashed in to tell them what had happened.

'Begod, John,' cried Broderick straight away. 'Aren't you the lucky one . . .' Then, looking at John's swathed head, he exclaimed, 'And has somebody gone and given you another one on the napper.'

John, being his usual self now, did not deign to answer but, pushing Broderick aside, walked slowly to the gate, through it and onto the pavement. When his eyes moved from one car to the other, it was Mr Fowler who pointed to the smaller and brighter one.

'There she is.'

John stopped an arm's length from the car as if afraid to approach nearer. His mind was telling him that this was his – he had won a car. The odd thing about it was he didn't even remember buying a ticket. This lapse of memory, he supposed, was due to the blow he had received from the ball. But him . . . him with a car.

'Don't be afraid of it; it won't bite.' It was the doctor's crisp tones and John, without looking in his direction, moved closer.

There were voices all about him now, all full of admiration.

'Oh, isn't she a beauty.' Linda could see herself and Pat side by side in the car going off for full days at a time. Pat could drive.

'Coo!' Frankie, now that his equilibrium had been returned with his birthright, saw himself doing seventy in her. Not that he wouldn't want his bike an' all but, coo, to drive a car . . . a new one.

Arthur was standing near his mother now and he wasn't thinking so much about the car as about her. He wanted to tell her that everything was all right, for he knew that she was glancing at him furtively from time to time. Even with all this commotion going on, he knew she was worrying about how he had taken the news. So being the lad he was, he put out his hand and slipped it through her arm, and as he pressed it to his side, he gave her all the assurance she needed by nodding towards the car and saying, 'A smasher, isn't she?'

Florrie was too full for words. She just looked at Arthur with a long look and, to stop the tears from flowing, she turned her eyes from him towards the car and nodded her approval. There was no excitement in the nod for she hadn't taken it in yet that they now possessed a car.

'Begod, she's small, but she's bonnie enough.' This was Katie speaking. Was there a trace of jealousy in Katie's voice?

'And you to win a car, John.' Broderick had his head back and his voice was loud. 'And you the one against cars an' all they stand for. Isn't it just like the trick that fate would play you? What will you do with it at all?'

The look John turned on Broderick was the old one, and his voice had the remembered cutting note as he said, 'What will I do with it? Give it to you?'

'Get inside and see what she feels like.' It was none other than the doctor holding the car door open for John.

John looked at the doctor, and he hesitated with one foot on the step.

'Go on, man, she won't bite you.' The doctor sounded quite different, quite human, in fact.

But for all his jocular manner, the young doctor still remained the enthusiast and, bending into the car, he looked at John sitting with the wheel almost in his lap and he pointed to a little effigy dangling from the front of the inner roof just above the windscreen to the right of the driving wheel. 'And you've got a St Christopher to guide you. Everything complete,' he said.

John's eyes swung up to the effigy, and as he stared at it the old antagonistic feeling against superstition arose in him and he thought, 'One of them; I'll have it out of that. I can do without that, thank you very much.' But on this there ran through his head a counter-thought; it was like an actual voice saying, admonishingly, 'Now, John; now, John.'

John blinked and looked again at the effigy, then quickly he closed his eyes and rubbed his hand across them. That blow had knocked him a bit off-colour . . . Why for a moment he thought the damned thing had winked at him.

'You're feeling all right?' The doctor's hand was on his shoulder.

'Yes, doctor, I'm all right.'

'Are you going to leave that there?' The doctor pointed to the St Christopher.

John looked again at the effigy and as he answered the doctor he kept his eyes on it. 'Well, if it doesn't do much good, I don't suppose it'll do much harm.'

The doctor nodded slowly, and as he watched John ease himself out of the seat, his face screwing up against the pain in his head, he said briskly, 'That's enough of that. Come along and I'll see to that head of yours.'

Like a family returning from a trip, they all went up the path – Katie and Broderick tagging on at the back. Florrie was leading the way, telling herself that she must get some fresh tea ready for this lot and also telling herself that she was happier than she had been for years. Then, as she entered the kitchen, a loud cry was dragged from her which brought John and the doctor and the rest of them crowding into the doorway for there, lying on the floor in a crumpled heap by the side of the table, lay Gran.

It was two hours later and Gran was in bed. She had been surprised to wake up and find herself there for she had fully expected to wake up and find herself dead. That's what came of willing things. When she had seen them all trooping out gaily to the car, a sense of loneliness had enveloped her that was frightening. She had wanted to cry out to one of them to come back. Even if she had wanted to go with them, she felt that her legs would not have carried her down the path. She started to upbraid them in her mind, each in turn, until she came to Lucy and John, and for them she wanted to achieve something that would bow them down with sorrow because of their treatment of her.

At one point she suggested to herself that she throw a faint. It would not be the first time that she had thrown a faint and given herself a few days' rest in bed. But then there was that doctor. He was as fly as a box of monkeys, that one. It would be no use doing an act and him about. Aw, she concluded, she'd be better dead. They'd all be sorry if she was dead. They'd find something decent to say about her if she was dead. 'Oh, Gran wasn't so bad after all, was she?' they'd say. 'She had a tongue but she was nearly always right in everything she said, and didn't she stop them from taking her son to an asylum. She hit him on the head with a rolling pin, on the very spot where the ball had bounced. She was cute, was Gran, and wise . . . Aye, she was. She knew what was good for him, and she was the only one with courage enough to do it.' Yes, that's about what they would say when she was dead this minute – that would stop their jollification.

A car indeed. And who went near daft just a week ago because the lad said he wanted a motorbike, and then seeing that Saint – the car saint. But above everything else, for him to have got married as soon as he got out of her hands, and her not to know it. Never till her last gasp would she forgive him for that.

This thought got Gran's heart to race unnaturally fast. It raced so much that when she tried to call out she found she hadn't any breath. It all seemed to be racing around her heart. She tried to hoist herself from the chair but found she couldn't. The racing became faster and faster, and Gran, deep inside herself, yelled at it, 'I'm not going to die like this, no I'm not.' But the more she protested, the more it raced. And then of a sudden she became quite calm. This was it then; this was the end. A deep sorrow enveloped her, sorrow and regret. For exactly what she was incapable of explaining, for in the sorrow she fell to the floor.

The bed was warm and soft and Gran felt sleepy. She felt she could lie for a week and that's what Florrie had said she must do. 'Now, Gran, you mustn't worry about anything.' Florrie had stroked her hair off her forehead. 'You've got to lie there at least for a week, the doctor said so.' And then she had bent and kissed her, whispering as she did so, 'You really did me a good turn. I'll never be able to thank you. You've put him on his feet again.' Then she smiled and added, 'And nobody but yourself could have done it.'

They had all been to see her, creeping in and creeping out of the room, and they had all been very nice, even their Lucy – particularly their Lucy. They all thought she was going to kick the bucket, but she wasn't. No, by jingo, she wasn't going to kick no bucket, not when Florrie had taken it like that. There was glory for her to wallow in for years to come. Every member of the family would talk for years of the day Gran had hit Dad with a rolling pin. All, of course, except her son. She blinked her eyes and realised that John was actually there before her, sitting by the side of the bed. His head looked twice the size so wrapped round was it with bandages. His face looked greyish and she said to him, 'You shouldn't be here, you should be in bed.' She was surprised that he had to bring his head close to her to hear what she was saying, and she made an effort to push him away, saying, 'Get yoursel' to bed.'

'Don't talk, Mother. Just lie quiet.'

The wave of sorrow and regret was once again enveloping Gran and she felt herself pulling him to her and it was very, very hard for her to say the words but she made herself do it as she brought her hands up to his face. 'I'm sorry, lad,' she said. She watched a light start up in his eyes as she spoke; a light that had never shone for her before. And then, with his hand touching her cheek, he replied softly, 'There's nothing to be sorry for, Mother, for from what I can gather from Florrie, you've done me a good turn. I can't take it all in yet, but I seem to have had a heck of a week and given all of you something of a time. The only thing for you to do,' he went on, stroking her cheek, 'is to rest and get better, and then you know what?' He was actually smiling at her just as she had watched him do at their Lucy. 'I'll take you for a jaunt in me car.'

The smile was covering his face and she returned it and asked with the semblance of a chuckle, 'St Christopher comin' along?' There was a puckered look of bewilderment on John's face as he replied slowly after a moment's hesitation, 'Aye, there's nowt for it. I suppose I'll have to take him.'

'And McNally?'

There came a quirk to John's lips as he looked at his mother. 'And McNally,' he said.

The thought of being in a position to give McNally a lift in his car had a strange effect on John – he felt he was actually swelling and it was a grand feeling. It went on and on until he felt more than twice his size. Then from somewhere deep inside him a voice exclaimed gleefully, 'I'll show him, I'll frighten the daylight out of him.'

NOTE FROM THE CATHERINE COOKSON ESTATE

We are indebted to our agent, Sonia Land of Sheil Land Associates, who has persevered in helping get this manuscript to publication. Special thanks and much appreciation to Emilie Marneur, Sammia Hamer, Sophie Missing, Gillian Holmes and Jill Sawyer, who have done a magnificent job in transcribing a much faded manuscript, which, without the presence of Catherine Cookson herself, might not have made this all possible.

And to Catherine Cookson, we are eternally grateful to you for writing yet another marvellous story and we hope you will be proud of this publication.

ABOUT THE AUTHOR

Catherine Cookson was born in East Jarrow near the mouth of the River Tyne, one of the poorest areas in Britain. Her childhood was deeply scarred by violence, fear, alcoholism, shame and guilt, and her books were inspired by her upbringing. She fought hard for a better life and was determined to be a writer. Her readership quickly spread throughout the world, and her many bestselling novels established her as one of the most popular of contemporary women novelists. After receiving an OBE in 1985, Catherine Cookson was made a Dame of the British Empire in 1993, and was appointed an Honorary Fellow of St Hilda's College, Oxford, in 1997. She died shortly before her ninety-second birthday, in June 1998. By the time of her death, she had written over one hundred books and was the UK's most widely read novelist, and remained the most-borrowed author in UK public libraries for twenty years.

The Cookson Estate recently discovered two unpublished manuscripts – a memoir and a novel – in the attic of Cookson's home. Amazon Publishing will be releasing these two unseen works and the author's backlist will be available through Kindle Direct Publishing, ensuring Catherine Cookson's legacy is available to readers across the globe.

20030798R00133

Printed in Poland
by Amazon Fulfillment
Poland Sp. z o.o., Wrocław